T0158794

THE HIGHLANDER'S
WITCH

Jennifer France

iUniverse, Inc.
Bloomington

The Highlander's Witch

Copyright © 2011 by Jennifer France.

All rights reserved. No part of this book may be used or reproduced by any means, graphic, electronic, or mechanical, including photocopying, recording, taping or by any information storage retrieval system without the written permission of the publisher except in the case of brief quotations embodied in critical articles and reviews.

This is a work of fiction. All of the characters, names, incidents, organizations, and dialogue in this novel are either the products of the author's imagination or are used fictitiously.

iUniverse books may be ordered through booksellers or by contacting:

iUniverse
1663 Liberty Drive
Bloomington, IN 47403
www.iuniverse.com
1-800-Authors (1-800-288-4677)

Because of the dynamic nature of the Internet, any web addresses or links contained in this book may have changed since publication and may no longer be valid. The views expressed in this work are solely those of the author and do not necessarily reflect the views of the publisher, and the publisher hereby disclaims any responsibility for them.

Any people depicted in stock imagery provided by Thinkstock are models, and such images are being used for illustrative purposes only.
Certain stock imagery © Thinkstock.

ISBN: 978-1-4759-3425-0 (sc)
ISBN: 978-1-4759-3426-7 (ebk)

Printed in the United States of America

iUniverse rev. date: 06/30/2012

CHAPTER ONE

Sarah inwardly cringed as the front door slammed and her sister stormed in. She pasted a smile on her face while removing brownies out of the oven as the junk drawer was yanked open and rifled through.

Carefully going about her business, Sarah tried to be as nonchalant as possible as she watched her younger sister pull out a pad of paper and start writing on it.

Knowing she and their aunt had gone overboard this time, Sarah observed Skye's normal cheerful behavior transform to a barely calm demeanor. One of her hands was running through her brown curls in frustration, muttering as she wrote things down, her light green eyes flashing in their intensity.

"What's that you're writing?" Sarah finally asked.

"A list." Skye glanced up to give her sister a meaningful look, the kind that involved a raised eyebrow.

Sarah had the grace to blush before she began cutting the brownies. The long minutes of silence, broken only by the sound of pencil on paper, made her curiosity get the best of her, something usually reserved for Skye.

"Why?" Sarah questioned.

Taking a deep breath, Skye looked up. "I am really tired of you and Aunt Gladys trying to set me up."

"All—"

Skye raised her hand to stop her sister.

"I know—believe me, I know." She went on as if speaking a well-rehearsed line. "Aunt Gladys feels terrible for pushing me into a relationship with my soul mate, only to discover he was your soul mate. So she spends her life trying to make up for it." She broke free from the litany to glare back at her sister when she opened her mouth to speak. "And it doesn't matter that I don't want her help—or yours."

Sarah nodded and gave a weak smile. "So this list of yours . . . ?"

"I'm pretty sure you know that Aunt Gladys' idea of an early dinner date was actually a setup for a speed dating event." Skye raised her eyebrow again and when Sarah's face grew red and her eyes darted away, she snorted. "Yeah, I figured as much. Anyway, my experience taught me that there are certain things you two obviously need to have a clue about, since common sense doesn't seem to be commonly used."

She pushed the paper towards the other side of the counter for Sarah to see. "This is the list of what I expect from any man I'd consider."

Sarah looked sideways at the list. "'Speak English'*?*"

"The very first guy I sat next to? It would have helped if he knew more than 'yes', 'no', or 'we go to bed now?'"

"No way!" Sarah exclaimed.

"Uh, way." Was Skye's droll reply.

"How tactless."

"Yeah, well, it was a speed dating thing. Who do you think was going to attend, Prince Charming?"

Sarah went to speak again then clamped her mouth shut.

"I didn't think you'd have anything to say." Skye smirked.

"Actually, you do know Gaelic." Sarah smiled encouragingly. "Any other language would be just as easy to learn."

"I cannot believe you just said that." Skye replied as she rolled her eyes. "For everyone's Christmas present, you cast a spell allowing all of us to speak and read Gaelic so Doug can read his dusty old manuscripts and you think I can just up and do the same?"

Sarah winced since they both knew that Skye casting a spell would only result in something disastrous happening like when she flooded the attic as she tried to make the temperature better for the herbs she once grew up there.

"Okay, soooo . . . I can do it for you." Sarah offered.

"The fact that he doesn't speak English doesn't bother you in the slightest, or that he thought the words 'we go to bed now' was at the top of his need to know words?"

Skye shot her sister another glare and Sarah bit her lip and looked back at the next item on the list.

"'Be financially secure'?"

"So I ordered my second drink and by the time I went on to guy number two, both our drinks arrived. He had the audacity to smile and say 'I know how women feel about being treated equal and all, so I'm going to let you buy mine as well,'" Skye mimicked in her worst holier-than-thou voice, "'to show that I respect you as an equal.'"

Sarah's eyes widened and she unconsciously rubbed her pregnant belly. "What an ass."

Skye took the list back.

"'Care about others more than himself.'" She read aloud before explaining to her sister. "Jerk three spoke of nothing but himself and his accomplishments, all while looking in the mirror behind the bar."

Sarah stood there in shock as her younger sister continued.

"'Have integrity'. Jerk four complained about how much more work he had because three guys were busted for stealing from the company, then let it slip that he was glad he hadn't gotten caught himself. Jerk five asked me my IQ before he even greeted me, hence 'Be smart, but have some humility.'" Her pencil paused at the next one as she looked at her sister. "And then there is number seven. Beyond a doubt he was the cutest guy there."

Sarah perked and grinned. "Yeah?"

"Oh, yeah. Hot with a capital H."

Leaning over to look at the list, Sarah asked. "So then, what does 'Love me for the way I am' have to do with him?"

"He wanted me to straighten and change my hair to blonde, lose a few pounds, and wear shorter skirts."

Except for Sarah's lighter shade of brown hair, being pregnant, and four years older, the two could have looked like twins. Both had green eyes, stood five foot eight, and were happy in their size twelve clothes.

Although they shared an innate sense of curiosity, which was why Sarah thought Skye would go for the speed dating fiasco their aunt had planned, it was really their personalities that set them apart. Sarah was the no-nonsense one, always planning with everything in order while Skye went by the seat of her pants and thrived on spontaneity.

"No way!" Sarah exclaimed.

Skye shoved away from the counter in disgust, not even bothering to reply. She picked up her discarded purse and walked away.

"What about this 'be a man's man, but be straight?'" Sarah asked.

"Since I'd had enough abuse for one evening and was so over the whole thing, I got up to leave and can you imagine my surprise when the next guy leaned over and said he was willing to do all that and more for number seven . . . and seven looked like he was considering it!"

"Oh, my God!"

Skye got to the basement door, turned the handle and looked back at Sarah's shocked face.

"No more, Sarah. I mean it." She ground out firmly through clenched teeth before closing the door behind her.

Heading down to the basement she'd set up as her own since Doug and Sarah's marriage, Skye tossed her hat, coat, and purse onto the nearest flat surface before curling up onto her favorite rocking chair as she played with the ring on her thumb.

It wasn't that she was truly angry with her sister and aunt.

Okay, she was, but she understood the meaning behind their actions, more than they gave her credit for.

It just seemed that since Sarah and Doug's marriage a little over a year ago, her life had become one huge circus with her aunt being the ringleader.

Magic always seemed the cause of it all.

Aunt Gladys had the ability to see connections between two people and insisted she and Doug were meant to be together.

When their professor had paired them for a project in their botany class, it was an instant camaraderie.

Doug was a very good-looking man with hazel eyes, black hair that always seemed to need a haircut, and a firm muscular body that belied his studious personality but it was the way he seemed to accept Skye's outlandish ways without taking offence when she said something without thinking it through that held her attention.

By the end of the week, Skye had brought him home for coffee and introduced him to her aunt, disappointed that her sister had been out shopping.

Later that evening, her aunt swore that she and Doug were bound together for eternity, as in from one lifetime to the next.

Since they got along so well, even though he was eight years older, Skye asked Doug if he wanted to go out on a real date.

Doug had laughed at the way she'd just come forward and asked but agreed.

Their date had gone exceptionally well.

Throughout dinner, he told her about the books he'd just inherited from an uncle in Scotland and was excited to read over and, since they were written in Gaelic, he was planning to take online courses to learn the language.

Never mentioning magic, Skye told him of her life with her sister, how her parents had died in a plane crash when she was seven and how her eccentric aunt had moved in bringing laughter back into their lives with her strange ways.

They laughed and joked for hours but the sense of familiarity between them was different from that of lovers and when Skye's need for answers got the best of her and she kissed Doug on her front porch step, trying for a real steaming hot kiss, they ended up breaking away feeling guilty.

It didn't take a rocket scientist to figure out they got along more like brother and sister than potential husband

and wife so Skye took Doug by the hand and brought him inside before he could walk away.

Realizing that if she didn't do something to take their minds off the awkward moment, she was going to lose someone she'd become close friends with, so she went looking for her sister knowing Sarah had a way about her that made most everyone comfortable.

The chemistry between them was instantaneous.

Skye introduced the two and stood aside grinning as Doug stared at her sister and Sarah blushed, offering a slice of pie she'd just taken from the oven.

Chuckling at the feeling of being in an old black and white movie, Skye made some lame excuse that neither heard before leaving the two alone.

The change in Sarah was immediate. She laughed more, her eyes sparkled, and she stressed over Skye and family matters less.

In a few short months, Aunt Gladys reluctantly admitted to being confused on how there was the same kind of attachment between Doug and Sarah as there was between he and Skye, only slightly brighter with Sarah.

Skye knew Sarah had always been scared of a relationship because of her specific powers. It wasn't every day that a person could look into flames in one place and see what was going on through them in another.

Not surprisingly, when they began to discuss marriage, Sarah had gathered her family together and they agreed that Doug needed to know.

As they all sat down to dinner a week later, they broke it to him calmly.

Beginning in hushed tones while watching his reactions, they explained how Sarah could manipulate fire with thought.

Doug quietly digested what they were saying but it wasn't until Sarah lit the candles by waving her hand that he truly believed.

He'd been silent for a long time while the women fidgeted in their seats. When he finally spoke, he mused aloud about how he'd always questioned the tales that spoke of witches in his ancestry but now he needed to reconsider the stories.

Then he raised his wine glass as he smiled at the three women watching him. "Here's to a never boring moment."

Skye rolled her eyes. "You're marrying Sarah who will keep you on your toes, but it's me who keeps everyone from boredom."

"I may be making Sarah my wife, but I am also hoping to have you as a part of the family I wish to start with her." He turned to their aunt. "That includes you, Gladys."

Everyone grinned and pretended the older woman wasn't blushing as they answered the questions Doug began to ask about witchcraft.

Sarah said they had plenty of time to go over her powers and nodded to her sister to start.

Skye explained her healing abilities. How, with a touch of her hands, she could remove any disease or heal any wound, explaining how she used the herbs she had moved to the newly constructed hot house in the backyard to disguise any mysterious recovery.

Laughing throughout her story, Skye told him it wasn't often that she could get a chant right no matter how simple, telling him of the time she wanted to get some ice cream at the store and wasn't going to make it before they closed so she used a spell and found herself at the bottom of their neighbors pool.

"I could go on and on, but let's not." Skye winked and laughed.

Sarah chuckled. "Well, that's not entirely true. She can shave without a razor, and light a fire with a touch. We covered those pretty well growing up."

"Okay, so I can do a couple things without causing mass destruction."

They brought up, to their aunt's embarrassment, how Gladys' ability to see connections had originally brought Skye and Doug together and they briefly tried to figure out why it had gone wrong before realizing the older woman's shame over the faux pas, quickly brushing it aside as a fluke.

It had become obvious during their courtship that Doug and Sarah was a true combining of soul mates and Skye couldn't be more thrilled.

Rolling her eyes at the memories, She pushed at the arms of her chair so it would recline then grumbled as her thoughts turned to her own attempts at a relationship and Sarah's unfailing involvement.

Her sister's abilities had interrupted every intimate moment Skye had with a man. Ruining the evening when Sarah "appeared" in the fireplace or whatever flame was around while a boyfriend was making wonderful advances toward having sex.

There was no easy way to explain to your boyfriend why you didn't want the candles lit or a fire going when they thought it was a great way to get her relaxed, only to be uncomfortable because you could see your sister watching.

Of course, nothing ended the evening quicker than having him return with a bottle of wine only to see her arguing into the flames.

She just wished it wasn't so cold in Salem so they didn't have to think getting a fire going needed to be a part of the romance.

She didn't have an element power like her sister, a very rare skill in their world, but she was proud of her healing abilities even if she wasn't able to use them as much as she wanted.

If the public found out what she was able to do and started talking, the wrong people could hear and no one in her family needed rumors flying and the media spying on them.

Because there was always the chance of Skye being caught performing the simplest of healings without something to use as an excuse like her herbs, she had to be constantly aware of what she did and how she did it because, if she was discovered, men in white lab coats would be doing all sorts of weird things to them.

Of course, that wasn't as bad as their ancestors burning at the stake because of misplaced superstitions but Skye still didn't want to push it.

Finally relaxing, Skye let her thoughts drift to keep her mind off the evening and they turned to a childhood memory when her gift was still new.

She'd been trying to save a dog that had been hit by a truck and her powers hadn't been strong enough.

When Sarah saw her falter, her sister touched her shoulder to see if she was okay. Gasping, the older girl tumbled to her knees, her face draining of color.

It was Skye who pulled away from her sister's touch when her strength came rushing back.

At that point, they both realized Skye had depleted Sarah's strength through simple contact to replenish her own.

It took three days before her mother's gentle coaxing brought Skye from the seclusion of her bedroom. Even still, she wrapped her hands around her waist instead of taking her mother's proffered hand as they went to the breakfast nook where her father and sister sat waiting.

Her father calmly explained how various powers came with side effects. Some learned of those discoveries the hard way.

He had assured her no harm was done and Sarah smiled as she agreed, telling her she was perfectly fine.

Brushing tears from her face, Skye pushed those memories back and sighed. She preferred thinking of her aunt and sister's interference much more than those last memories of her parents.

Glancing at her father's wedding ring that she wore around her thumb, she smiled wistfully. "I miss you, Daddy."

Heaving reluctantly from the recliner, Skye headed for the shower, lit the candles sitting on the counter with her fingertips, and wished she had a bathtub to climb into to take away the frustration that simmered just below the surface.

Stepping into the hot stream, she let her head fall back and enjoyed the heated water splashing over her skin and down her back.

For years, she'd been waiting for someone to sweep her off her feet and bring about her darkest fantasies.

What she couldn't understand was how the average male thought about sex every minute and she had the hardest time getting them to *do* it.

Shivering under the hot water, Skye flashed back to her last date.

When asked to go to the movies, she'd thought it was the perfect opportunity to enjoy the evening without having her sister interfere. It was also the first time she discovered she had a dark side to her powers.

Skye ignored Sarah's warnings about her date's anger issues a friend had shared, dismissing them as being frivolous.

Refusing to hear anything else her sister had to say, Skye stormed out yelling that she wasn't going to be back until Sarah let her live her own life without interference.

When her date had nearly raped her after dinner because she refused to "do it" in his truck, her fear had turned to rage as he forced himself on her.

Pressing her hands pressed against his chest, she tried to shove him off.

When her hands began to tingle and his face went white as her anger grew, she became confused. Never having used her healing powers to inflict damage before, the heart attack she caused shook her worse than the attempted rape.

She vaguely remembered calling her sister in a state of panic as she drove his truck to the hospital and being overwhelmingly relieved when Sarah and Aunt Gladys were waiting in the emergency room when she arrived.

Refusing to touch or be touched, Skye had no idea what they told the doctor or how they managed to get her out of the hospital, all too grateful when she climbed into the back seat of her sister's car.

Heading home, she curled up into a ball on the seat and ignored any attempts made to get her to talk, crawling into bed when they got home.

When Skye finally came out of her room on the third day and entered the kitchen, there was silence as Sarah and Aunt Gladys sat around the counter, watching her.

Calmly explaining what happened as she made toast, she finished by saying she didn't ever wish to discuss that night again.

That was eight months ago and Skye hadn't gone out again.

At least, not until her family began their recent crusade to set her up with someone.

Gritting her teeth, she stepped out of the shower not feeling a whole lot better.

All she wanted was incredible sex with someone who wouldn't make her feel cheap afterwards.

Snorting, Skye admitting it didn't even have to be incredible. All she wanted was one time.

One time to be able have sex before learning something that would turn her off.

Because of her family's meddling, Skye had remained a virgin.

A very knowledgeable virgin because of all the books she read, but a virgin nevertheless.

At twenty-three, it had become embarrassing.

Pulling on flannel pajamas, Skye sighed as she wondered what to do.

* * *

Gladys peeked around the corner after Skye left, chuckling as she slipped into the vacated seat.

"Well, that didn't work out as planned."

Sarah looked at her aunt with a raised eyebrow.

"Ya think?" She arranged the brownies onto a plate. "I've never seen her so pissed."

"Who?"

Gladys and Sarah looked up guiltily as Doug sauntered in.

He stopped and looked from one to the other. "Uh oh."

"Nothing." Gladys said, not looking at him.

"Then why do you both look like you've just been caught doing something illegal?" He asked as he went behind the counter and grabbed one of the sweets, placing an arm around his wife's swollen belly.

Sarah laughed as she leaned into her husband's embrace and kissed him. "Not illegal."

Doug gave her that look that said he wasn't buying it before he took a bite of the brownie.

"Aunt Gladys set Skye up—"

"With your wife's knowledge." Gladys chimed in.

"On a speed dating . . . thing." Sarah finished.

Doug stopped the sweet in midflight of his next bite.

"Speed dating?" He stared between the two of them. "Speed dating?"

"Now Doug—"

He looked at his wife incredulously.

"You knowingly let your sister go to one of those? And didn't try to stop this plan of hers?" He said as he pointed to her aunt.

"Hey." Gladys said in affront.

"I just thought that if she had choices . . ." Sarah blushed and let the sentence die.

Popping the rest of the brownie into his mouth, he wiped his hands.

"Bet she loves the two of you lots now, huh?" He threw over his shoulder as he made his exit.

"Pffft." Gladys made a face. "What does he know?"

"Enough. More than us." Sarah pushed the list towards her aunt. "The kind of men she met caused her to write this."

"'Speak English'. 'Be financially secure.'" Gladys muttered through the rest of them. "What is this?"

"That is her list of common sense things she looks for in a man."

Gladys looked from the list to Sarah and back again, getting that look in her eyes.

Sarah shook her head and protected her belly. "No. Whatever it is that you are thinking, I say no."

"You say Skye wrote this, right?"

Not even waiting for a reply, Gladys held the paper in her hand and walked away, talking to herself.

Sarah rushed around the counter and stepped in front of her aunt, blocking her exit.

"No." she repeated to her aunt.

The older woman looked up, confused. "No what, m'dear?"

Sarah tried to grab the list from her hand, but Gladys was faster.

"I don't know, but I do know that look in your eyes and you can't do whatever *it* is. Give Skye a chance to get over this latest disaster before trying something else. Please." Sarah begged.

Gladys' look of determination melted under her niece's pleading look.

Shoulders drooping, she sighed. "Alright, we'll give her some time."

"Thank you." Sarah sighed in relief.

Gladys' determined look resurfaced. "But this piece of paper is going to give me a clue as to what to do next. When I come up with something, I will let you know and this time we'll work out *all* the kinks."

Sarah reluctantly agreed. "As long as we both agree on when the time is right."

"I will let you know." Gladys replied with a thoughtful expression on her face.

Sarah watched her aunt nod emphatically then huff and walk off, not seeing the gleam in the woman's eye.

Shaking her head, she sighed, knowing the knot in her stomach wasn't from the child lying sleepily inside.

*   *   *

Skye looked up from the erotic novel she was reading when she heard a meowing from outside and groaned.

Getting up, she muttered the same litany she always did when this happened.

"I don't understand why Miss Kitty has to howl at my door so she can come in instead of going upstairs."

Opening the sliding glass door, she waited for the cat to race in from the cold.

When Miss Kitty didn't do as expected, she looked outside and saw her sitting a couple yards away in the snow.

Skye slid the door closed and muttered louder. "Stupid cat."

Stomping away only to sit down just as the meowing resumed, she growled in annoyance. "Damn pest."

Trying to ignore the cat was impossible with the beast's persistent meowing, so she went back to the door and slid it open, once again without the appearance of Miss Kitty.

She looked outside and saw her in the same spot.

"Come on, Miss Kitty. It's a damn basement, yanno? Heated, but still a basement." She growled. "Get in here before I freeze to death."

The cat meowed.

"Don't just sit out there—move it!"

The cat stood and took a hesitant step forward, glanced towards the second story, looked back at Skye, then sat down to continue to howl.

"What the hell?"

When Skye stepped outside, the cat turned, took a few more steps, peeked over its shoulder, and waited.

"You have *got* to be kidding me."

Thankful for thick wool socks, she wiggled her feet into her slippers as she tucked her still damp hair into the ugly knit hat her aunt had made from the peg next to the door then went after Miss Kitty.

Tightening her robe and swearing in Gaelic so it didn't sound as bad, Skye cautiously approached the cat, following the path she'd dug out early to get from her room to the hot house her herbs were stored in.

Half way there, she stumbled as her vision suddenly went blurry.

"*Faigh muin*, it's cold out here. Too cold to even see!"

Snatching Miss Kitty up, Skye stumbled, her ears ringing.

Shaking her head to clear it, she hurried back to the house.

Before she got to the opened door there was a strange sound in the distance, like something crashing through the brush. Miss Kitty jumped out of her arms and into her room as Skye swung around, but her peripheral vision blackened and the noise mixed with the ringing.

Her eyes wouldn't stay focused and her stomach heaved as she started falling, reality hitting her.

$

Chapter Two

"Aunt Gladys!" Skye gasped as she fell to her hands and knees, the wind knocked out of her.

Remaining still until the nausea and ringing in her ears faded away, Skye began devising ways on how she was going to get even with her aunt for utilizing whatever spell she'd cast.

Carefully glancing up after the queasiness eased, she abruptly sat up in shock as she looked at the surrounding trees and brush lightly covered with frost.

This looked more like a forest than her backyard.

Skye slowly eased onto her haunches to stand, biting back the bile the motion caused as she turned slowly, taking in the tree as well as the circle of flowers and mushrooms that surrounded her. Easing her back against the trunk, she waited for her equilibrium to return fully and took stock of her surroundings, as difficult as that was in the dim lighting.

"I k-know you have some-something to do with this Aunt Glad-d-dys." She stuttered through her chattering teeth as the cold seeped into her bones.

Clenching her teeth, Skye focused on a familiar sound of something running through the forest, only this time it sounded closer.

Too close.

Trying to see through the dimness in front of her as she clutched the robe tighter, she tried to breathe through her growing fear. She furtively glanced around and up, trying to find a place to hide.

The sound grew increasingly louder. Something was running through the forest and heading rapidly towards her.

Shit. Shit. Shit.

Racking her brain for a spell, even though that was just as terrifying, but not nearly as much as whatever it was that headed her way—and fast.

Too late.

Crashing through the brush in front of her was a large cat with foam dripping from its mouth.

A cougar!

Not Miss Kitty, not Miss Kitty!

"Leave, leave, leave!" She screamed as it ran right for her.

Leaves tumbled from above and Skye whimpered. "Leave, not leafs!"

She did what she scorned every girl for doing in a horror movie; she froze.

Eyes wide with horror, Skye watched it gather momentum, its gaze fixed on her.

A scream lodged in her throat as it jumped in the air, claws extended.

Stumbling back, Skye fell against the tree, fear clogging her throat and denying her room for thought.

A blur came from her right, slamming into the cougar.

The cold forgotten, Skye looked as the two animals rolled, snarls and sickening crunching sounds filling her ears.

"Oh, God. Oh, God. Oh, God." She whispered repeatedly as she watched in horrified fascination.

It was over almost as fast as it began. The cat lay lifeless on its back, the jaws of a massive dog clamped around its bloodied throat.

Disgusted by the sight, Skye still couldn't tear her eyes away. She gasped for air as soon as she realized she had been holding her breath, one hand clutching the tree she was leaning against, the other at her throat.

Another growl had her head snapping around and pressing back against the trunk.

There, crouched to spring, was another huge dog with a man on horseback behind it.

Then her peripheral vision caught more movement to her right and she slowly looked, terrified to take her eyes off the beast and man in front of her.

Skye whimpered as another man on horseback stood where the animal that saved her from death had come from.

Her mind was trying hard to sort through her fear and comprehend what she was seeing.

They looked like they had come from a medieval movie about berserkers as hair streamed in tangles past their shoulders, matted beards covered their faces, and grime coated their clothes and skin.

"Co thusa?"

Swinging her head around when she heard the first man speak, Skye was too afraid to comprehend what was going on so she just stared; her eyes riveted on the dog as it growled menacingly.

Facts rapidly fired through her brain.

Big men.

Big dirty men in leather pants with long gross hair.

Big dirty men on large horses with huge hairy dogs that killed a cougar.

She did what she should have done as soon as she heard the noises from the forest; she ran.

Twisting, she took off around the tree opposite from the man on her right and away from the beasts to her left, running as fast as the darkness and her slippered feet would allow.

She ducked branches and skirted bushes too large to leap over as the pounding of hooves grew closer.

Too afraid to look, she kept running, her chest heaving with adrenaline and fear.

Skye could feel the horse's breath as it came alongside her, its smell invading her nostrils and she darted to the left.

Oh, shit. She thought, just before a monstrous weight slammed her into a frozen puddle, her breath forced from her lungs by the figure on top of her.

She struggled, but it didn't take her long to figure out she wasn't doing much of anything but getting a mouthful of icy mud as she labored to breathe, so she stopped.

"I can't breathe." She rasped when he didn't move.

He lifted himself off her, grabbed a hold of her robe by the neck and hauled her up.

He stared at her hard. "Ye be English."

Even though it wasn't a question, she nodded, spitting out the mud caking her chattering teeth as she wiped the grime from her eyes, wondering where the hell she was and how she was going to get out of this.

"What be yer name?"

21

"S-s-Skye. My n-n-name is-s-s Skye." She rasped, hacking until she could spit out the mud in her throat.

He eyed her with distaste before hauling her bruised body over to his horse and started pulling rope from a sack.

When she saw his intent, she forgot about the fact that her left foot was missing a slipper and tried to break free, causing him to raise an eyebrow at the futility of her attempt.

Gritting her teeth, she watched in silence as he bound her hands together, wincing when they cut into her skin, but refusing to make a sound.

Stiffening to control the shivers racking her body, she took in the long black hair braided on each side of his temple falling in matted waves past his broad shoulders. The heavy beard covered most of his shadowed face but she could sense the anger simmering in him. Not used to having to look up so much to a man because of her height and the heels she normally wore, she was shocked at his build. Even his loose sleeves didn't hide his massive arms.

She watched as he climbed onto his horse taking in the way his leg muscles bunched under his pants.

Steroids. Had to be. No way could a man have such a body without them.

She looked away just before he reached down and hauled her up and over his lap as if she were nothing but a grain of sand. Before she could voice her distress, he pushed down on her back to keep her in place as he turned the horse and headed back.

Moments later, Skye found herself stewing in silence as she stood next to the huge horse testing the rope that went from her wrists to the beast's saddle.

Thankful the leaves had stopped falling, she concentrated hard on stopping the tremors that racked her body as the men made a pyre around the cougar. When it began to burn on its own, they constructed a litter for the injured dog, attaching it to the other man's horse when done.

Amazed at the size of the two men as they worked in silence, she wondering at their appearance, trying to figure out who they were and where she was.

They didn't wear normal jeans and shirts and there wasn't a button or zipper on either of them—at least from what she could see under the grime.

She remembered the smell of leather as her face swung uncomfortably over the side of the horse next to the man's leg. If it weren't for the shorter blond locks that barely touched the other man's shoulders, she wouldn't have been able to tell them apart.

Wrinkling her nose at the smell the fire put off, Skye once again focused on loosening her bonds.

When the blaze had destroyed the cat, they buried the remains and turned towards her. Fear caused her throat to clog as she backed into the stallion when the two monstrous men eyed her, causing the beast to turn its head and nip at her.

Before she could gather her wits, her kidnapper hauled her once more over his lap.

An hour later, they broke out of the forest into a cloudy day.

Shaking her head in confusion, Skye thought on how only an hour or so ago it had been late evening.

It was too soon to be seeing the sun now.

What she did know was that her body ached from the unpleasant position and the man wouldn't let her move to get comfortable, not caring that his hard thighs and rigid knees were digging into her ribcage to the point of constant pain.

Pushing herself up, she tried to get her bearings, but a hand pressed her back down, leaving her with only images of barren trees and brown hills dotted with patches of snow.

The sun was high in the overcast sky before they stopped.

Her captor used her robe to haul Skye off the horse and she stumbled, falling to her knees because she had no feeling in her legs after the hours of cold and forced into an awkward position during the ride.

Noticing she'd lost her other slipper, Skye glared up at the man as he dismounted, but he ignored her to check on the wounded dog.

Scratchy from the dried mud that made her itch in places she'd rather not be thinking of, she concentrated once again on loosening the rope that bound her hands together, freezing as the second dog approached her cautiously.

Towering over her, it growled low in its throat just before it sniffed her robe. It was like a huge hairy greyhound, only she never thought of greyhounds looking so ferocious. When it was finished smelling her, it went over to the litter where the men were tending to the other dog.

Since they continued to ignore her and spoke too low for her to hear, Skye looked around hoping to find a way to escape but they were in a large clearing. She didn't think she'd be able to find a place to hide before they noticed her gone and came after her. Of course, she couldn't know that for sure unless she tried. Placing her hands on her legs she concentrated, willing blood back into all her limbs.

Moments later, she was easing herself carefully to her feet when she noticed a body in front of her. Heart threatening to break free from her chest, she tilted her head, not happy that she had to, to look at the man who captured her.

She came to her full height and stared at him, trying to hide how his stature and strength intimidated her.

In the light of day, she couldn't help but notice his eyes. They were the purest blue she'd ever seen, ringed in a deeper blue, almost black.

Damn, he was big.

He stood there with his arms crossed and it angered her that he could so effortlessly frighten her. A shirt of some kind under his thick cloak barely concealed just how well built he was. Inwardly, she realized she was staring at him and it probably wasn't a good thing, but she couldn't help it.

Then it hit her; he had spoken in Gaelic earlier! What had he said? She couldn't remember.

She stood there shivering, refusing to look away or look as pitiful as she felt.

He returned her gaze, except he took in her appearance with a look of disgust.

"Ye be the filthiest lad I have ever deemed to look at." His lip curled. "An ye stink."

Skye glared, not knowing if she was more furious at being called a boy or filthy when it was his fault she was caked in dried mud, and it wasn't her fault she wasn't large chested.

Crossing her arms as well, she sneered. "Have you smelt yourself lately?"

That got a surprised look, but before he could respond, a yelp from the litter drew his attention, a worried look flashed over his features before disappearing as he turned back to warn her.

"Runnin be useless. Twilna do anythin but cause me to punish ye harshly."

She watched him walk away until a soft whimper brought her attention to the injured hound and she could not help but frown in sympathy.

That dog had saved her life. It may have been unintentional, but it remained a fact.

When the men settled to eat without offering her anything, Skye eased her way to the wounded dog.

Knowing the two men watched, she knelt before it, whispering soft words of assurance even as it growled weakly at her.

Blood matted so much of the fur, she couldn't tell where the wounds were.

"I know, baby." She cooed as she felt the warmth in her hands when her powers gathered strength.

Cold and weakened from the day's events, as well as the recent use of her powers to get her blood circulation going, Skye still knew she had to do something for this poor animal that had saved her life. She wouldn't do anything noticeable just enough to make sure it would survive.

Placing the back of her hand in front of its nose, she allowed it to sniff her, hoping its animal senses would pick up her abilities and understand she was here to help, not harm.

The growling stopped and Skye sighed in relief knowing the hard part was about to begin.

With her hands tightly bound, she could just barely close one hand in a loose fist so she could place the fingertips of her other hand on the dog's skin.

Concentrating, she focused her energy inwards.

"What be the lad doin, Aiden?

"I doona ken." Scratching the irritating beard, he glowered. "But he harms me wee Seelie an he won't be seein the end of this day."

"Mayhap he be prayin the way his head be bowed over her?"

"Damn Christians." Aiden replied in a distracted voice, his eyes never leaving the boy who showed him no fear.

They watched the stranger for a moment, absently biting the salted dried meat.

"I canna put me finger on it Collin, but there be somethin about the lad . . ." Aiden sighed in frustration. "I doona ken it."

"Twould be wise to keep an eye on him, to be sure." Collin placed a hand on his friend's shoulder. "Ye ken Seelie won't last the journey home?"

When there was no reply, Collin nodded and left the man to his thoughts.

Skye removed her shaking hand.

"I don't know how you survived this long, little girl. There was more damage than I thought." She shook her head in amazement as she spoke quietly. "But I got the worst of it."

She was cold and her body was quivering with the energy she spent. Unable to hold herself up any more, she sunk to the ground, curling into a ball, trying to heat her worn out body.

Aiden found her that way when he came to harness the litter. What gave him pause was seeing Seelie licking the lad's bound hands.

"Would ye look at that?" Collin whispered in awe as he drew his horse alongside.

Aiden clenched his teeth and hauled the boy to his feet, shaking him. "Wake up, ye lazy welp."

Skye fell as soon as he let go of her. On hands and knees, she lifted her head and glared at the man. "Dammit, give me a second, will you?"

"Ye have until we get this hooked, no more, ye ken?"

Skye scrunched up her face, trying to follow along with the heavy accent.

He crouched beside her and pulled her head back by the knit cap, tugging her hair with it. "Ye ken?"

"Yes, dammit, 'I ken'."

Aiden gave his friend a sour look when he chuckled.

By the time they had the litter attached to the other man's horse, Skye was barely able to stand on her feet.

Her throat hurt and her voice was horse from swallowing the grit in her mouth and a lack of water to rinse the sand out put her in a foul mood, but she'd be damned if she showed any more weakness to these men.

Aiden came alongside and patted behind him. "Get on back. Ye smell too foul to be in front."

Feeling the grit crunch when she clenched her teeth, Skye patiently held up her bound hands.

"And how do you propose I do that?" She croaked.

Too swift for Skye to step back, Aiden leaned down, grabbed her upper arm and then hauled her up behind him.

She would have shrieked in surprise but it came out a croak and then she was too busy grabbing his cloak to keep from falling when the horse took off.

Scared of what could happen in her condition if she fell asleep while touching him, Skye struggled to remain erect but was exhausted and found herself, more than once, leaning into his broad back, only the tickle of his matted hair on her nose brought her alert.

Unable to stop her thoughts about her captors, she wondered at the brute strength they seemed to wield with ease. Everything about them exuded power and control, from their height which towered almost a foot over Skye's five foot eight frame to their body mass, which was pure muscle from head to foot and everywhere in between.

She was thankful that the one she was riding with was big enough to block most of the wind and kept her slightly warm. From his neck down, he had the body of a god. From the neck up, he looked wild, untamed, fierce—and ugly . . . except for his eyes, they were breathtaking.

She should be afraid of him, but the way he treated the injured dog made him seem more human and less god-like.

Skye's stomach growled and she wondered how long it had been since she'd eaten. Because she thought she was meeting her aunt for dinner and not going to a speed dating event, she hadn't worried about food, then she'd became too disgusted to even think about eating.

Looking around, she tried to forget about her angry stomach as she worked on figuring out where she was.

From their language, she figured Scotland. Probably the backwoods because they hadn't passed any towns. They were scruffy, had bows and arrows, and that thing that kept hitting her thigh when she was lying across his lap earlier was probably some kind of holster for a gun.

Hunting season in the backwoods of Scotland.

Just great.

The language they spoke wasn't the Gaelic she knew but it was close enough that if she concentrated she could figure most of it out, like when they were discussing if they should stop for the night, their main concern on if Seelie, the wounded dog, could make it.

Her stomach growled again and she winced. A moment later, she felt him poke her and she looked up to see something in his hand.

"Eat." He commanded.

29

Too hungry to be offended by his rudeness, she took the piece of dried meat and forced herself to chew slow, not knowing when she would eat next.

Skye told herself that as soon as they stopped, they would probably start a fire and then she would have a chance to get a hold of her sister to get her out of there.

Then, by damn, she was going to have a one-sided conversation with her family.

No more of this trying to set her up with someone because, obviously, Aunt Gladys had lost her marbles sending her here. She knew it was her aunt, because Miss Kitty only listened to Aunt Gladys and the cat only used Skye or Sarah when she deemed them worthy, like letting her in from the cold.

Finishing the meat, Skye was jerked out of her thoughts as they came to a halt.

Looking around, she watched the second man walk behind his horse and crouch by the litter, checking the dog.

"How be she?" The man in front of her asked in Gaelic.

Collin looked up. "I think the wee lass will make it." He stated with surprise written all over his face.

Skye relaxed slightly. She'd been worried she didn't have enough strength to do all that was needed to make sure the dog would live.

The other man looked around. "So, do we make it home or stop at the auld shepherds place?"

"Tis gonna rain."

"Aye."

"We could make it no long after night fall."

The other man grinned. "We would be wet but we would be home in a warm bed."

"Cover her up an let us get. I be tired, an the thought of a night with the smell comin from the lad isna apealin."

It wasn't until they were on their way that Skye figured out what he'd said and snorted.

CHAPTER THREE

Skye collapsed against her captor's back.

She couldn't help it. Worn out, freezing, and soaked to the skin from the chilly rain that had started a couple hours ago, her body finally shut down.

Aiden felt the lad fall against him and he twisted around carefully to keep him from falling.

He should have given the boy some kind of cover but he didn't know who the lad was or where he came from and too many years of battle had taught him to err on the side of caution.

Concern was the last thing he would show the intruder.

They were close to their destination. It was already dark as the rain began to fall and would be pitch black when they reached the castle gates but he was tired of being away and looked forward to the comfort of his own hearth.

Aiden's thoughts centered on his home and not some small campfire out on the march or in a field surrounded by men who didn't know there was better than the present.

He was tired of war and the worthless spilling of blood.

Tired of the nobility's failure to unite to strengthen Scotland for all, instead of the individual.

He, Collin, and their men, had just returned from the brutal battle in Edinburgh where they battled alongside Robert Stewart against imprisonment of the young Duke of Rothesay. A man whose actions threatened to destroy the very aristocracy Aiden was weary of.

All he'd wanted was to be left alone, laird of his own keep. Concerned with nothing but the improvement of his people and the land they lived on.

Not even given a moment to remove the grime from his body or the hair from his face, his people had begged him to hunt down and kill the cougar that was destroying their cattle and had killed the last man sent after it the previous night.

When Collin, his longtime friend and younger sister's husband, had seen Aiden readying himself to do as his people asked, he had kissed his pregnant wife and saddled a new horse.

Now he was returning to his castle.

He should be happy.

Instead, he was concerned.

He knew that there was alarm over recent fear of the English crossing their boarders and aligning with Reivers to steal land and slay those they couldn't make into slaves.

Now, here was this English boy caught just inside his property.

He was going to get answers before he would be able to rest. Mayhap they should have stopped for the night at the old hut. He sighed, knowing Collin wished to return to his family as much as he did.

* * *

She was dreaming about a chant to get her home, confused by the water that seemed a part of it.

Then she was falling again.

"No!" She cried out hoarsely, struggling to reach the surface.

Arms held her tight as she fought with all her strength, her bound hands unable to break free against the grip on her.

"Stop!" Came a vaguely familiar voice, stern in its demand.

Skye stilled in shock before sagging in relief as she realized it was pouring rain and she'd only been hauled off the horse's back and hadn't actually cast a spell sending her to the bottom of the ocean.

A small amount of light came from somewhere behind her, making it difficult for her clouded mind to make out details so when he grabbed one of her fists and felt something cold slice between her wrists she stiffened even as her body shivered from the god-awful cold.

Gritting her teeth, she looked up at him, the heavy downpour causing rivulets of water to course from her cap down her face.

Aiden stared down at the barely illuminated face in front of him, eyes narrowed as something tickled his brain.

Hauling the lad up the stone stairway by the arm, he ignored the cries of protest and dragged the boy inside where torches lit the entryway.

Ignoring his mother and sister's welcome, he glowered at the person before him.

"What?" Skye croaked in frustration.

She cringed when his meaty hand reached out, yanking off her cap.

There were gasps and then silence as her hair unwound from its twist in thick clumps.

"Yer a lass." Aiden accused.

"Well, duh."

Realizing this was not the appropriate time to get snide, Skye snapped her mouth shut feeling her teeth grind against sand.

Aiden shook his head and walked around her, poking here and there. When he returned to stand in front of her and poked a breast, her hand lashed out to slap him but his reflexes proved faster than hers.

As he caught her wrist, Skye glared up at him.

"You are an ass." She spit out, enunciating each word as if she was talking to a simpleton.

When she made to go on, he leaned into her space and whispered fiercely. "Hold yer tongue!"

Straightening himself, he called out to one of his men and when approached, he pushed her into his arms.

"I want her washed, presentable, an before me in one hour." He demanded as he stormed off, his family following.

Led to a place resembling a kitchen that would have fit in perfectly in medieval times shocked Skye and she stumbled to a stop.

She didn't remember seeing where they were before they got to wherever it was they were because of the night rain and she'd been sleeping, but the things she saw now was cause for concern.

She began to tick off clues.

Torches, tapestries, the gowns the women were wearing, the kilts and trousers the men wore.

"No way." She remarked.

Looking at the woman gathered, Skye noted some were watching her curiously as they chopped, kneaded bread, or stirred pots hanging over fires. Two were filling a large metal cauldron in the center of the large room while an older woman eyed her with intent as she rolled up her sleeves.

Her eyes widened in disbelief.

"No . . . way."

*   *   *

An hour later, with her body scrubbed raw, hair washed three times and braided, a dress too short and tight covering her, Skye was led on bare feet into a large hall by the same man who had promptly left her with those evil woman who gave no pause to the humiliation they put her through.

She felt defeated, mortified, and small in a world she had no knowledge of but she walked with her head up, willing her tired limbs to keep going. Her only sign of unease was how she played with the ring on her thumb.

Led through the great hall with over a dozen men standing on either side to allow her to pass through, Skye watched them watching her and worked hard at not biting her lower lip, trying instead to keep her focus on the man who seemed to dwarf everyone around them even as he sat in a larger wooden chair.

He wore a green, red, and yellow plaid kilt that showed off muscular legs and a loose, cream-colored shirt covered his chest that did nothing to hide its broad expanse. A wide belt exemplified a lean waist and she licked her lips nervously at the male specimen in front of her.

Embarrassed that her mind was drifting and not wanting to see that he had caught her staring at him, she glanced at the roaring fire and thought of her sister.

So close.

She glanced at the men between her and the fire.

So far away.

"What be yer name?"

Skye frowned at the sound of his voice and turned back to the man before her.

Looking into his face, she took in the gleaming black hair that flowed past broad shoulders as braids on either side of his temple kept it from his piercing blue gaze.

It was a strong face. A face full of angles that had her swallowing hard and thinking wicked thoughts she had no right to think of.

Then she frowned and looked closer.

It was him! The same brutish thug who'd captured her and made her suffer.

His hair now washed and combed and the beard removed but his eyes where the same vivid blue ringed in a deeper color and slanted with determination.

Damn, he was beautiful.

The square jaw, high cheekbones and straight nose had her staring again.

"What be yer name?" He repeated slowly, demanding an immediate answer.

"I already told you it was Skye."

"What kind of name be 'Skye'?"

"Something about being born outdoors on a bright clear day and all that. I suppose it inspired my mother to give me such a name." She clamped her mouth shut, knowing she'd been blabbering nervously.

"Where be yer clan?"

That made Skye pause for a moment.

She shook her head. "I don't know."

"How can ye no ken?"

"I'm not sure."

"Ye dinna ken the question?"

"No. Yes. I just don't know how to answer the question."

"What be yer clan name, lass?"

"Clan name?"

"Yes." An older woman stepped around a group to her right and walked up to her, placing a comforting hand on her arm. "Your surname, love. What is it?"

Skye looked at the small woman who was an exact replica of the man in front of her, only smaller, and was surprised at the perfect English accent spoken with a gentle squeeze of encouragement on her arm.

She nodded her understanding and looked back at the man. "Bennett."

"Skye Bennett?"

"Yes."

"What where ye doin in the forest, Skye Bennett?"

She looked around at the men gathered, a very scary lot, and wondered if they burned witches at the stake. Many excuses came to mind, but she never got away with lying.

"I can't answer that."

"Ye canna? Or ye wilna?"

Swallowing hard, she straightened her spine when her body trembled, surprisingly thankful for the comforting feel of the woman's hand on her arm.

"I am not sure which works best in this situation, so either or, it doesn't matter." She turned red when her stomach chose that moment to rumble its loudest but she didn't waver.

Much.

She wasn't feeling well either.

The woman patted her arm before walking over to stand next to the man, speaking softly to him.

Skye couldn't hear the words but it was apparent he didn't agree with whatever she'd said because the woman laid her hand on his arm as she made one last comment, squeezed his hand, and walked away. She smiled encouragingly as she passed Skye.

"What where ye doin passin yerself off as a lad?"

Sighing, she locked her knees and squared her shoulders. "I did not pass myself off as a man. It was an assumption on your part."

His eyes narrowed. "Ye covered yer hair an wore trews under yer cloak."

Her vision blurred and she shook her head to clear it. "So? I didn't dress like that to look like a boy." She could hear her voice break even as it began to sound far away. This wasn't good. "I was just trying to be warm."

Things began to spin and she stumbled. Strong hands held her, and she tried to focus on the face but blackness overtook her.

Aiden looked at the woman before him and pondered a hundred different things at once. Her beauty, the proud way she held a body too voluptuous for a man's piece of mind—wondering how he missed that—the valiant attempt to hide her exhaustion, and the way her eyes skittered when she spoke.

The last, and the fear in her voice when answering only certain questions, held his attention most.

Aiden frowned at her behavior. He watched as she shook her head as her face began losing color.

He pushed from his chair and took the few steps to her side, catching her as she collapsed.

As he carried her away, one of the men called out, "It may be a ruse, Laird Aiden."

"Tis no like the lass can get far." He threw over his shoulder without breaking stride.

Chapter Four

Skye woke up disorientated. Blinking, she frowned at her surroundings, trying to bring the unfamiliar room into focus.

It took her a moment before she remembered everything that happened since she found herself in the forest.

"This cannot be real." Groaning she pulled the covers over her head. "Maybe it's a medieval fair type thingy."

She waited a moment then peeked over the covers. "This so cannot be happening."

Swinging her feet off the bed, she tested her balance and found that she felt a lot better. Looking down at the dress she still wore, she looked at the somewhat coarse material and saw the hand stitching.

"Okaay. So . . ." She let the word trail as she assessed her surroundings.

A tapestry hung over a tall narrow window that had no glass, furs covered the floor and a candlestick with a pewter holder sat on the bedside table.

"My first question would be; '*When* am I?'"

A knock sounded at the door. Skye's gaze swung up as the handle turned and slowly opened enough for a girl to peek inside.

"Ah." She saw Skye standing and swung the door wide. "*Tha i 'na dùisg.*"

With an eyebrow raised, Skye watched as the girl, advanced in pregnancy, closed the door behind her and spoke slowly in English.

"'Tis sorry I be, but I see ye be awake an thought we could visit a spell."

Skye cocked her head, trying to follow the girl as she talked. When she understood the gist of the words, she smiled and nodded.

The girl let out a sigh of relief before waddling over to a chair and eased herself into it.

Sighing again once she was comfortable, she smiled at Skye's curious look.

"I be Anna, Aiden's sister an Collin's wife." She smiled and rubbed her stomach. "An this little one will be our first bairn."

Skye smiled in return and sat on the edge of the bed. "I'm Skye."

"Aye, that I heard. Me brother said he caught ye sneakin around the woods."

Before Skye could take affront to the accusation, Anna held up her hand.

"Doona worry yerself, me mother doesna ken ye to be of a bad sort. 'Sides, ye dunno have the look about ye."

Skye laughed. "Thank ye—you. I am going to take that as a compliment."

The door opened and another girl came in bearing a tray loaded with food. Her hair was kept under a bonnet and most of her gown was covered with a white apron.

"I hope ye dunno mind, but I be hungry an thought ye wouldna bother breakin yer fast with me?" She winced before grinning at Skye. "Och, me poor feet. I ken they have to be there since they ache sorely, but I canna see them."

"Maybe I can help?"

"Ah, lass, there beint anythin ye can do for me, tis just the way of thins, ye ken."

Skye smiled and grabbed a pillow to place over her lap before sitting at the girl's feet.

Looking up, Skye smiled and waited.

Anna sighed, toed off her slipper, and let Skye look at her feet.

"Swollen." Skye stated in sympathy.

"Aye, an the pressure be a terrible feelin too."

"A massage would help get the circulation going." Skye began to massage the girl's bloated feet and ankles, allowing enough of her healing powers to help.

Knowing Anna was a little embarrassed, Skye kept the conversation running smoothly. They ate and chatted about Anna's mother being English and teaching them her native language as well as how Aiden became Laird when their father had been killed in battle before discussing Anna's concerns over her pregnancy.

Skye shared how her own sister was pregnant and how excited she was to be an aunt.

"Is she skeert?"

"Skeert? Scared? Why?"

"Why? Because of the complications that arise."

"Ahhh." Skye nodded her understanding. "Yes, there could be that. But Sarah refuses to spend her pregnancy worrying over what might or might not happen."

"Sounds like a smart women, yer sister."

The door opened and Aiden entered, making the small room feel even tinier with his size.

He looked at the tray and then his sister.

"*Dè tha thu a dèanamh?*"

Anna smiled up at her brother, unruffled that he was questioning what she was doing, and gave her reply in English.

"I be enjoyin a nice speak with our guest."

Aiden finally looked at Skye before returning his gaze back to Anna, also speaking so Skye could understand. "Ye need to be restin, sister."

"I *am* restin, brother."

Skye stiffened and stopped rubbing Anna's feet when Aiden entered the bedroom.

Gently easing the girl's feet from her lap, she scooted up and sat on the bed, doing her best to keep her eyes off him.

Skye was embarrassed that she had fainted and scared because he wanted answers she couldn't give.

When he was finally able to escort his sister out, demanding she return to bed, Skye became nervous when he turned his attention back to her.

Acutely aware she was sitting on a bed, she hurried to her feet, realizing her reaction brought his attention to the same fact.

Gritting her teeth as he took in her appearance, she suddenly thought of how her hair must look and forced herself not to smooth the tousled curls, hating the flush that stole up her neck to her cheeks

When she backed up, he frowned before speaking. "The council has questions that ye will answer."

"I don't know what answers I can give that would help."

"We shall see. Make yerself presentable an I will send someone to fetch ye."

Too soon, Skye found herself back in the large room. The flames in the fireplace teasing her while she stood in the middle of a group of now seated men.

This time, all of them asked her questions with Aiden translating.

Her inability to satisfy them caused their anger to rise.

She told them she was born and raised in Salem—it being in Massachusetts was not something she cared to add. That she was twenty-three and no; she was not married. Her parents had died when she was young and an aunt raised her and her older sister.

However, the questions she would not answer riled them.

"Why where ye found near the border on MacGregor land?" They asked for the umpteenth time.

Before she could give the same answer, a man entered and approached Aiden whispering in his ear.

He pushed away from the long table and stood. "We must stop here an continue later."

He repeated it in Gaelic for the council, further explaining that raiders had been sighted close to the outer gates. He turned his attention back to Skye and frowned at her.

"When we begin this again, ye need to ken the importance of yer answers, or the lack thereof."

Skye was tired and her brain hurt from the unaccustomed worrying over the repercussions of what she could or couldn't say.

In the end, all she'd really done was make them believe she was an enemy with something to hide.

The crackling of the fire drew her attention as the council disassembled. She went over and stared into it.

"Sarah?" She whispered tiredly. "C'mon Sarah, hear me."

Grabbed from behind and pulled away, Skye lost her balance as she was twirled around.

"To the doogun with ye."

Too afraid to protest, she still dragged her feet as panic rose in her.

Dungeon? This was not going be good.

The man took her around the corner to a dark alcove. It smelled of waste as he led her to the end, opened a door made of bars, and tossed her inside.

"Ye won't be makin an escape from here."

Too freaked out to utter anything more than a squeak, she stared as the bars shut and locked before the man ambled off, placing the key on a hook by an empty sconce.

With only the dim light from the fireplace glowing from around the corner, there was barely enough for her to see.

As her eyes adjusted, she saw the iron cuffs hanging from the walls across from her about eight feet away with something looking like a cot near the far left corner.

Squinting, she went over for a closer look but half way there, she heard the clitter clatter of rats scurrying about and she hurried back to the bars.

"I hate rats. I hate rats. I *hate* rats!" Skye muttered as she shuddered in disgust.

Pressing her back against the bars, she stared into the dim room barely bigger than a small storage space, hoping this nightmare would end soon.

A long time later, she heard a whine from the hallway behind her.

Heart pounding as she swung around, Skye relaxed when she saw Seelie, the injured dog, limping towards her with a chewed off rope around her neck.

Crouching down, she encouraged the dog to come near, her hand stretched through the bars.

"Come here, baby girl."

It seemed to take forever for the hound to reach her as Seelie sank to her belly and crawled until her head just reached Skye's fingertips before collapsing to her side, exhausted.

"Ah, *bein tu go.* Yes, you poor, poor, baby girl." Skye crooned, patting her head with her fingertips, using soothing endearments. "*Truagh leanabh.*"

In moments, Skye forgot about the rats as her senses began to tingle.

Shifting her body so her shoulder could get through the bars, Skye laid her fingers on the hound's head.

Centering herself, she concentrated.

"Oh, no." A tear slipped down her cheek as she realized rabies was forming in the animal's brain.

Determined not to let that happen, Skye gritted her teeth and nudged the animal.

"I need you closer, Seelie. Please, just a little more."

The dog whined weakly but didn't budge.

Tears flowing freely, Skye kept badgering her to move.

Hearing another noise, Skye started.

Looking up in surprise, she saw the male dog stepping around the corner and held her breath as he cautiously approached, sniffing and growling low.

Reaching them, the huge animal sniffed at the prone dog and whined. Seelie opened an eye and whimpered in return.

"Listen." Skye whispered in Gaelic to the male as she lifted a hand towards him, wincing when it growled at her but determined to try anything she could. "I need to reach Seelie. You need to help."

Skye let him sniff her, praying the dog's sixth sense could sense her abilities like Seelie had before.

*   *   *

"What do we have here?"

Skye sleepily turned her head from her sitting position against the bars to see Collin approaching with torch in hand. He was also clean-shaven and looked very handsome with the dirt washed from him.

She looked at the two dogs on the outside of the cage, her hand rested on the male's head, absently smoothing over the rough curls while Seelie lay in a healing sleep.

"It's a tea party, can't you tell?" She answered through a yawn.

Collin stopped in his tracks and stared at her in shock. It took a moment to realize that, although she'd spoken in English, he had not.

She dropped her head in self-disgust and defeat.

"Alright, lass, ye be needin to explain yerself quick."

She shook her head. "I can't. Nothing I say will make sense and if it does, my life will be over."

He placed the torch he was holding in the sconce then approached the bars menacingly.

"Ye be a spy?"

Looking him in the eye, she gave a halfhearted smile.

"No spy here. I just happen to know Gaelic." Shaking her head, she continued. "As long as you speak slowly because what I understand doesn't seem to be the same dialect as yours."

He stared at her a long time as if trying to figure something out, frowned, glanced over his shoulder, and then returned to face her.

"I happen to believe ye, lass."

"You do?" Skye asked disbelievingly.

Collin sighed before kneeling on one knee.

"Aye. Me mother-by-the-law believes in ye an me Annie swears ye have magical hands. Besides, these mangy beasties go nowhere near anyone but the Laird, an yet here they be, allowin ye to pet them like lap dogs." He shook his head. "These beasties would no if ye be a bad sort."

Skye swallowed when he mentioned magical but he seemed to brush it off as if he didn't mean it literally.

"Please, Collin. I don't belong here. Is there some way I can be taken back to where you found me?"

He frowned as if he'd discovered what he said might have been wrong. "Why?"

"I just know that if I can get back to where you found me, I can get home."

He crouched down in front of her. "Where be home, lass?"

She sighed and turned away, wrapping her arms around her bent legs. "I can't tell you."

"Why canna ye tell?"

"Because no matter how much I would like to believe nothing will happen if I did tell you, I could be wrong."

"I be sorry, lass, I doona ken of what ye speak."

"I know." A tear slid down her cheek.

"Och, doona cry."

"I'm sorry. I'm not really a crier. I just never felt so . . . lost."

"Aye, a terrible feelin that can be." He rubbed his face. "Maybe I can get a letter to yer clan?"

Skye snorted. "No thanks."

"I be tryin to help but ye keep hinderin me ideas."

She looked at the man and tried to read his shadowed face.

"I know and I thank you for the help, really, but there is nothing you can do." She sighed, turning her body away from him and slumping further against the bars.

Collin nodded. "Except to return ye to that place we found ye."

"That would be ideal." She said watching the corners nervously for rats.

"Returnin ye is no up it me."

"Let me guess, it's up to the council."

"Nay, tis up to me."

They both turned to see Aiden standing in the passageway.

Heart pounding in her chest, Skye slowly stood, braving the hardened look and the set lines of his angry face, like a determined angel of war.

"What else have ye lied about?"

Her chin went up. "I have tried my hardest to not lie."

"By withholdin information." He curtly responded.

Skye pursed her lips together and refused to comment.

Stepping forward, Aiden placed a hand on Collin's shoulder.

"Ye tried. Now it be my turn."

Skye gasped as she looked at the telltale blush on Collin's face.

Turning away from both, not caring that Collin left her alone with Aiden, she tried to deal with the feeling of betrayal even though she knew the reason for it.

"I want answers."

"I want to go home." She replied angrily, turning to glare at him. "Who do you think will get what they want first?"

Aiden seemed to notice Seelie for the first time. He frowned as he knelt beside her and checked on her breathing and examined the chewed rope he used to keep her tied in his study.

"She's only sleeping." She crossed her arms in defiance. "What? Did you think I was a murderer too?"

Aiden kept his shock to himself. Never before had someone stood up to him like this woman did. Except for the brazen ones who wished to share his bed thereby gaining some form of power within his household, most maidens cowered from him.

This lass was either daft or brave. Of the two, he had to find out which, soon.

"The council believes ye to be a spy sent to breach our gates an weaken us to attack."

"I know." Seemingly deflated by the facts, she rested her face between the bars, hands clasped on either side. "If I didn't know me and was in your position, I would have little choice but to believe the same thing."

Aiden watched as she turned to step away then catch sight of a rat as it scurried across her cell and press her back involuntarily against the bars, recoiling in horror.

He was surprised at the need to touch her, to remove her from the smell this place emitted, but he had his clan to think of.

"I just want to go home." She whispered, turning to look at him. "I don't want to harm anyone. I am a *good* person."

Aiden watched as she turned away, swiping at her eyes before facing him again, her jaw clenched.

"Just take me back to the place you found me."

"I canna do that."

"Then give me a horse and directions and I will go myself." She pleaded.

He crossed his arms in silence, watching her revealing features as she battled with something inside herself.

Realizing it was useless, she let go of the bars she'd grabbed and licked her lips.

He watched her closely, not knowing if she had no clue her emotions showed so easily or if it she was purposely showing an inner struggle.

Skye felt lost, scared that she was losing a battle that would lead to certain death no matter the outcome.

Her shoulders sagged for a moment as she gathered her thoughts before she straightened her spine and stood tall again.

"I am a good person."

"To whom, lass? To the greedy English who attempt to weaken us so they can take our lands? To the Reivers that kill livestock without reason but the simple pleasure of butcherin? Both of which have killed, crippled, raped, an enslaved our women an children."

Never taking her eyes from him, although filled with pain, she reached out and touched him.

When he stepped out of her reach, she took a hold of the bars and looked him in the eyes as she spoke.

"I am sorry this happens here. However, this is not how I was raised. To know this kind of fear or to cause fear . . . or pain, or death."

She refused to think of the heart attack she'd given the man who had tried to rape her, knowing it wasn't the same thing.

"Pshht lass, tis no sech place."

"I am not saying it doesn't happen, Lord Aiden. I am saying I do not live with that as a part of my environment."

"Tell me where this place is that ye live."

She looked down, knowing she couldn't give him the answers he wanted and afraid of burning at the stake if she did.

What would happen if he didn't believe her? She could well imagine the loony bin in a time and place like this.

Skye shivered at the vivid image that brought about as much as the fear of what could happen if he did believe her.

"Just get me back to where you found me." She pleaded again.

"I wilna do that."

Skye searched his eyes and when she found no leniency, she nodded. "Then I am to be a prisoner, kept in this cell until when? I die?"

"I canna ken what the council will decide."

"You have no say?"

His chest puffed out. "I be Laird."

As if that said it all, he gingerly scooped up Seelie and walked off.

Watching him walk away and taking both dogs with him made Skye feel more alone than before.

Then she noticed he'd left the torch behind!

"*Sarah!*"

* * *

Dammit! She'd been trying for what felt like hours to contact Sarah until the flame dimmed before flickering out.

Sliding down the bars in the near darkness, Skye whimpered in exhaustion.

Lying her throbbing head on her bent knees, Skye wondered if it was her imagination, but she could have sworn she had heard her sister just before the torch had sputtered out.

Her stomach had stopped growling about the same time she heard the servants clearing the dinner table in the other room. They were going to either starve her to death or make her so hungry she would tell them everything.

There was no way she was just going to sit here in failure.

There was a spell that would work. There had to be!

She just had to think of one, make sure it was fireproof and waterproof, and then she'd be home.

Her head snapped up as she heard the scurrying of rats on the other side of the dank, dark cell. Wanting to climb on top of the cot to get off the ground crossed her mind but it was on the other side in the darkness where the rats seemed to like staying so she curled and tucked her toes under her dress, fighting the tremors that racked her body.

Rabid cougars and rats were at the top of her list for creatures that petrified her.

Sometime later, the dim glow at the end of the passage from the fire in the main hall extinguished leaving her in complete darkness.

Shivering involuntarily, Skye tried convincing herself it was from the cold, not fear.

The clicking of tiny nails grew closer only to dart away when she moved as the night dragged on endlessly.

There was a time when she had fallen asleep and her body slouched against the wall, only to wake up to sharp teeth gnawing at her toes. She shrieked and scrambled to her feet, head dizzy at the sudden movement. She tried in vain to see but there was only blackness.

Skye whimpered, feeling her bare feet exposed but too afraid to bring herself closer to the rats by kneeling again. It was too late to climb onto the cot since she couldn't see her hand on front of her face.

Her imagination went wild, picturing them coming out of every crack in the walls to feed on her.

Why couldn't she have Sarah's powers of fire so she could create a flame to keep the rats away?

Whiskers tickled her toe just before she felt little paws balancing on the top of her foot making her screech in horror, thankful when it ran off.

Sobbing, Skye sunk to the floor, once again covering her feet with the dress. She thought of the corner to her right. It was only a couple of feet away, she could brace herself there and have more of her body protected.

Once in the corner, she actually felt a little relief.

Knowing movement kept the rats away, she rocked, humming to keep the terror from overtaking her as she listened to the creatures scurrying on the other side of the cell.

All throughout the night, the rats kept her awake. She would shriek and wave her arms in front of her, sometimes touching one as it hurried away from her attacks, and then she would go back to rocking and humming.

*   *   *

Aiden found her huddled in the corner, feet hidden under her skirt, arms tucked between her legs and chest, head resting on her knees.

She didn't move when he unlocked the cell and came in and didn't raise her head when he approached but when he reached out to touch her shoulder, she came alive, her screams piercing the dimness as she lashed out blindly.

He tried to calm her, not understanding where this behavior came from but she didn't hear him as she screamed and cursed.

Then he heard her say something about rats and realization dawned.

He grabbed her arms and pulled her up, holding her close to his chest so she couldn't claw at him.

"Skye. Calm down, lass. Tis Aiden." He held her tighter, continued to use soothing words, until she finally recognized his voice.

She latched onto him, crying uncontrollably as she looked around the cell.

"Rats! Oh, my God, rats. They were everywhere, biting me!" She clutched his tartan.

"Tis alri-"

"Please, please, anything, I'll tell you everything! I swear. Please, just get me out of here." She pleaded as huge tears rolled down her face.

"I did it." She hurried on when he didn't do anything, her face twisted around to watch for the rats.

He stiffened. "Ye did what?"

"I don't know. I don't know! Everything! Anything! Name it. I did it! I planned it all, everything!"

Aiden realized she was rambling with fear and lifted her into his arms and carried her out of the cell.

She wouldn't let go of him, even once grabbing his face to make him look at her as she pleaded. "Please, just make it fast."

"Make what fast, *leanabh?*"

"When you kill me, make it fast. Just please don't burn me."

She searched his face then buried her head against his chest, arms locking around his neck whispering repeatedly against his collarbone that she had done whatever it was they wanted to think she had done.

He stumbled on the stairs as his heart felt like it was being cleaved in two.

Her tears soaked thru his shirt as her body trembled violently.

He kissed the top of her head, his chest feeling tight.

"I dinna ken, lass. I swear to ye, I dinna ken." He crooned as he came across Collin at the top of the stairs where he motioned for him to follow.

His friend held the door open as they got to his chamber and closed it behind him, leaving Collin outside. He crossed over to a chair and sank into the cushions.

When Skye felt the downward motion, she started crying out, gripping him harder, believing he was putting her back in the cell.

"Nay, tis alright. I no be puttin ye down." He soothed as he settled her over his lap. "Tis alright, *ghaol*. I wilna be leavin ye."

He stayed like that, her head tucked under his chin, arms wrapped around her and speaking gently until her body stopped trembling, never once showing the anger he felt.

Not anger towards the woman in his arms, but at himself.

When he left her after discovering she was able to speak and understand Gaelic, Aiden had been livid, having believed in her innocence and his mother's assurance she was telling the truth during the interrogation that he'd told the council to wait until morning to discuss what to do with the girl. Unable to sleep, he went over every detail from the moment he had seen her until the conversation the night before and his battle-hardened instincts told him, no matter how he looked at it, she was no enemy.

He had gone before the council, warriors themselves, and had listened to their concerns of an English girl appearing as she did and unwilling to answer questions.

As Aiden listened to their arguing, he became frustrated that his own clan elders could not come to an agreeable solution.

Having heard enough, he stood up and said he was going to remove her from the dungeon.

When that raised concern, he explained that they would keep an eye on her, and if she were involved with the enemy, catching her would be easier if she was free to move about on her own.

They hesitated in their agreement but he was finally able to extricate himself from the meeting and hurried off to get her, unwilling to think about why he was going instead of sending another.

Shaking himself out of his reverie as he felt her body relaxing, he took a deep breath and tried to control the reaction he was having to her nearness.

She smelled of the dungeon and still his cock swelled. From the moment she'd walked into the hall, hair plaited like a Scotswoman, gown hugging her woman's curves, his cock had been erect, another reason he'd become so angry when he'd discovered what he believed to be betrayal.

He whispered things in English and Gaelic of no significance, smoothing over her tangled hair even after she fell asleep.

* * *

Skye lifted her head and looked unseeingly at the face in front of her.

Feeling depleted, her mind was unable to sort out the dream she was having and just how it went from a nightmare to the feeling of being safe and secure. Too tired to know anything else but the feeling of being wrapped in a warm cocoon, she lazily adjusted herself and rested her head back down, inhaling the comforting sent of earth and man before drifting back to sleep.

Aiden watched in curiosity as her eyes tried to focus then barely held back a groan when the lass rubbed against him causing his cock to swell again. Gritting his teeth, he waited for her breathing to even out and then waited for his manhood to ease, promising himself he would seek out Mairi from the kitchens to relieve his lust.

*   *   *

It felt like forever before Skye could open her eyes and find out what that delicious smell was but when she did, she found herself weighted down by the warmest comforter she'd ever had. Rising up on her elbows and letting the comforter fall from covering her face, she saw someone familiar supervising servants as they filled a small tub with hot water.

"Good morn to ye, lass. I thought ye would enjoy a light repast to break your fast and then a bath. When ye are done, perhaps ye would enjoy having a larger meal with Anna and myself?"

Skye blinked several times and looked around covering her nakedness. "Anna?"

"My daughter." She paused and looked up. "Unless ye prefer to be alone?"

"Ummm." Pushing her hair from her eyes, she gave herself a moment to remember where she was. "No, I would enjoy the company." She smiled tentatively, still confused.

"Excellent. My name is Elizabeth." She said, returning her smile and went back to overseeing the bath. When it was completed, she motioned to the table. "There be some pastries and jam. The loo for ye to . . ." She searched for the right words and blushed. "relieve yourself in, is down the hall."

"Thank you."

Ekizabeth indicated a beautiful girl with large breasts beside her. "Mairi here will show ye where it is."

Skye thanked her again.

"Anna and I shall join ye in, say an hour?"

Skye nodded and watched as the woman left.

Mairi standing at the door waiting impatiently once they were alone.

"I have thins to do an no time to get it done." As if in afterthought, she added grudgingly. "If ye please."

Skye made quick work of the 'loo' and returned to the bedroom where the girl left her alone. She hastily downed the jam and pastries, enjoying the splash of sugar that filled her mouth while she quickly removed the borrowed robe.

Making sure the pastries were in easy reach, she climbed into the tub not caring that the bath was only a large basin that she had to kneel in. She was just glad to be getting rid of the smell on her body and hair.

Looking around the room as she scrubbed, feeling shame that the bed had been clean when she'd slept in it, Skye eyed the furs piled on top and figured that was what she had thought had been the comforter.

He must have brought her here.

She cringed, recalling how she thought a rat had crawled up her arm, lost it, and began blubbering on about how she'd admitted to any crime they wanted to accuse her.

Shit. She hoped he knew she had been out of her mind then.

After washing her hair and body repeatedly, she climbed out of the mucky water and used the last bucket to rinse off her body and feet.

Looking at the gown she'd worn, Skye shuddered in protest at the thought of having to put it back on.

Lost in that terrible thought, she jumped when someone knocked on the door and covered herself as best she could when she heard Anna on the other side.

"Skye, might I come in?"

"Y-yes."

Anna opened the door and peeked in, grinning.

"Good, ye be finished." Her eyes widened. "Och, look at yer hair!"

Skye touched the clump that was her hair and grimaced. "I know, but I couldn't help it, it was so dirty and it's so long and curly."

"Aye, tis that." Anna giggled as she made her way to the chair and sunk down. "Me mother be fetchin yer gown an shoes, an I will have Mairi fetch somethin for yer hair."

Feeling relieved that she wouldn't have to put on the dirty dress, she smiled and tightened the thin towel around herself.

"Thank you! I so did not want to put that thing back on."

"Doona be *sgaog*." She blushed. "Och, I dinna mean that in a bad way, but I dunno ken what word I would use in its place."

"'Silly'. And I understood." Skye smiled as she stepped out of the basin.

"Ye do understand Gaelic!" Anna clapped her hands.

Just then, Anna's mother made her entrance.

"Here we are." She said as she held out the gown. "Let's put ye in this so we can get this water removed and food brought in, shall we?"

With that said, there was a flurry of activity and before long, Skye was massaging Anna's feet while chewing on the food set out and having her hair carefully brushed of the tangles by Elizabeth.

It wasn't until Collin came looking for his wife that they realized how much time had gone by.

"Oh my, I need to see to the preparation of dinner." Elizabeth muttered, standing up as Collin scooped Anna into his arms and carried her out, ignoring her insistence that she could walk on her own, even though she smiled hugely and wrapped her arms about his neck.

Watching them walk out, Skye was startled when Elizabeth turned around and looked at her questioningly.

"Would ye like to come with me?"

"I can?"

"Of course, luv. Ye are not a prisoner."

"I'm not?"

Elizabeth laughed and motioned for her to follow.

"Now pay attention to how we get to the kitchen so ye know yer way back to yer chambers."

Skye was fascinated as she spent her time following Elizabeth around. They went from the kitchen to the dining hall to ensure everything was running smoothly.

When she commented on how well things seemed to run, Elizabeth smiled.

"Tis true, evenings seem to be better. The daytime is of a different tune, but I like this time best, or right after the evening meal. It gets quiet, the children are calmed down, and the noise from hurrying to accomplish this task or that is over. Tis very nice indeed."

Skye was thinking of the lack of vacuum cleaners, dishwashers, and laundry machines as she gazed at the furs covering most the stone floors. "It must be difficult."

"It can be, aye, but I have Glenys. She was the first person I met when my husband brought me to his lands and she made my life so much easier to bear." Elizabeth smiled fondly at the memory. "Twas not easy back in those days."

"I can imagine." Skye agreed.

"But I learned to love my husband and he me." Elizabeth smiled. "And his people as well."

"You didn't marry him for love?"

"Nay, not in those days any more than now. My family was nobility and Dougal had been rewarded this castle for his help in the battle of Otterburn back in eighty-eight, after the previous owner had been found a traitor."

"Eighty-eight?"

"Aye lass, 1388. Ye were just an infant back then, still in nappies I am sure."

Skye followed Elizabeth's explanation in a stupor as the woman continued.

"The English and the Scottish are always trying to form alliances but never truly forming an understanding of each other." She looked at Skye and smiled sadly. "Tis like that no matter where one is, I suppose."

Skye nodded not even hearing what had been said.

Oh, my God! America hasn't even been discovered yet!

"Ah, lass, I have troubled ye with this talk of war and such. I apologize." Elizabeth said as she gently squeezed Skye's arm. "Let us turn our thoughts to other things, shall we?"

Good idea, let's begin with when they started burning witches at the stake.

Skye looked around the room, taking in everything with new eyes, marveling at what must be the beginning of the fifteenth century when she caught a man following them at a distance.

"Elizabeth?"

"Yes, dear?"

"Why is that man following us?"

"Follow—oh him." She smiled and touched Skye's arm. "You mustn't think you are a prisoner. I had the same thing happen to me when I first arrived. It satisfies the counsels' concerns tis all."

"Oh."

She frowned at the man and then shrugged. "He is also there for yer safety. Tis not like I need remind ye that these are troubled times."

Looking at the man and the fierce way he held himself, Skye shuddered.

"Not like I have a choice." She snorted to herself.

Later that evening, as she sat eating out of a small silver trencher with a knife and spoon given to her by Elizabeth, Skye watched in amazement at the activity that took place during a meal. There were small bowls of salt and platters of meat and fish, bread and something like butter within arm's reach, and so many more things coming and going that she couldn't keep up, and it all tasted delicious.

Nothing was as she had imagined the fifteenth century would be like.

Not that she had ever thought about the fifteenth century.

Doug would be so envious of her!

She loved the wine most and knew she needed to drink it sparingly because her third glass had her face feeling flushed and her nose and cheeks were starting to go numbish.

She giggled at the thought of 'numbish'.

Not wanting anyone thinking she was laughing at them, she concentrated on her food and watched the people around her in awe.

Although Skye tried not to look at Aiden, she found herself doing so throughout the meal.

He was wearing the kilt again and she so wanted to lean over and see what was past those manly thighs of his and hidden under the tartan. Gritting her teeth, she looked away again and began tapping her foot to the music when the couple next to her leaned over and began talking.

Aiden hated that he kept staring at Skye and hated more that other men looked as well.

Her hair hung loose this time and its curls made his fingers itch to wrap around them. Her face was glowing and her eyes sparkled as she chatted with the couple beside her.

"Fair pretty be the lass when cleaned up, aye?" Collin asked, laughing.

Aiden narrowed his gaze on his brother-by-the-law. "Ye be married to me sister, I no be rovin with yer eyes, if I were ye."

Collin threw back his head and roared with laughter, causing several people to look at the main table.

Aiden glared at Collin before realization struck and he had to chuckle. "I dinna wanna hear nothin from ye, do ye ken?"

Turning away, Aiden caught Skye watching him and he sobered, drinking her in until she blushed and looked away.

Collin patted him on his shoulder. "Aye brother-by-marriage, I ken. Mayhap more than ye do." When he noticed the girl blush and look away he grinned further. "More than the lass ken, as well." Collin chuckled.

He is beautiful, was all Skye could think when Collin's laughter had caught her attention and she turned to look at the two.

When the scraggly beard never reappeared, she was glad. Aiden's face was strong and manly, only his eyes, so vividly blue, could go from fierce to mesmerizing when he smiled.

Caught staring, she blushed furiously and jerked her gaze away, staring unseeing in front of her but not before she had seen his smile showing even white teeth framed by a mouth she instantly wanted to kiss.

﷽

CHAPTER FIVE

Skye woke up to pure darkness and squeaked, stiffening in fear as her mind imagined being back in the cell before she forced herself to accept that she was no longer with the rats.

Trying to see the dim room with what little light came from the glow beneath her door helped her see the candle on the bedside table had melted to nothingness.

Unable to stop thinking about rats, Skye slid out of bed, grabbed her dress from the chair, and leapt back on the mattress to dress.

Shoes in hand, she called out to the guard.

There was a noise on the other side followed by, *"Gu dé?"*

When Skye asked in Gaelic if she could come out, there was another long pause before the door opened and a strange guard looked in with a frown on his face.

"I'm sorry, but I can't go back to sleep."

She hated how her voice quivered when she spoke, but thoughts of rats nipping at her feet as she crossed the room would not go away.

His face remained emotionless. *"Dé tha thu-fhéin ag iarraidh?"*

Realizing she'd reverted to English, she cleared her throat and answered him. "Ummm. Can I get a glass of water?"

She breathed easier when he nodded and they headed to the kitchens. She was surprised to find it a buzz of activity, which promptly stopped once they saw her.

She blushed at the attention until an older woman stepped forward. "Ye be the English lass, aye?"

"Glenys?"

When the woman looked surprised, Skye went on. "Elizabeth spoke so highly of a woman named Glenys and then you spoke English, I just assumed. I am sorry if I'm wrong."

"Nay, ye have the right of it." She turned to the other women and clapped her hands, commanding them to go back to work. "What can I do fer ye?"

"I couldn't sleep, and I thought I could get some water. If it's okay with you?"

"Aye, follow me."

After handing her a mug with water in it, she sat her at a table, away from the women working.

Not wanting to go back to her darkened room, Skye watched as the women prepared for the coming day. Conversation was slow to start amongst them with her there but gradually picked up, although is a more subdued manner.

When Skye heard they were one short due to a sickness, an idea occurred to her.

It took some doing, but she convinced Glenys to let her help and before long, she was peeling potatoes and grinning happily. By the time the sun began to come through the open door, she was chatting away with the other women and laughing as they gave a young girl tips over an upcoming date with a boy that had come calling the previous day.

That was how Aiden found her, with an apron around her gown and her head covered with a kerchief while slicing potatoes and laughing.

He stood unnoticed listening to the sound of her mirth and his gut clenched, his manhood hardened, and all he could think of was covering her mouth with his own while he plunged into her wet depths and turning her laughter into moans of desire.

He left before he made a fool of himself.

Glenys placed a hand on Skye's shoulder. "Tis time for ye to leave, lass. Folks be arisin an ye need to be out there eatin an no in here cookin."

Skye looked outside to see the sun rising and smiled.

Taking off her apron and the kerchief she wore to cover her hair, she thanked Glenys.

"May I return tonight, if I can't sleep?"

Glenys looked at the girl in front of her and saw the need to be accepted. She'd worked next to her girls as if she was one of them, never acting mightier, nor did she slosh in her duties, always there to do what was needed next.

"Aye, ye be more than welcome."

"*Tapadh leat.*" Skye grinned happily, holding the other woman's hands as she thanked her before walking out with a smile.

She stopped short when she saw a handsome man standing waiting for her, instantly taking in his dark blond locks as long as Aiden's.

"Change of the guard, huh?"

When he didn't speak, she spoke slowly in Gaelic, trying to say the right words.

"I'm not really hungry and I'm not sure what I can and cannot do." Sighing, she looked around. "Is there somewhere I can go to just get some fresh air?"

A short while later, Skye held back a thick tapestry in an alcove, enjoying the beauty of this foreign land. She knew Scotland was beautiful because of the detailed descriptions Doug gave them from his visit a few years back, but this was breathtaking.

Ignoring the chill, she watched as the sun rose over the distant hills, casting an orange glow across the open land and showing the deep violet hue of the hills.

She took in the breathtaking scenery and sighed.

"Missin home, lass?"

Skye jumped and turned to see Aiden standing close by, the guard a number of steps away with his back to them. She looked at his hardened face wondering how she could be so attracted when he was so primal and forbidding in appearance with all the hard angles and set mouth.

Drawn to his even white teeth, she wondered how he looked when he smiled.

A sudden grin had her heart leaping into her throat as heat spread throughout her body. She tried to swallow it down as her breath caught at the sight of a simple smile.

Beautiful

Lost in the way creases appeared around those to-die-for blue eyes, softening every angle on his face. Even the slight dimple in each cheek captured her attention before drawing her eyes to his mouth.

"Or tis dreamin ye be doin?"

Skye jerked her eyes up to his as she realized she had been staring and licked her lips only to watch his smile disappear when he lowered his gaze to her mouth.

Her heart flipped and she felt achy in all the wrong places at that darkened look. She turned her face away and looked back out the window silently demanding her body to regain control.

"Which be it, lass?" Came the low sensual question.

Think Skye, what was the question?

Oh yeah.

"Miss home?" She shrugged and gave it consideration, glad for the distraction. "It's hard to explain really."

"Will ye try?" Came the soft request.

Skye looked at the man before her and everything inside her cried out to tell him all, wishing he was a witch so she could explain away how his voice made her insides melt and longed to step inside the power of his embrace even after everything he had put her through.

Instead, she looked out over the landscape holding back the desire to stare at him as well as to spill her life story, completely confused over her feelings.

"My sister, Sarah, and I grew up with loving parents. They took us everywhere with them so we were pretty used to traveling."

Sorting through her thoughts and taking a steadying breath, she pushed aside the hurt feelings of being left behind when her parents took their final vacation to celebrate their fifteenth anniversary and the plane had crashed, killing everyone.

"When they died, my aunt came to live with us. She was very much different from my parents. More of a loner I suppose." She quickly looked at Aiden. "Don't get me wrong; she loved us, brought laughter back into our home, but she was . . ." She searched for the word and then just shrugged and looked back through the window. "just different, eccentric, I guess. Unless there was something to teach us, Aunt Gladys kept to herself and left Sarah and me to ourselves. So my sister and I did everything together. Even though she was four years older than me, we were inseparable."

She shook her head as the memories flooded her mind.

"And then along came Doug. My aunt swore he and I made the perfect couple." She laughed not seeing Aiden stiffen. "But it became very clear that we only made good friends and that it was he and Sarah who were really supposed to be together. Now they are married and expecting a baby."

She drifted off.

"They have each other."

Letting the curtain go, Skye crossed her arms and leaned a shoulder against the wall. "They have each other." She shrugged through her agreement.

Aiden watched the flames from a torch play over her features in the now darkened alcove, seeing the resolve in her features that still didn't cover the sadness.

Skye shrugged through the misplaced hurt. "You have to understand that I love them both and I am so very happy for them because they *are* meant to be together."

When he came closer, she swallowed and looked away, nervous at the way her stomach twisted and her breasts tingled. She hurried on, covering her emotions with chatter.

"So, yes; I miss my family and I do, um, need to go home. Just—" She couldn't think anymore, he was too close and the air had become so warm.

Skye might not have felt the coldness of the stones on her back as she cast him a quick glance but she did feel the heat that pooled between her thighs and spread up to her breasts that warmed her when she found she couldn't look away.

He was a predator and she the prey and it excited her.

This man, who was so hard and tall, that could move with such stealth and grace with a voice that made her yearn to reach out for him while making her feel extremely feminine when he was so close, her breasts heavy and needy for his touch.

He placed a hand above her and her breath hitched as the smell of things earthy and primal invaded her lungs. He was going to kiss her and she knew she was going to let him.

His head lowered so slow, too slow.

All those years of craving to be touched centered on this man.

She could not wait.

Always thinking in the now, she fisted her hands into his shirt, pulling him to her as she moved to press her body to his.

Ecstasy coursed through her veins in molten waves as his mouth captured hers, a hand large and sure reached around her waist and pulled her in close as she willingly accepted his dominance.

Feeling the ache between her legs as her clit swelled in need, she pressed against his firm thigh.

She reveled in the control he had as his embrace heated her flesh, his mouth sliding from her lips to a neck she never knew was so sensitive. In the recesses of her mind, she knew this was different from any other attempt she had ever experienced with someone else.

Whereas before, she had enjoyed the touch of another and looked forward to finally having sex, this was a hunger for more. A need that took away all thought but the ones of his one hand at the small of her back and the other clenching her hair at the nape of her neck keeping her from moving away, something impossible to comprehend as she softly cried out when he gently bit her. Feeling his restraint to bite her harder made her rub her aching pelvis into the hard muscles of his thigh, seeking relief as his mouth slanted back up to her mouth and forced her to open for his tongue.

Aiden did not understand the lure of the woman in front of him but he trusted the instincts honed in battle, they had kept him and his men alive on too many occasions to doubt them now.

The need to have her, to place her before him naked so he could feast on her skin, and then make her a part of him gnawed at his gut even while sleeping. He woke up hard, his dreams filled with taking her hard, hearing her cries of passion as he rammed his staff into her wetness.

Now it was her unspoken fear of being unwanted, alone, that drove him to shelter her, to wipe away the sadness in her eyes and heart.

He drew near her like a hunter approaching his prey. He watched as her breath quickened causing her breasts to swell with each intake, her eyes darted everywhere as she pressed her back against the wall, but she didn't try to run and that made his cock jerk in hunger.

Aiden felt his control slipping. The way she responded to his touch, submitting to his need to control, to take, and encouraged with her mews of pleasure and frustration for more made him want to push her, lift her skirt, and fuck her there against the wall.

Instead, he took a deep breath knowing now was neither the time nor the place.

Inhaling her light scent, he tilted her head up, placing a soft kiss at each corner of her mouth before slowly easing away.

His cock twitched at the glazed look in her eyes, the way her mouth slightly opened to allow needed air into her lungs, and how they curved down when he broke from the embrace.

He stood there forcing himself to remain apart from her but teasing himself by remaining close enough to feel her heat reaching out to him as he watched her eyes clear, then her mouth closed and she swallowed.

"Wow."

He couldn't help the grin at her dazed comment.

Watching her hand reach up to smooth over her lower lip, plump from his kisses, had Aiden gritting his teeth as he pushed away.

"Me mother requested ye to break yer fast with her an me sister."

He turned and nodded for her to follow, grabbing the torch as he led the way back down the stairs the guard had previously brought her up.

Wow was all she could think as she absently followed Aiden.

Never before had a kiss made her lose all thought. All previous kisses dulled in comparison.

She'd always been thinking about how the kiss was, how she should be kissing, where it would lead, and would her sister be popping up to ruin it all. This time she could only feel and need.

Oh Lord, and want.

Cannot forget want.

And she so wanted more!

Everything in her still tingled, from the vee between her thighs to the neck he had bitten on.

Wow.

By the time they reached Anna's bedchambers, Skye forced herself to stop behaving like a fool and push aside her erotic thoughts to mull over later.

She entered without looking at Aiden and smiled at the look of pleasure Anna had on her face when she entered.

"I be so glad ye came, Skye! Have some sweet bread an cream, it be delicious."

The door remained open as Skye stepped forward to take the offering. Taking a bite of the bread coated heavily with cream, she closed her eyes in bliss.

"Mmmm, this is good!"

"Told ye." Anna grinned.

It didn't take long for Skye to realize this was a morning ritual between the two since Anna had started staying in bed most the day because of two previous miscarriages.

That brought back to reality the harshness of the time.

People here died of simple diseases, a cut untreated or a bad piece of meat, even childbirth.

"When are you due?"

Anna's eyes got dreamy and she smiled sweetly as she soothed her extended belly with both hands. "The bairn should be here in two fortnights."

A month. In her time, a baby could survive if born now.

"Och," Elizabeth patted her daughter's hand. "The baby will be just fine."

Anna smiled at her mother but Skye could see the concern in both their eyes.

In her day, her powers were useless.

The possibilities of someone finding out, detained, analyzed, and then have the rest of her family put through the same only allowed for smaller healings so she wouldn't draw unwanted attention.

Since those were always unfulfilling, the need to cure was something she always had to battle.

Her powers were a part of her and the need to use them was as strong as the need to breath. Taking anatomy and botanical classes had made it possible for her to help others, and when there was the added need of her abilities, she was able to do so while allowing the herbs to become the reason for a speedy recovery.

Skye became torn.

She wanted to go home desperately but knew she could ensure the safety of this baby if she remained, but to what cost? Would they be thankful or superstitious?

Moreover, did superstition equate to burning at the stake?

Even though she itched to touch Anna and find out what was going on with her body that she couldn't seem to carry full term, she kept her hands on her lap and forced herself to join the conversation.

Elizabeth stood an hour later, prompting Skye to do the same.

"Come now, daughter. Tis time for ye to nap."

"But me feet arna swollen an I feel wonderful."

"I am sure ye do, but it still would be best. I am sure Skye will return to spend time with ye—after ye have rested."

"I would love to."

"Then tis settled; ye rest and Skye shall return later."

As they were leaving, Anna called to Skye. "Please, go outside an tell me everthin ye see."

"Deal."

When the two women frowned, Skye chuckled. "I mean, sure."

As Elizabeth and Skye left, Their guard followed them silently down the stairs behind them.

As they approached the front entrance, a woman stepped up to Elizabeth and curtsied, waiting for the woman's attention.

Elizabeth handed Skye a shawl then told her to wait as she took the woman aside to speak with her.

Skye turned to the guard, taking in the long, curly, sun streaked brown hair.

"What is your name?" She asked in Gaelic, thinking about the man who watched her at night and wondering just how many good-looking men there could be in one place.

He frowned and looked at her curiously.

She smiled and asked again.

"Keir."

"Thank you, Keir."

He nodded and she turned back around as Elizabeth approached.

"We need to stop at the laundry, there seems to be a bit of trouble."

Walking outside, Skye took her first breath of fresh air.

When Elizabeth saw her shiver at the cold, she laughed, "It will not be long until it begins to warm, just be thankful it hasn't rained since yer arrival, a rare thing indeed it seems this year."

They made their way around to the side of the keep where Skye saw large barrels with women washing and wringing clothes out, making her think of the washer and dryer in her home.

A stout woman approached and nodded in respect to Elizabeth before telling her of the troubles they were having with two of the girls sick and the children needing attendance since the mothers were constantly being interrupted by the 'wee ones'.

When Elizabeth frowned in concern, Skye couldn't help but volunteer.

"I can help with the children."

At the look of worry on Elizabeth and distrust on the other woman's face, Skye continued.

"I love kids and Keir will be around in case anything happens."

After a brief amount of thought and a small nod from Keir, the other woman still looked unsure but nodded.

"Are ye sure, Skye?"

"Absolutely. How difficult could it be?"

Famous last words.

What did one do with a dozen children between the ages of four to nine?

"Duck, duck, goose!" She cried out to the surprise of the children running around her.

In very little time, she had them scattering straw on the ground and sitting in a circle as she slowly explained how to play the game and then demonstrated it, smiling in relief when they caught on quick.

She spent her time cheering them on, jumping up and down as one would leap up and run after the other.

When several older children came to watch, she took some of the more mature ones from the first game and showed them and the new group how to play *Red light, Green light.*

She kept an eye on the little ones while standing a couple yards in front of the group of older kids, turning her back as she yelled "Green light!" then waiting different amounts of time before spinning around right after she cried out "Red light!" and good naturedly booting the ones who got caught moving back to the beginning.

The few 'unbelievers' joined in the next round when she'd been tagged by the first teenager to get to her.

Skye was happy to see the mothers coming to check on their children, showing up with barely concealed worry only to leave with beaming smiles. A few men came by, even a couple of the elders, some spoke quietly with Keir before going about their business.

Skye was having a great time and when the adults came to get their children, they even thanked her and one of the youngest grabbed her about the knees and gave her a hug before running off with her parent.

"What a terrific bunch of kids." Skye said standing next to Keir as the children left one by one.

She forgot she'd spoken in English and repeated it for Keir, then sighed as she tried to figure out what to do next while the ever-silent Keir waited patiently.

Her growling stomach told her exactly what she needed to do next.

"I can't believe I'd forgotten to eat!" She exclaimed. "You must be starving too, Keir. Let's go grab something!"

They headed towards the entrance with Skye's excitement about the day bubbling over as she babbled on about how much fun it had been. When they turned the corner on the opposite side of the keep, she came to an immediate stop at the sight before her.

Dozens of men were in the fields practicing with swords or hand-to-hand combat, but Aiden was the man to capture Skye's attention.

He and Collin were bare-chested, leather trousers and boots being the only covering they wore, and the sight fascinated Skye.

Her hunger forgotten, Skye stood there and took in everything.

Wincing in concern as they fought with real weapons, she still couldn't take her gaze off Aiden's chest and stomach. Something every twenty-first century man would kill for.

A fine dusting of dark hair covered his chest and tapered to a thin line, disappearing into the waist of his pants. The pure hardness of his body, and the way the sweat glistened, made her mouth water.

Skye chewed her lower lip, biting back a groan at the muscles that rippled when he blocked a blow, feeling her body react in a very primitive way. She squeezed her thighs together when her womb clenched in need.

Several times, she tried to move, to turn away, but it was useless. Even as their practice ended, she couldn't tear her eyes away. She watched as they pounded each other on the back good-naturedly and still could not turn away.

The moment his eyes met hers, she knew she had made a mistake by staying but it was too late, he was heading towards her.

Eyes widening at his purposeful approach, her nipples hardened and her breathing hitched at his intent gaze, and still she stood waiting.

So fixated was she on his face, she didn't catch the short wave of his hand as he dismissed Keir.

His first touch ignited Skye's desire and her hands came up on either side of his head, holding onto his hair, pulling him closer as she opened her mouth to his demands.

She felt wetness between her legs and rubbed herself against him, reveling in the hardness, whimpering into his mouth, needing more as heat pooled low in her belly and spread over her in waves of need, everything else forgotten as he wrapped her in his hard embrace.

She didn't realize she was moving backwards until she felt herself pressed against a wall.

Aiden had seen Skye earlier when the sound of laughter distracted him from his journey to the practice fields. She had been mediating some kind of argument between two boys, both of which had nodded at the decision before running back into some kind of game in progress. He watched her laughing and cheering on another group of smaller children.

Once again, her laughter kept him in place.

It wasn't until Collin patted him on the back that he remembered where he was headed. He ignored Collins ribbing in silence, instead concentrating on getting his cock under control, again.

When he saw her standing there watching only him as other men practiced, he forgot everything but how she'd felt in his arms earlier that morning and how she had responded eagerly to his lust.

He ignored whatever Collin was saying and headed for her. Everything else faded away as his cock came to life and his hot gaze focused on the need to have her, possess her.

Drinking in how her curves filled out the gown, the way her gaze widened at his approach, how she licked her lips as her eyes darkened to a mossy green, and a flush blossomed over her skin had him waving Keir away and then he was in front of her, reaching for her as she fell into his embrace.

He pulled her into him, his mouth claiming hers as a hand came up behind her head to cup her neck and pull her impossibly closer, another sweeping over her lower back pressing her against his engorged length as he walked her backwards, cocooning them between two sheds.

She moaned when he pulled away from her, forcing her hands to let go.

"Please, don't stop." She begged, rubbing her sensitive breasts against his chest.

"Och, lass, we need to be stoppin or I shall take ye here, an I doona wish to be watched when I take ye."

He felt the shock course through her as she stiffened in his embrace.

"Oh, my God." She whispered as her face and neck flushed red with embarrassment.

She pushed away and slipped under his arm before backing up.

"I'm so sorry. I can't believe I . . . I don't know what came over me."

Grinning to himself, Aiden watched as Skye looked around before looking relieved no one seemed to have seen what had happened.

"I won't let it happen again." She promised just before she ran off.

Aiden watched her go and followed to see her slip into the keep.

"That, lass, is no one promise I intend for ye to keep."

* * *

"Was it a beautiful day?" Anna asked when Skye came up for a visit.

"It was."

"Nan said that ye took care of the wee'ans an had them playing games no one had ever seen before."

"They were games I grew up playing. We all had a blast."

"I doona ken this 'blast'."

Skye laughed. "It means we had the best kind of fun."

Anna sighed. "I have been told it hasna rained. I miss the fresh air an canna believe I will be in here for sech a long time."

"Maybe you can go out if you are careful."

She soothed her hands over her belly, a wishful look in her eyes.

"I had terrible pains in me back earlier. The midwife says me time out of bed is even more restricted, as if it wasna bad enough before." She rolled her eyes.

"For the rest of your pregnancy?" Skye asked.

"Tis for the best." The girl said even a forlorn look stole over her features.

"Anna—"

She held up a hand. "Och, it disna matter. Besides, what I want to be talkin about is why yer face is still flushed an yer eyes be all shiny."

"What?" Skye's hands went to her cheeks.

Anna nodded sagely. "Tis from more than playin with the children I be sure."

Before Skye's scattered mind could come up with something, Collin entered laughing.

"Och, *mo ghaol*, leave the poor lass alone."

"But why, husband? If I am to be stuck here, I must find amusement somewhere an Skye amuses so easily this afternoon." Anna grinned at Skye playfully. "See how her face grows even more red?"

"Tsk, tsk, Anna. Have ye no shame?"

"Nay. None."

"Well then, I be sorry to be the one to tell ye this."

"Doona spoil me fun, Collin."

Collin kissed his wife's forehead and smiled softly. "Then I wilna tell ye that Riona be here."

"What? That be two whole days early." She pouted to Collin's back as he walked out.

"Is this a bad thing?" Skye asked as she watched Anna's face crunch up.

"Bad be no the word for it. Riona be . . ." She searched for the word. "I doona ken the English word for *galla*."

Skye looked shocked when she heard the term 'bitch' come from Anna and then she laughed.

"Well, she is." Anna pouted, trying to remain serious and then she too laughed.

"I consider myself warned." Skye assured her.

"She be devious to be sure." Anna glanced at the open doorway then leaned forward to whisper. "I ken she be lookin at marriage to Aiden, an no simple hand-fasting will do."

That sobered Skye up. "Marriage?"

"Aye."

"And what does Aiden think about that?" Skye probed Anna.

"Who kens the thinkin of me brother's mind? She be a bonnie lass," Anna shrugged. "An would make an advantageous marriage, but no a very happy one."

Skye didn't understand why this conversation caused her stomach to twist in knots. It was only a simple kiss. Okay, not so simple and it was damn good, her womb still clenched in need when thinking about it and she could feel the flush rising up from her breasts as she remembered the way he had taken her into his arms.

Or had she leapt into them first?

She mentally shook herself away from those thoughts and concentrated on what Anna was saying.

"Her brother, Finley, is just as braw as can be, except for me Collin that is." She winked at Skye. "I had me eye on him at one time, til I saw him beat his horse. He tried to sweet talk me after but I lost me interest, ye ken?"

"Absolutely."

Anna snuggled down into her pillow. "The *galla* will be makin her way up here to pretend concern but I will act as if I be asleep."

Skye stood and smiled. "I understand. I will see you tomorrow."

She turned to leave and ran into a petite young woman just as she got to the door.

"*Gabhaibh mo leisgeul.*" The girl apologized, and then noticed that Skye wasn't someone she knew and frowned. "*Cò thusa?*"

"My name is Skye."

"Ye be the English girl I heard of."

"That would be me."

"Ye canna even speak proper Gaelic." The girl sneered, looking her up and down as if she were a bad piece of meat.

"Riona, Skye is a very good friend of mine."

They both turned, Skye surprised that Anna decided not to fake sleep, Riona surprised someone had witnessed her distain.

Having no way to explain her behavior, Riona chose to ignore the incident and brushed by Skye, her eyes wide and innocent.

"Och, Anna, I heard ye were up here an thought I would come to visit."

Anna looked beseechingly at Skye as Riona made herself comfortable, so Skye returned to the room after giving Keir a shrug.

"Oh, doona let me keep ye, girl." She waved Skye off. "Ye were headed out an I be sure Anna an I can get along fine on our own."

Anna's face turned down and Skye could see her sink in misery, causing Skye to chuckle. She waved at them as she headed back out.

"Enjoy your visit."

They turned the corner and Skye caved into a real laugh, she turned her head over her shoulder towards Keir.

"Poor Anna."

"Ye have no idea."

Skye almost missed her step down, she was so shocked to hear him speak, but Keir caught hold of her arm and steadied her.

She smiled up to him. "Anna gave me a clue."

"She was bein nice."

That caused Skye to laugh even harder.

*   *   *

"I want ye to find out everthin about that English girl." Riona whispered to her brother before they headed down for the evening meal.

"I have already found that she was captured at the boarder an thought to be an English spy." Finley said as he sat watching his sister brush her hair.

"Why is she no in the doogun?"

"I doona ken the why of it since she couldna answer many of the questions asked of her by the council."

Riona seemed lost in thought.

"Have ye seen her?"

"Aye."

"I hear she is a truly bonny lass."

That angered Riona. "She be fat, an tall like a lad. Very unbecomin in a woman."

"Sounds to me as if ye be jealous."

She waved the topic off. "What I want to ken is why be she here an why she has the run of the grounds with only a guard who trails her yet disna restrict her access."

"Ye be vexed about her a bit much, no?"

She threw the brush down as she stood and turned on her brother, eyes flashing with anger.

"Tis wise to be knowledgeable about what one disna fully ken." She leaned in closer and whispered fiercely. "We do not need anything to ruin our plans *this* time."

They walked down the stairs and came across Aiden as he was entering the keep.

Riona smiled and glided over to greet him. "Tis wonderful to see ye, Aiden."

Aiden watched as Riona approached, noticing the way her gown clung to her figure and found himself comparing her to Skye.

The woman's straight blonde hair was always smooth and in place. Her perfectly clothed petite figure coming only to his chest made Aiden feel as if he could hurt her without thought, or worse, muss up the hours it probably took her to prepare.

Skye, on the other hand, had light brown curly hair that always looked sleep-tousled, making him itch to grab a handful as he pulled her towards him and a body curved in such a way as to make a man think of bedding her then keeping her by his side throughout the night. Skye's height only added to his desires as he thought of her long legs wrapped around him when he took her.

"Aiden." Riona chided.

Shaking himself of his thoughts, he centered his attention back on his guest, giving a brief nod to Finley. "I be sorry, Riona. What was it ye said?"

Wrapping her arm through his, she smiled becomingly, batting her lashes. "I asked if ye were headed to supper an, if so, mayhap ye could escort me."

Smiling patiently, Aiden disengaged himself. "Nay, I need to clean up before headin to the evenin meal. Ye go ahead. Ye must be ready to eat after sech a long journey. I shall see ye soon." He nodded again to Finley and left.

Riona huffed in her disappointment.

* * *

Skye settled into bed for the night, exhausted from the day's events and very satisfied. She placed the candle on the small table and laid the spare Elizabeth had given her beside it, and then she concentrated.

"Come on, Sarah, be there."

They had always been able to connect through Sarah's powers no matter how far they were from each other as long as there was a flame.

She just didn't know if it was possible with over six hundred years separating them.

Over an hour later, Skye was exhausted and the candle was half-gone. She rubbed her eyes and wiped away the hair from her face, sighing in frustration.

"Skye?"

Blinking her eyes back to focus, she sat up straight.

"Dammit, Skye, are you there? Answer me!"

Hearing the fear in Sarah's voice made Skye smile.

"I'm here, Sarah. I was about to give up."

A moment later, a portion of Sarah's face came into view. "If it wasn't for the baby kicking me awake I'd still be in bed. Geez, Skye, it's got to be around oh dark thirty."

"It probably is there." Skye snorted.

Sarah squinted into the fire. "Couldn't you find a bigger flame? Light a fire or something?"

"I'm lucky to have what I do, thank you very much." Skye answered saucily.

"Where are you? Aunt Gladys and I have been searching for you for days!"

Skye harrumphed when Sarah mentioned their aunt. "Sweet Auntie sent me to the beginning of the fifteenth century, Sarah."

"She what?"

"Yep, and you think *I* suck at casting spells."

"Oh, my God, Skye."

"Yeah—" Skye stopped when there was a knock at the door. "Shhh, Sarah, don't say a thing until I come back."

The door opened and Skye watched the guard come through. He stopped abruptly and looked around.

When he asked whom she was talking to, she smiled.

"Sorry. I have a tendency to talk out loud when I am trying to sort things out."

He looked at her before checking her room to make sure she was alone then he nodded and left.

"Okay, Sarah, I'm back, but have to keep my voice down."

"If you had a bigger flame I could see more."

"Stop with the flame thing and come up with a spell to get me home."

"Now that we know where you are, I'll talk with Aunt Gladys and see what we can come up with."

"No!" Skye whispered furiously. "She's the one that got me here in the first place."

"I'm sorry but I need her help, especially now with Doug . . ."

"What about Doug?"

Sara sighed heavily. "We don't know."

"What do you mean you don't know? What about Doug?" Skye repeated frantically.

"He hasn't been feeling well lately. The doctor doesn't know what's wrong with him either."

"Doctor? You had to take him to the Doctor's office? Dammit, Sarah, get me home."

"I will, I promise. Aunt Gladys was visiting friends for a few days and will be back in a couple hours. Let us put our heads together and see what we come up with. Can you contact me tonight?"

"Tonight, my time or your time?"

"Oh, umm . . . what time is it there?"

"Oh geez, let me just take a look at my watch—well, lookie there." She snapped at the flame. "It's the fifteenth century for Christ sake, Sara. There are no watches here and I left home without mine."

"Okay, okay; no need to get snappy."

"Wanna make a bet? When's the last time you used a *cludgie*?"

"*Cludgie*?"

"Yeah; *cludgie* . . . you know: medieval chamber pot."

". . . Sorry?"

Skye sighed, raking her hand through her curls. "No, I'm sorry. Please; just get me back to where I belong."

"We will, I promise. I have a doctor's appointment today and Aunt Gladys and I will come up with something after that. Contact me this time tomorrow, or as close as you can get, okay?"

"What's the appointment for?"

"We decided to find out the sex of the baby." Sarah grinned.

Skye smiled as well. "About time."

When they ended their conversation, Skye undressed and got under the layers of skins, shivering in the cold.

She was worried.

Something was going on and she knew she had the power to fix it.

Chapter Six

Skye woke up when she thought she felt something tugging at her feet. Once again, it was dark and she swore she could hear rats scurrying on the floor.

Heart pounding in her chest, she quickly dressed before calling out to the guard.

When he opened the door, she had enough light to see and she tried to walk quickly out of the room without embarrassing herself.

Smiling up at him, she noticed it was the same guard from the previous night.

"I couldn't sleep. Can we go to the kitchen?"

Having been through this before, he followed in silence, standing at the kitchen door as she made her way in.

The morning quickly flew with everyone seemingly more accepting of her. Even Glenys welcomed her with a kerchief for her hair. She spent the morning cutting vegetables and helping with the dough for bread and was surprised at the time when Glenys shooed her off.

Walking out of the kitchen, Skye met Keir with a smile.

"Stuck with me again, aye?" She asked, pleased to see him return her smile.

They were heading towards the stairs so she could join Elizabeth and Anna for breakfast when she saw the two dogs through the open door of a room.

"Seelie!" She cried out in happiness as she slipped inside before Keir could stop her.

Skye dropped to her knees before the animals, laughing as the male licked her chin, scruffing his fur.

"Hey, girl." She softly patted the female and ran her hands over her body, noticing the chain that ran from a collar to an attachment on the side of the fireplace. "No rabies. How wonderful."

"It takes a wee bit longer to ken if she will be gettin rabies, lass."

Skye swung around to see Aiden standing in front of a desk.

"Oh." Damn but her body reacted quickly to his presence. "I . . . uhh . . . didn't know you were in here."

"Tis me study." He replied raising a brow.

She looked around at the furnishings and blushed. "I see."

She petted both the dogs and got to her feet, wondering how she had not noticed the scent of him when she entered. He smelled of leather and earth, mixed with something wild.

It called out to a part of her she never knew existed.

Like dinner the night before, Skye tried hard not to look at him, afraid she would give away how much he affected her.

"I'm sorry, I saw the dogs and I—I just wanted to check on them." She stepped towards the door. "I shouldn't have just barged in here. I'll go."

"Be ye afraid?"

"Wh-what??"

"Be ye afraid?" He asked in a low velvet voice, far too sexy for Skye's piece of mind.

"When I kissed ye yester eve," He took a step towards her. "I be wonderin if ye was tryin to flee or if ye came into me arms freely."

Her womb clenched as she thought about the kiss, heat suffused her face as her breasts tingled at the memory. Skye tried to say something but found herself staring at his perfectly full mouth and promptly forgot what it was he wanted from her.

He watched as her eyes darkened and the emotions play over her features, so easy to read, and struggled to keep a smile from curving his lips.

"Och, but the feel of ye in me arms, lass, the way yer tresses curled about me hand as I pulled ye closer."

Aiden's voice mesmerized her. Another step and her heart rate increased.

She tried to hide her trembling hands behind her but when she felt the gown stretching over her sensitive breasts, she clasped them in front instead.

So tuned to his words and the arousal of her own body, she didn't hear the door close softly behind her.

"I can still feel yer body against mine. Me staff pressed against yer belly."

Skye barely swallowed a whimper, biting her lip as she felt the moisture on her thighs.

Somewhere in the back of her mind, she was shocked at how intensely she craved his touch, wanted everything that was primal about this man to master her.

He took another step towards her, his gaze darkening. "Do ye ken how much I wanted to cup yer breast with me hand?"

Aiden lifted a hand towards her as if to do as he said only to stop in midair.

Seeing that large callused palm reaching out to catch her breast caused it to tighten in need. Unable to stop herself she took the final step, her hand reaching out to cover his and draw it against the swollen mound, moaning as his mouth covered hers, his other hand slipping behind her back to press her body into his.

Her hands grabbed his shirt, pulling him impossibly closer to her as she opened her mouth to his tongue, needing it all. Her hands wandering eagerly over his hardness, whimpering when she couldn't get any closer. She had no idea he had turned them until she felt the back of her thighs against the desk.

Aiden pulled away and she clutched his muscled shoulders. "No, no. Please don't stop this time."

"Nay, lass, no this time."

He sucked at her lower lip as he pulled her skirt up, wanting her skin bared to his touch, clenching his teeth against the urge to rip the cloth from her body and feast upon her skin, making her surrender to him.

When he had her dress around her waist, he lifted her up to sit on the desk before spreading her legs apart with his knee, his hand sliding up her inner thigh.

Skye sighed, her body arching as his fingers found her lips.

"Och, ye be wet."

"Please, it hurts."

Grinding the ache in her pelvis against him, she cried out when he slipped a finger inside.

"Yes!"

Her body shook as arcs of electricity coursed through her veins, liquid heat spreading in waves of pleasure from where his fingers took possession of her, and she rocked against him.

Wanting desperately to feel him, she reached between their locked bodies, moaning in need, cupping him through his pants, his hard length making her unbelievably wetter as she imagined taking him inside her.

"Not enough. Please, Aiden, more."

The way she begged and pressed herself against him as she keened was making him loose control.

Aiden gritted his teeth as he spoke. "Ye be so tight. Do ye ken what ye be doin to me?"

Moaning, she tightened her hold on his shaft.

"I only ken what you be doing to me." She sighed as she unconsciously mimicked his brogue.

When he inserted another finger, she cried out as she felt her juices coating his fingers.

"Oh, my God, Aiden, you're killing me!"

Suddenly, he pulled away and Skye gasped at the loss.

"Ai-" she stopped when she heard the noise too.

Someone was arguing on the other side of the door.

"Oh, my God." She scurried off the desk as he held himself rigid.

Straightening herself, Skye stood shocked for a moment trying to understand why she lost all sense of reasoning when this man was near.

Taking a deep breath, she walked to the door wondering if she should be embarrassed at her behavior or accept the fact that she was highly attracted to this man.

As she reached for the handle, she turned, her body still trembling from his touch.

"Well, I'm not sure if you still think I am scared, but if you have any more concerns, I am sure we can try figuring it out again."

She winked then turned the lever and walked smack dab into the last person she wanted to see.

"*Dhut!*" Riona snarled.

"Yep; it's me." Plastering a smile on her face, Skye walked away.

Half way up the stairs, Skye paused with her finger tapping her chin in mock thought as she looked at her blond guard.

"I don't know how that door to the study ended up being closed, but I am very appreciative that it was."

At the lifting of one corner of his mouth, Skye smirked and continued on her way.

After stopping at the *cludgie* to clean up and catch her breath, she entered Anna's bedroom determined to get her body under control and enjoy herself, succeeding until there was a shuffling at the door and voices.

Opening the door, they all looked at the young boy standing there fidgeting with his head down, Keir smiling next to him.

"Brian?" Skye asked.

"Aye."

"What is it, lad?" Elizabeth asked when he didn't explain himself.

"Well . . ." He stuttered to a stop.

Skye motioned him over, took his hand, and smiled. "We can't read minds, Brian, so you'll have to tell us what you need."

"Tis rainin, ye see?" He went on in a rush. "An I was chosen to ask if ye had any games we could play inside."

"Is that right?" Skye stood and faced the other women. "Well, ladies, it seems as if my break is over. Off to work I go."

She grinned at the two women, who smiled their understanding, and took Brian by the hand before heading downstairs.

Aiden and Collin stood at the study door, perplexed as to why there was a group of children at the base of the stairs when they heard a cheerful voice.

"Well, well, well. What do we have here?"

Upon seeing Skye, the children started talking at once.

"Alrighty then." Laughing, she held up her arms to quiet them. "Entertainment is needed, I get that. So what will it be? Shall we play a game, or do you want me to tell you a story?"

The children's voices raised in their excitement as they each made their thoughts known, trying to out-voice the other.

"Okay, okay! Seems as you all are a bit too rambunctious for a story so let's start with a game and go from there, shall we?"

When she asked where they could play without interrupting the adults, Skye found herself immediately surrounded by the lot, a hand taken by the two littlest ones, and led away.

As Aiden watched in awed silence, he began to wonder how his world had become turned upside down so easily.

It wasn't until he heard Collin chuckling that he remembered he wasn't alone and glared at his friend, cursing when that only made the man laugh harder.

*   *   *

"We need to get rid of her." Riona shrieked.

Finley glared at his sister as she went on a tirade about the English girl.

"An ye need to keep yer voice down, sister mine." He stressed the accent in a furious whisper.

Hissing between gritted teeth, Riona cleared her throat and continued.

"She came out of Aiden's den all askew, an the door had been closed, her guard defendin it like it was full of treasure. Then Aiden refused to talk to me, made some excuse, then ushered me out."

"Ye need to calm down before ye get a wrinkle from frownin so."

Riona twirled around, angry with her brother before catching herself and clearing her features. "Ye sit there as if ye have nary a care in the world. Do ye no ken that if he marries her all our plans were for naught?"

Finley's calm exterior turned cold. "I ken, sister, I ken. However, as ye stomp around in a huff, I have come up with a plan an have someone workin on it now."

Riona's eyes widened and she clapped her hands with glee. "Tell me of this plan, brother."

*   *   *

Gladys put her book of spells down when Doug and Sarah came through the door, immediately feeling the tension.

"How did the ultrasound go, m'dear? You were gone longer than expected. Did you go out for lunch?"

Doug guided his wife to a chair before turning to Gladys. "The heartbeat stopped for a little bit."

"Dear heavens."

"The doctor doesn't know what caused it." Sarah whispered. "He wants me to go in for more tests."

"Oh no." Gladys covered her mouth with a trembling hand.

"Tell her the rest, Doug."

Doug sighed before continuing. "I passed out as it happened. The nurse just thought it was from anxiety but when they checked my pulse there was none."

"It's my fault. If I hadn't used magic, Skye would be here and everything would be fine." Gladys lamented.

They sat in silence, each lost to their own worries.

"Skye will be contacting me in the morning. I suggest we think of a way to get her back by then." Sarah said with determination, one hand caressing her belly the other holding tightly to Doug.

* * *

Once again, Skye forgot about lunch while playing with the children and, as a parent carried the last child away, she headed for the kitchen.

"Think they will take pity and feed us, Keir?"

Before he could answer, they saw Elizabeth standing on the last step lost in thought, her features pensive.

"What is it, Elizabeth?"

Elizabeth broke out of her thoughts to look at Skye.

She stood undecided for a moment before sighing. "Tis Anna. She had some terrible cramping."

"Oh no." Skye made to go up the stairs. "Is she and the baby okay?"

"She's fine. So is the baby." Elizabeth stopped her. "Collin is with her and wants time alone."

Skye looked up the stairs, every nerve ending pushing her to go to Anna and help.

"The midwife says that Anna must stay completely bedridden until tis time for her to deliver."

Skye took a deep breath. "I can help."

Elizabeth patted her hand.

"Yes, dear, but we need to let Anna rest now." Then she walked away distracted.

Skye looked back up the stairs and then to Keir. "I *can* help."

"Aye, lass, but ye heard the mistress. Let her rest." He steered her towards the kitchen.

Skye sat at the long table in the kitchen, pushing the food on her plate around, feeling torn in two.

Keir finally pulled her from the room so they could get supper served without her in the way.

Bringing her plate with her, Skye entered the dining hall and sat down noticing the empty chairs at the head table and the somberness of the room.

Other than a few murmurs, no one seemed to want to break the mood.

Having no desire to eat and tired of the way Finley and Riona kept looking at her, Skye left the hall and grabbed two candles before heading to bed with her decision made.

She could not leave knowing she might be able to save a life and was going to tell Sarah that she needed to stay a little longer before coming home.

That stopped her in her tracks.

Did she trust her standing in this place to take care of Anna and the baby and then be able to go home?

She couldn't help the doubts she was having. Being out of her element, let alone her own time, made her feel vulnerable in ways she couldn't explain. There was a very real possibility that they were a superstitious lot and feared what she could do to them.

In her own time, people feared the unknown and Skye could only imagine how much worse it was here.

Maybe she could do it without anyone's knowledge.

The door was always open when she was in the room but the guard never looked so, as long as there was nothing to attract his attention, she should be all right.

She continued walking as she played with her father's ring, her step slow as she considered all aspects. The hardest part was being able to concentrate without others becoming worried at her silence. It wasn't like she couldn't talk but she needed to be able to see without distractions so she wouldn't miss anything vital.

There was also the possibility that she could do it while alone with Anna. Could she trust the girl to keep it to herself if she told her what she could do?

Growling in frustration, she entered her bedroom, smiled crookedly at the guard who stared at her strangely, and closed her door.

Walking over to the bedside table, she placed her two candles on top, keeping one lit on the stand before calling out to her sister.

They had been waiting for her.

"Good to see this is getting easier." Skye laughed softly. "So then, what in your original spell got me here?"

"I don't know." Gladys admitted. "I created a spell for you to find the man of your destiny and thought your list would help to pinpoint that man. How it sent you to the stone ages I haven't figured out yet."

"I suppose that doesn't matter now since we need to know how to get me back."

"Exactly." Sarah piped in. "We went over the original spell and looked at variations to get it reversed with as simple an incantation as possible and believe this will work."

"That sounds promising." Skye sighed in relief.

"Are you ready?" Sarah asked.

"No, I can't come now."

"What?"

"There's a young woman here who is pregnant too, Sarah, and it looks like she's going to lose the baby. I need to help her."

"Fine, so help her and then cast the spell."

"What if it doesn't work?"

"Believe me when I say we made it simple so it will work. Aunt Gladys and I went over it too many times for it not to."

"Good, because it has to work the first time or I may be in deep shit."

"What does that mean?"

"Oh, something called fifteenth century mentality."

"You have to speak English, Skye. I don't get what you're trying to say." Sarah replied in frustration.

"I don't know, but something about burning witches at the stake comes to mind."

"For saving a life?"

She gave them a moment to think about it.

Gladys sighed. "They might start wondering what else she can do. What if she gets mad or someone pisses her off? They may start thinking she would use her powers to harm another."

There was silence as Skye let her sister digest that information.

"We need you home, Skye."

"I know, Sarah, I . . ." Then it hit her on how her sister had spoken, quirking an eyebrow she frowned into the lit candle. "What's going on?"

More silence.

Before Skye could ask again, her aunt spoke up. "The baby's heartbeat stopped during the ultrasound. At the same time it happened to Doug."

Skye's thoughts went pinging in all directions, all of them centering on '*at the same time*'.

"Has this happened before?"

"We don't know." Gladys admitted. "This was the first doctor's visit Sarah had for an ultrasound or to listen to the baby's heartbeat."

"Sarah, you mentioned Doug before too. Was this it? His heart?"

"Yes." Came the soft reply.

Skye's heart ached at not being able to remain to save Anna and her unborn child but there really was no choice.

"Okay, no worries. I'm coming home now."

Skye got off the bed and stood in the center of the small room. She took deep breaths to center herself then said the spell her sister had given her.

> *"Through time and distance, let me arrive*
> *without hindrance.*
> *To right the wrong so I may return to where I*
> *belong."*

Skye waited for the queasy feeling but all she got was a moment of blurriness.

Trying once more gave the same results.

Sinking to her knees, she shook her head in disbelief as she stared at the same four walls she'd been in for the last couple of nights.

"Skye?"

"It didn't work."

"Where are you?"

Shaking her head in despair, Skye rose to her feet and turned in a circle.

"I'm still *here*." She said in disbelief. She sank onto the mattress and looked in the flickering flame. "Dammit."

Her aunt piped in. "Maybe we should do the spell."

"Man, I suck as a witch." Skye whispered.

"Don't say that, what you can do will save Doug and our baby. Modern medicine doesn't seem to have a clue and if so they might be too late."

"I'm sorry. A moment of self-disgust got the better of me. You two go ahead and try."

She climbed off the bed and stood in the center of the room taking calming breaths as they repeated the spell.

Nothing.

"No way." Skye ground through clenched teeth.

"Did anything happen, dear? Anything at all?" Gladys asked.

Flopping back on the bed, she clenched her fists, trying to keep herself from making a noise that would draw the attention of the guard.

"A quick moment of blurriness, but that happened when I did it."

"And what did you feel when I sent you there the other day?"

"I got nauseous and almost blacked out."

"So we're on the right track. I just cannot fathom why it is not working. Sarah and I went over the spell with a fine tooth comb, so to speak."

Closing her eyes as something occurred to her, Skye asked, "Would a fairy circle have anything to do with this?"

"There was a fairy circle? Where? On the other end?" Sarah asked excitedly.

"Ummm, yes. Does that make a difference?"

"It may very well be why you were able to go into the past, child." Her aunt mused from behind Sarah. "I was wondering how that happened since normally you go from point A to B with no time involved or at least that was my intention with my enchantment. This house is a magical spot in itself, add the fairy circle at the other end, and it makes sense. A portal of sorts I suppose."

"This is not good. Do you know how far it is?"

"We'll try to think of something here," Sarah smiled weakly. "but try to get there if you can and I know that is easier said than done.

"Yes, dear, do try. I'm thinking the spell works because you do feel some of the same things, just not as strong, so being in that circle would give you the added *oomph* to get you back."

Feeling hopeless, Skye tried to keep from thinking of the impossible and changed the subject.

"How is Doug doing?"

"He has finally taken some vacation time and is holed up in the spare room looking over his family history. Keeps him busy and his mind off things he has no control over. Which you know is a very difficult thing for that man." Sarah actually chuckled. "He's dy—excited to talk to you about the Scotland you are in now."

Skye heard the change in words and acted as if it had not occurred. "Tell him I'm up for a long night of storytelling."

They ended the conversation soon after and Skye slipped into bed wondering how in the hell she was going to get back to the fairy circle.

*   *   *

Skye cracked open the door after Aiden called out for her to enter when she knocked on his study door.

"May I come in?"

"Aye, lass."

Not daring to look at him, she crossed the room, taking a moment to pat the dogs before standing in front of the desk Aiden sat behind, trying to steady the pounding of her heart.

Having been absent-minded all day, she fretted over how she would say what she needed, waiting for a rare moment like this when Aiden would be alone.

Skye took a deep breath. "Am I a prisoner?"

Aiden straightened and paused in his perusal of her and took in her tight features and the nervous way she played with a ring on her thumb.

"Why do ye ask?"

"I need to go home."

Aiden ignored the way his gut clenched at her words.

"Ye can go home any time ye wish, just tell me where home be, lass." He answered carefully.

Glancing up, she saw his face, hard in its intensity and her heart cried out at the wall she was creating.

"I just want to go back to where you found me is all."

"An do what? Leave ye there?"

"Yes."

"Do ye ken how dangerous that be?"

Skye searched for an answer while her heart hammered so loud she worried he could hear it.

"I just need to go home. Now."

"Aye, ye have said so before. What makes it so urgent that ye seek me out now?"

"My sister is pregnant too and the problem with Anna is making me concerned for her." She couldn't help wringing her hands as she silently willed him to just let her go. "Please."

"I need a better answer than that."

Squaring her shoulders, she forced herself to straighten her spine and hold her head up.

Begging hadn't worked. Not like she thought it would, but no other option had come to her.

"So I am a prisoner."

Silence.

"You are keeping me from my family."

"Tell me who they be an I shall send a missive informin them of yer stay here."

"I cannot do that, and you know it."

He stood and placed the palms of his hands on the desk and leaned towards her.

"Nay, I doona ken, but ye will be stayin put til ye can give me answers to the questions I have."

"I don't have answers I can give you." Skye cried out.

As his face cleared of all expression, she gritted her teeth, fighting to hold back the tears, knowing his trust in her had taken a step backwards but she didn't have any other choice.

"Then this conversation is moot." His voice was deathly soft.

"I really wish you would reconsider."

"Doona think of leavin, Skye." His voice was slow and precise. Its unyieldingness surprisingly made her insides clench in desire. "Ye wouldna get far."

Aiden watched her walk out of his study, his belly tied in knots. He couldn't help but wonder why she came to him now with her wish to return home. Although mentioned before, this time it seemed more urgent.

He began to doubt the very instincts he had relied on in battle. There was no help for it. He had too many simple questions she refused to answer.

Now he wondered if she had been here long enough to gather whatever information she needed and was ready to turn that over to someone.

"I saw Skye leave an now here I see ye with a stone mask over yer face. This doesna bear well, I be thinkin." Collin commented from the doorway.

Aiden looked up at his brother-by-marriage and shook his head. "Tis no good, Collin. The lass wishes to go home."

"What makes this request so disturbin, Aiden? She has wanted that from the beginnin."

"She was very adamant this time."

Collin watched as Aiden brooded for a bit before he smiled and sat in a chair.

"Ye be thinkin once again the lass be a spy."

"What else can it be?"

"Then give her what she wants an put an end to yer worries."

"What be ye suggestin?" Aiden asked as he watched the man's roguish smile.

"Return her to the glen, if she be a spy ye will ken then. If she isna, then it will put yer worries to rest."

"An set meself up fer an ambush, man?"

"Nay, brother, ye take yer time gettin there. Stay the night at the old shepherds place. I will take some men an pass ye. We will get to the place before ye, check it out an stay hidin til ye call us. If she wishes fer ye to leave then so be it." Collin shrugged. "Ye can double back an join us as we wait to see what the lass does."

Aiden looked at his friend with mild amusement. "Why be it that I dinna think of this?"

"Because ye be smitten with the lass an yer heart be overridin yer brain too much to be thinkin clear."

That caught Aiden in the chest. Were his feelings that strong in such a short time?

He quickly brushed it aside, knowing his desire was to take Skye to his bed, nothing more.

Smiling, he nodded his agreement. "I will speak with the council today an plan on leavin on the morrow. Gather three good men, more will just attract attention—if there be attention to be attracted."

Collin nodded before leaving the room.

Skye left the study with her heart pounding heavily in her chest.

When she looked at Keir's unyielding face, she knew he had heard.

Placing her hands on her hips and refusing to let the tears fall, she frowned at her guard.

"We all have secrets we can't tell. But mine won't destroy any one other than myself." She huffed. "All I want is to go home, to be surrounded by those who trust and love me. Who wouldn't want that?"

Not seeing Collin standing off to the side, she turned on her heel and stomped away, not caring who followed.

Frustrated and unsure what to do next, she wandered aimlessly until she noticed a light coming from under Anna's door. Tapping lightly, she slowly entered when Anna answered and noticed the girl's pale face.

She walked up to the bed smiling though her concern. "How are you, hun?"

Anna reached out and clutched Skye's hand. "I no be doin too good, truth be told."

Skye swallowed back her uncertainties. "Tell me what you are feeling, Anna." She encouraged as she fought these new fears.

"Tis the bairn." Tears formed and fell freely from her face as she gripped Skye's hand harder. "I doona ken why I canna carry a babe."

"Did you call for the midwife?"

Anna shook her head vehemently. "I doona want her, she does nothin for me or the bairn. Keep her away from me, please!"

When Anna's voice caught and sweat broke out, Skye forgot everything and clutched the girl's hand.

Leaning forward, she whispered. "I can help you, Anna. Let me help you."

Anna's body stiffened in pain.

"Please help the bairn." She gritted through clenched teeth.

"I will, I promise." She said as she forced her hand from Anna's and lifted the covers, barely covering a gasp at the blood starting to spread across the sheets.

Warmth suffused her body as her powers quickly gathered, removing the chills the sight of blood had caused as she lifted the bloodstained gown and touched the swollen belly.

Not removing her gaze from the first hand, she lifted the other to touch Anna's forehead and sent calming thoughts as she focused her energy.

The room became hazy, her eyes narrowed, faced flushed, and Skye felt like she was floating as she followed the controlled energy into the womb. Her powers fanned out, stopping the bleeding and doing a general healing. All the while soothing Anna, telling her all would be well, feeling the girl's body slowly relax as the pain eased and surprise and hope took over.

The bleeding stopped and Skye focused on the baby.

Smiling down at the perfect little boy, she wrapped him in gentle warmth and love before searching for the cause of Anna's continuous miscarriages.

Muffled noises distracted Skye and she frowned, trying to concentrate on the colors her healing powers used to show her where she needed to be.

She was following the womb when she suddenly felt herself falling.

Dizziness distorted the sounds around her and as she felt her body smack against the floor and wall, her stomach reacting violently to the sudden movement and disconnection from her healing.

She grabbed her head with one hand as she struggled to her knees, the skirt making it difficult.

"Get her out of here!"

"Nay!"

Unceremoniously hauled to her feet, Skye felt herself pushed into unyielding arms.

Fighting the urge to throw up as her equilibrium was thrown off balance from being jerked in too many directions.

Unable to speak or resist as someone pulled from the room and down the stairs, she barely felt the shoves as people passed her to rush up the stairs and into the room, Anna's cries echoing in the distance.

Thrust onto a bench, she would have fallen over if rough hands hadn't heaved Skye back up.

Head spinning and stomach ready to rid itself of everything in it, she squinted her eyes and found herself next to a table and carefully laid her head down as her body began to tremble from the effects of her transition and handling.

When things stopped spiraling and bile wasn't fighting its way past her throat, she eased up and looked around, surprised that Keir or someone else wasn't at her side.

Still wobbly, she stumbled to her feet and made her way to the opening of the room, wiping Anna's blood from her shaky hand on her skirt.

Hearing the commotion upstairs as people rushed around, it suddenly occurred to Skye that she was alone, and no one was paying attention to her.

Gritting her teeth and stiffening her spine, she turned for the front door knowing Anna would be fine for now.

Grabbing a cloak from a peg, Skye covered herself and eased out the door, promising her body rest as soon as she was free.

Surprised how easy it was to go through the village, she concentrated on figuring out how to get through the gates when she saw a caravan being ushered through.

Skye quickly became a part of the procession, holding on to a wagon to steady her shaky legs and keeping her head down, she forced her breathing to stay controlled.

Not breathing a sigh of relief until they had a good hour between them and the gates, Skye detached herself from the caravan and made her way towards the forest only knowing she needed to keep the sun at her back as it sunk closer to the distant hills.

Nausea and vertigo gone, she still urged her weak body on, knowing it wasn't wise to be out in the open.

* * *

"What do you mean she be gone?" Aiden stormed.

Keir stood his ground, deserving his liege's fury and more for leaving his charge.

"Tis no his fault."

Aiden whirled around face red with rage. "Explain."

Collin stepped forward. "Ye need to be askin Riona why she had one of her guards replace Keir in his duties."

Thunder crashed and lightening flashed causing his anger to grow as he paced while waiting for Riona to be found, unsure whom he was angrier at, himself for assuming everything with Skye was taken care of, or the sight of the blood on his sister's body and bed.

It didn't take long to find Riona and Aiden glared at the girl before him, waiting for an answer to his demand of why Keir had been removed from the care of Skye.

"We n-needed help, an my man had no clue where to go to get what was n-needed, an Keir d-did."

Aiden frowned at the girl quivering in front of him as her tears streamed down her face in fear.

"So ye thought twas best to exchange them?"

"A-aye."

Shaking his head in amazement, he looked at his man. "An ye did it?"

"I t-told him ye told me to do it."

"Ye what?"

Riona's face paled and her hand came up to fan herself. "Och, I think I am gonna faint."

Aiden turned away from her in disgust, waving his unconcern as he stormed out, calling for Collin and Keir to follow him.

"Ye have yer men picked?" He asked Collin.

"Aye, Keir an two others."

"Nay, ye stay here with Anna. Pick another in yer stead."

Collin grabbed his arm to stop him from walking away. "I be goin if for no other reason than to stop ye from killin the lass."

"Ye still ken her innocent?" He asked incredulously.

Collin stood firm. "Aye, Anna wouldna be askin for her if she wasna."

"The girl was covered in me sister's blood when she was caught by Riona an the midwife. God kens how me sister in her pain could have deduced right from wrong. She was so upset she had to be givin a dram to get her to sleep."

They glared at each other, neither giving ground before Keir cleared his throat. "We be wastin time, m'Laird."

"I know!"

Collin arched an eyebrow, waiting for his brother-in-law to make a decision.

Aiden turned to Keir. "Have some men look around the grounds, just in case she didna make it out the gates an we missed her, then meet me—" He glared at Collin. "Meet *us* at the stables."

*   *   *

Skye fell under the onslaught of the storm, causing her to stumble until she fell against a tree. Darkness had fallen, quickly obscuring the fast approaching storm.

Even though the increasing winds had warned her to start looking for shelter, her fear of capture and death had kept her going until it was too dark to see.

Soaked to the skin, her body stiff and shivering from the ice-cold rain, she knew her mind had ceased to make sense of anything.

It became impossible to try to gain distance between her and Aiden or to find the forest because she no longer knew which way she headed.

None of the trees, bushes, or rocks had provided shelter from the rainstorm and now she leaned heavily against the trunk and cowered as her mind kept urging her to keep moving so she could get home.

As her gown grew heavy in its sodden state and Skye's legs grew too tired to hold her up, her knees gave out, her whimpers unheard as she slipped to the muddy earth.

Teeth chattering, arms trapped in the saturated cloak, legs in the cumbersome skirt, she gave up trying to crawl to the other side of the tree to keep some of the force of the storm from her and just collapsed as the howling wind and beating rain pressing her exhausted body against the base.

That was where Sileas found her, alternating from licking her face to wake her, to barking for his master to find him.

Heart pounding, Aiden jumped from his horse and rushed to Skye. He removed the wet hood from her head and ran his hands over her face.

"Skye, wake up. Ye need to wake up." He patted her cheeks, ran his hands up and down her arms. "Come on, wake up."

"Home." Came her weak reply.

Collin took her as Aiden climbed his stallion, lifting her into his arms before he turned his horse sharply and headed off as fast as he could push the animal.

In mere moments, he was at the shed where Collin had forced him to wait out the storm, insisting they would do Skye no good if they went in the wrong direction. Keir had stayed behind when the storm showed the first indication of easing up and Aiden had brushed past Collin to resume his search, angry at staying in the confined space for even a couple hours.

Keir was holding the door open as he slipped from his saddle with Skye and rushed inside only stopping when he was in front of the fire, Sileas slipping past to lie at the side of the hearth, out of the way.

"She was so close to here." He muttered to Collin as his friend crouched beside them. "If it hadna been for the storm she'da been safe inside. She was so close."

Collin said nothing knowing she would never have needed the shed if it had not been for the storm. Placing a hand on Aiden's shoulder, he squeezed.

"The storm be passin. Ye need to get her out of those clothes an dry. I will take the men, scout the area, an meet ye where we agreed on."

Aiden nodded.

The men filed out. Collin stood at the doorway and looked at his friend. "She felt like she be feverish so I will wait a couple of days, if I doona see ye . . ."

Letting the sentence die out, Collin watched his friend's distress and sighed before continuing. "Are ye gonna be—?"

Aiden nodded.

When Collin made his way to the door, Aiden called him, his eyes never leaving Skye's face as he admitted to what he felt in his heart.

"I was wrong."

Collin waited.

"It doesna make sense, what was explained. Somehow, some way, she thought she could help." He looked up. "Me mother told me Skye said she could help the other day an me mother believed her. She has always believed her but she was too aggrieved to be thinkin proper. Maybe Skye has knowledge in the healing arts."

Nodding, Collin agreed. "Maybe she does."

Aiden shook his head in disgust. "Me mother believes her. Why did I no?"

When Aiden looked back down and brushed his hand across her face, Collin nodded and left, knowing everything was going to be fine if she could pull through this.

As soon as the door closed, Aiden cleared his mind and went to work.

Taking the bedding from two of the bunks, he placed them before the fire then gently peeled the gown from Skye's shivering body. Clenching his teeth at the blue tint of her normally light golden flesh, he covered her in layers of fur before placing her gown out to dry.

He had just positioned his own wet clothes beside hers when he heard a moan.

Rushing to her side, he eased her into his arms as he sat beside her.

"C-c-cold." She muttered through chattering teeth, barely conscience.

Pulling the skins tighter around her, he tried to return the warmth to her chilled skin but her body continued to rattle in his arms.

Making a quick decision, Aiden slid under the skins then gathered her into his embrace, using his body heat.

The torture of holding her naked in his arms was far worse than when he held her after removing her from the dudgeon.

So was the fear.

He spent the next two hours skin to skin, even using his breath to warm her as he whispered words of assurances whenever she made a noise or frowned.

It wasn't until her fever lessened that he was able to breathe evenly and when her shivering diminished, he waited a bit more before easing away to add wood to the fire, thankful that Keir had taken the time to gather lumber from the attached lean-to and pile it beside the hearth.

He checked the clothes and readjusted them to help them dry before sitting on a chair to keep an eye on her, not daring to tempt his demanding cock any more than necessary and angry with himself for even wanting to take her as she lay ill.

Running a hand over his face, he tried to sort through his thoughts.

What was it about the lass that made him concerned that she may be a spy and yet constantly fighting his desire to bed her?

Was she a spy? If so, how could Skye have gotten word to anyone when his best men had been watching her?

Even though she was from the same country as his mother, her accent was unknown to either of them. If she was innocent, why could she not tell him who she was or what she was doing here? If she were guilty, why would she try to save his sister?

The excuses the midwife and Riona had made of trying to kill Anna had not made sense.

There was no weapon.

Her hands had not been around Anna's throat. Keir said one had been on her forehead the other on her stomach.

Was she trying to find out what was wrong so she could help?

The midwife had laid hands on the belly to feel around during his sister's last two pregnancies as well as this one, and no one had questioned that.

Maybe she was forced to spy.

Perhaps a member of her family was being held hostage until she returned with information.

His head was spinning with too many questions and not enough answers.

"I either lost my mind or I am dreaming."

He swung his gaze to Skye's and froze as she moved beneath the furs.

She closed her eyes and sighed. "I didn't make it and all I can think about is how handsome you are."

When she opened her eyes, he watched as she took in his naked form, causing his shaft to rise up in pride.

"Am I stupid or what?"

Ignoring the blood pooling downwards and seemingly uncaring of his nakedness, he smiled. "Ye need to sleep, lass."

She watched him watching her, failing to ignore his unabashed nakedness. "I was trying to help Anna and her baby."

"Aye, lass, I ken this."

"You believe me? Thank God." A tear fell.

She smiled as her hand quickly wiped it away.

His heart squeezed in his chest.

"How long have I been here?"

"No long."

She sighed at his evasiveness. "I suppose you'll be taking me back."

"Nay."

She frowned and lifted her head. "No?"

"Nay."

He almost came to her assistance when she struggled to sit up but the way the skins rolled away exposing her firm breasts with large pink areolas to his gaze had him gritting his teeth and staying put, even as his cock twitched its own demands.

Snatching up the furs, she ignored the blush that stole over her face and sat up, forcing her eyes to remain on his face and not lower.

"Are you going to explain?"

"Explain?"

He frowned as she raised her arm to push back the hair from her face causing her breasts to threaten to spill over, even as she clutched at the coverings. He focused on the golden skin, remembering the silky smoothness as he had held her close, trying to warm her with his body.

How he wanted to warm her in other ways.

"Well?"

He blinked at how strong and irksome her question sounded.

"For someone who was in a rainstorm for hours an feverish, ye sure do sound hearty."

He watched her blush deepen and wondered at it.

"I'm a fast healer." She shrugged.

"Ahhh." He said as if that answered all.

"Are you going to explain now what you are going to do with me?"

Why that question caused his groin to swell he refused to think of, but his mouth watered as he remembered the satiny curves he had held in his arms a short while before and knew exactly what he wanted to do to her.

Skye's mouth opened as she watched his eyes darken and then her gaze dropped to his shaft straining upwards between thick thighs lightly covered in dark hair and she swallowed, her breasts growing heavy and painful as her nipples hardened, feeling dampness between her thighs.

She really didn't care that he hadn't answered her question when all she could think of was touching him, her mouth watering for a taste.

She raised her eyes, taking in the hard plains of his darkly tanned, lean stomach. Fascinated with how his chest hair went from a narrow strip up his flat belly to spread out over his broad chest.

Skye's fingers itched to spear through that hair to feel if it was as soft as it appeared and her breath quickened at the thought. Her gaze traveled upwards taking in his muscled arms and shoulders and further to a face kept masculine by a strong chin, cheekbones, and nose. It was his blue eyes, fringed in thick black lashes, watching her intently that had her barely holding back a whimper of need.

She instantly knew what she wanted. Not knowing if this chance would ever happen again, she lifted her chin and lowered her hands.

Aiden sat still through her perusal of him while clenching and unclenching his jaw but he straightened when she let the covering fall from her breasts to her lap. His eyes narrowed as he watched her nipples harden in the warmth of the room and her breath quicken.

"Lass." He cautioned as she removed the furs from her completely.

Her determined eyes never left his as a flush spread over her face and down her neck just before she rolled over and slowly made her way toward him on hands and knees.

Every muscle in his body tightened when her hand touched his ankle and traveled slowly up his calf, the other tracing the same path over his opposite leg.

Aiden watched her swallow as her eyes left his face and fixated on his staff. Unable to move, wondering, waiting for what she would do next.

She eased between his rock-hard thighs, her fingers sliding over his legs, enjoying the way the crisp hairs tickled her fingertips before coming up the inside of his thighs to cup the base of his cock.

Licking dry lips, she peeked at his face and bit her lip. When he didn't move to stop her, she lowered her head slowly, her tongue flicking out to capture the drop of cum that leaked from the head, her eyes never leaving his.

He went to swallow but froze as her hot mouth opened and sunk over his eager cock, gripping him in heated wetness as she tried to suck him in, her mouth indenting as her tongue swirled around the underside.

She tried to take him all in, but he was too big and she moaned in disappointment.

He grabbed her hair in his fists when vibrations from her whimper tempted his resolve.

"Och, *leanabh*." He gritted out as his neck strained and his head fell back only to swing back down in his need to watch, trying to keep her from moving so he would not explode like a lad at his first bedding.

His hands holding her still caused her nipples to tighten and she sat up straighter, rubbing herself against him, locking her knees together to stop the achy swollen feeling growing in her. Needing to keep touching him, she laved him with her tongue as she cupped his sacs in one of her hands and lightly squeezed as the other hand slipped around his outer thigh, squeezing.

"Och, *leanabh*." He repeated, his voice strained, lost to the feeling of her hot mouth stretched over his cock as her hand moved from his balls to the base, gripping it in her small fist.

Before he embarrassed himself, he hauled her up by her shoulders, trying not to bruise her as he pushed her back onto the furs. His mouth silencing her cries of protest as his hands ran down her body to the vee of her legs and then to the wetness between them.

Skye cried out against his mouth as nerve endings came to life at his touch, her body arched in need. She welcomed his tongue eagerly, opening to its invasion as she pressed upwards, needing to feel him on her, in her.

She gasped when his fingers sunk inside her. "Oh, God, yes."

Her legs opened of their own accord and she panted as she wrapped her hands around his back, demanding he close the gap by grabbing his muscled forceps and pulling him closer.

His fingers spread through her juices, sliding over her swollen clit then back to her pussy. "So damn tight."

"Please." She begged, the heels of her feet helping her to press into his hand as his fingers plunged inside then back out.

"More." She sobbed. "Please, Aiden, more."

Skye squirmed under the onslaught of his hands and mouth. Her body grew tighter as consuming need speared her core, turning her body into an inferno of heat.

Taking his cock, he swirled it around her opening, coating the head in her juices before slipping his hand under her waist and thrusting inside her tight sheath.

Her body stiffened as she cried out in surprise.

His heart entered his throat and he stilled.

Looking down at her face, he watched a tear slide down her cheek as she bit her lower lip. "Ye where a virgin."

She squeezed her eyes shut and swallowed before opening them and nodding.

"Why did ye no say something?"

Her hands where clenching his shoulders, whether to pull him closer or push him away he could not say, so he waited, not moving.

"I didn't . . . I wasn't . . . thinking about it." She searched his face. "I'm sorry, I just wanted you so much, it didn't cross my mind, I mean—"

Embarrassed and hurting, she shook her head, not knowing what to say as her eyes skittered away from his.

He leaned forward to kiss her and she winced at the pain.

"Och, lass. Ye be killin me." He said softly.

"I'm sorry. I knew it was going to hurt, just not this much." She looked back at him then quickly away, mortified that she was acting like an idiot but he was larger than any other man she had ever seen and she should have considered that.

"I think maybe you're too big." She whispered.

He tried hard not to chuckle, but failed.

She glared at him and tried to push him off but flinched at the pain.

"Shhh." He slowly eased forward and kissed her forehead. "Doona move. Just relax."

He spoke softly as his brogue thickened in his need, placing gentle kisses along her temple, down her cheek to her mouth, where he nibbled at the lip she was biting.

"Tis alright, *ghaol*."

Her breathing hitched at his gentleness and she accepted her body's reaction as it began to relax.

"An toir thu dhomh pòg?"

She let go of her lip and opened her mouth, kissing him as he asked.

It was slow; this seduction of her senses, and her body began to respond.

He touched her cheek with his fingertips before sliding down her neck to cup her breast letting his thumb scrape back and forth over her nipple.

She could not help the way her body arched at the contact and gasped.

He stilled. "Does it hurt, wee one?"

She looked at him and blinked as she assessed her body then smiled shyly and shook her head.

He returned her smile and went back to kissing her.

"Aiden." She cried softly, moving under him as desire again began to course through her, testing and unsure.

His mouth found the place where her neck and shoulder met and he lapped at it with his tongue, adding pressure when she cried out, her body thrust up of its own will but he remained still, nibbling up her throat to her earlobe.

She moaned as the pain receded and the feeling of fullness became pleasurable.

Moving, she again tested the sensitivity and sighed in approval as he pushed in deeper.

Still confused at how this girl responded so easily and with great desire for being a virgin, Aiden kept his body still, sweating at the restraint of not plunging deeper into her tight heat, allowing her to grow accustomed to his invasion.

His teeth skimmed over her full lower lip before tugging at it. When she moaned and opened to him, he slipped his tongue in and caressed the recess of her mouth.

Pressing herself against him, Skye pleaded. "Please, Aiden. Move. Do something . . . please."

He groaned at her words and pressed slowly into her.

Her whimper of frustration teased his ear as she eased her hand down over his back to his buttocks, her nails digging in as she pressed up using her heels and widening her knees.

Her begging tested Aiden's control as he eased out unhurriedly before pressing in deeper.

"Easy, lass." He cautioned setting a slow pace as a bead of sweat slipped from his hairline to his clenched jaw.

Always preferring the experienced so his dark desires were easier to accept, he had stayed clear of virgins. Now he held one under him. As he was straining to keep control, goose bumps skittered across his damp skin where her fingernails skimmed, gritting his teeth as he swelled inside her and thankful when she whispered in his ear, biting as she told him how wonderful it felt and still he took his time.

More sweat broke out on his forehead as her pussy tightened around him, squeezing an already tight fit. She had found his rhythm and met his thrusts, her head tilted back.

She could hear how wet she was as he eased himself in and out, the feeling of emptiness as he pulled out only to stretch her when he eased back in drove her need higher.

Grinding against him, Skye frowned as she began to feel closer to the orgasm only her hands had brought her before.

"What do ye need, lass?"

"I don't know." She gasped. "More. Please, Aiden, I just need more. Now. Faster. Something."

She wept, her breath caught as he thrust harder inside.

He pulled out to the tip then plunged in, watching her for signs of discomfort.

On the second thrust, she cried out. "Yes, that's it."

She moved, squirmed under him, pulled at him with her hands, ground her heels to shove her hips up and he watched as her face flushed and the need to bury himself deeper consumed him. He placed a hand under her waist and pulled her tight against his pelvis, his mouth claiming her breast and he suckled as he drove in and out of her, pulling at her nipple, biting at the underside of her breast, constantly watching her reactions to ensure she found pleasure.

Skye was lost in sensation.

Every touch, every time he pushed harder inside her, deeper, she felt the pressure, the need growing in her womb. When he suckled her breast it shot to her core, when he bit, licked, or plunged inside, the pressure grew. Her head tossed from side to side as she opened her knees wider. Shoulders pressed against the floor, she ground her pelvis against him causing the tempest in her body to rush to her womb.

"Please, Aiden, please." She cried in need. "More. Harder. Please, harder." The last word drawn out as her neck arched.

"Cum for me, *leanabh*." He demanded as he descended on her bared neck, thrusting harder.

Skye felt him suck at the vein just above the juncture of her shoulder and her breath caught as molten lava erupted deep inside her cunt, coursing in waves through her.

Her orgasm gripped his cock as he pumped harder, lost in her tight hot sheath, scraping his teeth over her neck as his balls tightened painfully, but it wasn't until Skye cried out his name that they exploded, shooting through his shaft, expanding it painfully before it spurted into her heated depth.

"Oh, God. Oh, God . . . oh, my God." Skye whispered when she was able to breathe, her body held tightly in Aiden's arms as she collapsed, limp and sweaty from her orgasm.

Aiden silently held her as their breathing slowed, amazed at what they had just done when such a short time before she was at deaths door.

Easing from her, he rolled to his back taking her with him. He brushed the hair from her face and saw her grin. Before he could question her, she lifted her head to see him.

"I waited twenty-four years for this." She said as if surprised by that fact.

"Ye waited twenty-four years for me." He assured her as he tucked her back under his chin, wondering who was more shocked at his words.

When he was sure she wasn't going to respond to his comment, he eased away from her and got up. He felt her silent gaze on him as he got out a flask and cloth before returning to her side.

"Tis cold, but will be better to be clean as yer body starts feelin the discomfort."

"I can do it." She whispered, embarrassed.

"Aye, lass, I ken this, but ye will let me have the honor."

He gently removed the covering she had used to keep warm as he gathered the supplies and wet the cloth before tenderly cleaning the blood and semen away.

Skye could not stop the heat that suffused her body at his administrations any more than she could keep her eyes from his face.

"How be it that ye doona have any hair on yer legs or under yer arms, lass?"

"Huh?"

"Ye have no a single hair on yer legs or under yer arms." He repeated. "An yer woman's hair tis so short."

"Oh, that. Ummm . . ."

How was she to tell him she could run her hands over the places she needed to and the hair would be gone?

"I shave there."

"Ye shave?" He asked incredulously. "There?"

Skye blushed even more and nodded. "Everyone does where I'm from."

Shaking his head in bewilderment, he dried her off before standing and cleaning himself, dropping to her side after putting everything away.

She watched his movements and was again in awe over the way his muscles rippled under his smooth skin, how his dark hair glowed in the shadows cast by the flames, and how his eyes held hers as he eased down beside her.

Forgetting her embarrassment, she reached out and touched his cheek feeling the roughened growth and the tingles on her sensitive chin from his attentions. She didn't stop the smile from showing as he covered them in the furs, pulling her back against his stomach, his hand coming around to smooth over her belly as she laid her head on his bicep.

Aiden smiled moments later when Skye's breathing slowed and her head and body fully relaxed as sleep overtook her.

He kept touching her, enjoying the softness of her skin.

Ignoring his growing shaft, he cupped her full breast, running his thumb back and forth over the side, then tracing over her ribcage and down to her thigh before delving in the curls between her legs.

He fell asleep with his cock pressed against the rounded globes of her ass.

*   *   *

Ye waited twenty-four years for me.

Skye woke up thinking those words as she found herself enclosed in the warm embrace of the man who had rocked her world.

Her leg curled over his lower abdomen, one arm tucked tightly between them and the other laying across his chest with his hand over hers while his other came up from under her, holding her to him.

Had she been waiting for him?

For this?

Lord knows, she tried to have sex before and it never worked. Thankfully, because she highly doubted any of them could have compared to how this man felt, and he felt good. She felt her body already reacting to his closeness and the memories of him stretching her, going from pain to a deeper, more pleasurable ache.

She could not help when she pressed herself closer as her nipples tightened over the thoughts crossing her mind.

The last thing she wanted to do was leave the feeling that his nearness brought as if nothing could go wrong.

She took a deep breath, her fingers curling under his hand as the foolishness of that longing hit her.

"I will be takin ye back to the glen where ye were found."

Shock caused her to catch her breath and stiffened. She tried to lift her head but his hand came up and held her to his chest.

"I doona wish to discuss it, lass. Twas planned before ye ran. Tis what ye want an ye shall have it."

What Aiden truly wanted was for her not to see the sadness in his eyes at the thought of sending her away but he knew he had to go through with their plans or he would never find peace.

Skye didn't know why she wanted to cry. She knew she needed to get home because Sarah and Doug needed her before things went terribly wrong but she was suddenly feeling hopelessly lost, something so much deeper than the feelings she had when she had collapsed against the tree.

Then, she felt lost and angry.

Now, she felt overwhelming despair.

"When?"

Even hearing the catch in her voice didn't stop his heart from sinking to his stomach. "When ye be ready."

She was never going to be ready.

Her hand ran down the surface of his chest before following the path down his flat stomach, marveling over the way it felt so hard and firm.

Shifting, she angled her body to be more on top, allowing her hand to wander slowly, memorizing how he felt, how he smelled. She felt his cock against her inner thigh and smiled as she shifted to straddle him, running her mouth over his shoulder, licking and nibbling as she rubbed her breasts against his hard chest, moaning when his hands came up to cup her ass and press her down against his hard cock. Her juices coated him as her pussy clenched in desire.

"We have time. Please tell me we have time." She whispered in his ear, trying to slow her racing heart as her hands kneaded into his skin.

"Aye, *leanabh*, we have time."

He went to roll her over and she protested. "Just let me touch you."

He softened his grip and relaxed—as much as possible for a man going insane at a mere girl's touch.

"As long as ye do no do what ye did last time."

Skye smiled against his collarbone, remembering taking him into her mouth.

"But why?" She pouted, moving her hand down his chest to wrap around his cock, its size causing her to shiver in yearning.

"A man can handle only so much, lass." He cupped her face and drew her eyes to his. "Where did ye learn sech things?"

She grinned. "I like to read."

"Ye can read?"

When she nodded, his frown deepened.

"What manuscript has knowledge of that sort?"

Her eyes widened at her slip and she worried her lower lip.

"Well." She dragged the word out. "It's from something called the *Kama sutra*. That's about all I know."

"That's all?"

She grinned wickedly and felt his cock jerk.

133

"It has pictures of different positions." She squirmed teasingly. "This is one of them."

Aiden groaned, his hips jerking against her.

Feeling the wetness between her thighs pleased him tremendously but he remained still, allowing her ministrations.

He was still cautious since she had been a virgin. His tastes ran dark and he preferred his women well accustomed to his type of sexual demands.

It had not taken him long to see the desire in her, she hadn't backed down from his touch or kiss.

Instead, she had met him head on, begging for more.

He had chosen to ignore the signs of her innocence because of his desire for her and now here he was, eager to plunge inside her wet tightness.

"Ye need to have a care, lass. Ye will be sore."

She seemed fascinated with his nipples, playing with them as they hardened, glancing up absently when she answered his comment.

"I am a fast healer, remember?"

"So ye say." He grunted as he wedged a hand between their bodies and touched her mound.

Her moans of encouragement had him plunging a finger inside, gritting his teeth at the tightness, his cock growing heavy as she slowly rode his finger, little mews coming from her throat. He rasped his thumb over her swollen clit as he took her hair and forced her head up to meet his mouth, thrusting his tongue inside when she cried out.

"Please." She begged.

"What be it, lass?" He asked, his words demanding an answer.

Unable to think past the need of him filling her, she could only moan.

His fingers caused sensations so pleasurable as to border on pain all around the opening of her cunt as his finger fucked her. Inserting another only made her arch into him as he stretched her, knowing he was preparing her.

"Tell me, *leanabh*, what be it ye want?" He asked as her juices ran down his hand.

"You, Aiden. Oh, God, you!" She cried as she rocked hard against his fingers, feeling the pressure building.

A third finger plunged inside and she trembled, lost to his will, wanting more.

"Put me inside, Skye, an ride me."

Yes! Her mind screamed, wondering why she had not done just that.

Skye took him in hand, her passion overriding some of her fears of his size and the pain she had felt the first time.

His hands on her hips kept her from thrusting his cock inside her quickly and she was inwardly pleased even as her body screamed for more.

When the head of Aiden's cock entered her, she gasped at the feeling, her hands moving to his chest as she raised herself up, slowly easing him in.

Her breathing quickened as he stretched her impossibly wider, amazed at the feeling of pleasure-pain his steady entry caused, craving more, asking him for more.

When he eased out, her eyes flew open and she looked at him, begging.

"No! No please, Aiden, inside."

She tried to force herself down over his shaft as she begged but his hands kept her at his will.

We watched her eyes darken with desire and a sheen of sweat formed over his skin at his restraint. No matter how much he wanted to ram into her, he had to remember she had been a virgin and needed to be eased into the pleasure slowly so she could grow accustomed to his size.

"We have time, *ghaol.*" He assured her even as he gritted his teeth.

"I know." She moaned as he slid in further and she wept at the feeling of being filled, stretched. Searing pleasure burned through her. "But it hurts, it hurts so good and I want more. I want more, Aiden."

She wiggled demandingly in his hands causing him to allow her to sink down further.

"Yes, yes."

She bent down and bit his chin, took his lower lip and pulled, her body trying desperately to find completion. She was burning and only knew that he could help ease the fires.

"Now, damn you." She sucked at his lower lip in frustration, no longer caring, angry then he wasn't giving her what she wanted. "Stop doing this to me."

"Aye, lass. To both of us." He thrust up and he took her hips, pulling her down to burying himself deep inside her.

Her body arched up and she cried out as her world disappeared into arcs of pure sensation.

"Oh!"

He stayed still, trying not to explode in the tight sheath of her womb but she was grinding against him, fighting his strong grip, mewling words he couldn't understand.

Gathering what was left of his control, he eased his hands from her hips, allowing her to move when she was ready.

She instantly swiveled her pelvis and gasped at the feeling of ecstasy when he hit something inside her.

She moved again, testing different ways, leaning forward to scatter kisses on his stubbled chin, sitting up a little as she rocked her hips, riding the tide of pleasure every movement brought her.

When he took her hips and lifted her then brought her down hard on him, she knew she was lost. She sat up using her knees and thighs to help him quicken the pace, her hands kneading like a cat on his chest, mouth open as she tried to draw in air.

Balls tightening in demand, he slammed into her, forcing her to take him deeper, the sound of her wetness as his cock rammed in and out drove him wild.

Aiden felt her spasms gripping him as she approached her climax and he slipped a finger between them to flick over a clit soaked with her honey.

She was on fire as sweat from her pores dripped down her arms while she strained against him, reveling in the way he controlled her and his powerful thrusts. The way he kept hitting something deep inside her making the throbbing pleasure almost unbearable and yet she still fought to have him deeper, fanning the flames that licked through her veins to gather around her sensitive cunt, expanding, contracting.

When his thumb scraped over her clit, she gasped as her breath left her and the flames swept through in an inferno of ecstasy.

She held onto his forearms as he pounded into her, causing her orgasm to continue to build. She cried out his name, unable to catch her breath as wave after wave of sensations pounded from her cunt to every nerve ending of her body.

Aiden felt Skye's contractions squeeze his cock and could not hold back his own, his balls tightened painfully and he thickened even more.

Fingers digging into her thighs, Aiden thrust once more into her womb and let go his seed, growling as he felt her hot core tighten around his staff.

Skye collapsed on him, exhausted and feeling wonderfully complete. She could still feel him inside as her muscles twitched in the aftermath of her orgasm.

She closed her eyes in contentment as his arms came around her, his heart tickled as it pounded against her ear, their sweat and juices mingling as their breathing returned to normal.

When the air cooled the sweat from their skin, she lifted her head and kissed him lightly on the lips.

"Thank you."

He looked into her eyes and watched the emotions flickering through them before she lowered her gaze and slipped off, hating every moment she felt him slide from her.

He caught her arm before she could rise to her feet.

"We have time."

She shook her head.

"It won't make it any easier." Looking into his eyes, feeling the warmth of his skin, she searched his face. "Will it?"

"Nay, lass, twilna."

Gritting her teeth, she nodded before looking away and unsteadily began to climb to her feet when he grabbed her upper arm and pulled her back to him.

"But it makes me feel good an tis all that matters right now."

* * *

They traveled in silence, Skye held between his legs as his tartan kept her close to his chest, his smell sinking into her pores while Sileas ran a short distance ahead, sniffing at everything before looking up to ensure they were close, then heading off to investigate more.

The sun barely peeked through dark clouds overhead, matching her depressed mood.

The closer they got to the distant woods the worse she felt and it had nothing to do with the rising fog.

Neither said anything.

He knew by her pensive nature and the emotions flashing across her face that she was sorting through conflicting thoughts, but every time she went to say something, she stopped herself.

Trying to remain relaxed, Aiden worried over her behavior, hoping it was as simple as she made it sound.

When she sought silence in his arms and pressed back into his loose embrace, he wrapped her closer as the fog thickened, not seeing the tears that began to fall.

Even though it took several hours of traveling, each lost in their own thoughts, all too soon they found themselves in front of the tree that Seelie had fought and killed the cougar.

Aiden saw the barely discernible signs his men had left for him as they approached their destination. His body felt laden down with discontent as he kept his eyes open to their surroundings and any sign from Sileas that there may be others not known in the area.

Stopping his horse in front of the mound they had buried the cougar, he sat still, his arms loose about her for long moments until she took a deep breath then shifted.

He helped ease her from the horse, jaw clenched to keep from saying anything, and watched as she walked to the tree, seemingly reluctant as the fog swirled around her body, and gingerly stepped over some mushrooms.

She stood there looking down, drawing in deep breaths. When she looked up, he wondered at the sadness in her eyes but refused to look around as long as the dog was quiet.

"You should leave now."

"Leave ye here, alone?" He asked incredulously.

"It won't be for long." She smiled sadly, wondering if she was right, hoping she was wrong, and hating herself for the guilt eating at her.

They stared at each other as the fog continued to grow thicker, then he nodded curtly, knowing his men were close in case something happened.

He turned his horse and slowly guided it away, refusing to look over his shoulder as he waited for Skye to call out for his return and explain all his questions away.

Aiden kept moving even when Sileas began growling.

The hairs on the back of his neck rising with alarm and his heart rate picked up as the dog started running around his steed then took off behind him. He tried to twist around to look but could not see clear enough in the fog.

Just before Sileas started barking in earnest, he swore he could hear Skye call him.

Aiden whipped around and raced back but she wasn't there.

Jumping off his horse and drawing his sword, he called out her name, damming the fog.

In moments, his men joined him having heard his shout.

"Watch where ye step, I want someone to see if they can find footprints—now!" He ordered as he tried to peer through the fog.

"What be wrong with Sileas?" Collin asked.

They stared at the hound as he continued to bark at the spot Skye had stood.

Aiden watched as Keir knelt down and picked something up to look at before the man stood and walked over to Aiden, holding it out in his hand.

Aiden took it. "The ring she wore on her thumb."

Then the words he didn't understand became clear.

"Pray I can return for this, Aiden."

Chapter Seven

Skye fell to her knees, her equilibrium off and stomach rolling. She covered her face waiting for it to go away, thankful it wasn't as bad as the last time.

Just when she was being grateful for twenty-first century heat, she glanced to the left and stared right into a stone fireplace, embers from the dying fire burning inside.

Frozen in place, she looked around, blinking back the dizziness and refusing to believe the things she saw even as his scent filled her lungs and made her body ache for his embrace and for a moment, she thrilled that she was still in Aiden's time.

Then guilt swamped her and reality set it.

"No way." Pushing up on unsteady feet, she took in Aiden's bedroom, turning in a slow circle. "No fucking way."

Her mind went blank and all she could do was shake her head. She stood there blinking, unsure what to do for long moments before she snapped out of it and quickly turned.

Sinking to her knees before the fireplace, Skye added twigs and hay from the box next to her.

As they caught, she added logs, lots of them.

When the fire was strong and she no longer worried it would go out, she cleared her mind and willed her heart to slow down, then called for her sister, praying as time went by that Sarah would hear her and appear.

"Skye!"

She jumped at the sound of her name. "Sarah!"

"Where are you?"

"It didn't work. I tried, Sarah, honest I did! I got to the forest with the fairy circle and I said the spell verbatim—I swear! And all it got me was back to the keep."

"That's okay, baby."

"No, it's not, the baby and Doug—"

"No, Skye, listen to me. It's okay. Doug needs to talk to you and you need to listen very closely."

Skye frowned more confused than ever. "Okaay."

"Skye?"

She looked as Doug's face came into the flames. "Yes?"

"Listen to me, Skye. You need to save the baby."

Throwing up her hands, she wanted to cry her frustrations.

"I know that, but I can't get home. That's what I was trying to tell Sarah, I tried, I did! But all it got me was a big fat nothing!"

Sarah stepped in to calm her. "And that's a good thing."

Wondering if traveling via magic had fried her brains somehow, Skye shook her head.

"You're not making any sense."

"We know, just listen and trust us."

Skye sat there as Doug explained he had been going back through the records of his family history. Because of Skye being in the fifteenth century, he went to the beginning of his manuscripts, just as something to do to keep him occupied with all the turmoil going on in their lives, and he'd found a reference to a woman who'd shown up out of nowhere and saved her unborn baby's life.

"The pregnant woman's name was—is—Anna Rander, wife of Collin Rander and the daughter of Elizabeth and Dougal MacGregor."

"Aiden's sister?" Skye asked in wondered shock.

"Yes!" Doug answered. "My family tree begins with the writings from Elizabeth Gordon who marries Dougal. I followed quickly to my great, great uncle, which was when the books ended."

He paused and Skye watched as he scooted closer to the flames in his excitement.

"We believe, if you can save the baby, you save my entire history. Without that baby there is no family tree."

The enormity of it hit Skye and she fell back on her haunches. "Sarah loses you and the baby."

"That is what we believe." He quietly confirmed, sitting back.

Skye nodded, still dazed by what she'd been told. Long moments passed as she absorbed the information.

"Okay." She said distractedly as she rose to her knees, her gaze fixed on the floor as her mind whirled with the new information before returning determinedly back to the fire. "I can take care if this."

When she saw Sarah visibly relax and Doug smile, she nodded, relaxing somewhat herself.

Standing, she told them she would contact them as soon as possible.

As they faded away, she strode to the door and slipped out of Aiden's chambers, thankful is was quiet.

Leaning against his bedroom door, she sighed. There was no way Skye could dare tell them what happened the last time she tried to save Anna's baby, she was hopeful everyone believed as Aiden did and that she was trying to help. The question of how they would react after it was done was still unanswered.

Or was it?

It had to be in the book. After all, he would have told her if anything bad happened to her.

Wouldn't he?

His child's life was a stake and that could make a man do many things.

Skye shook her head.

Not Doug.

He would tell her, or at least warn her . . . give her options.

She was turning to reenter the room when a voice stopped her.

"You!"

"Oh, Lord." Skye muttered when confronted by Riona.

"Where do you think you are going?" Riona demanded as she pulled Skye away from the door.

There was no way she could explain this.

"We were told you ran away. Aiden and his men went after you. You were hiding here the entire time." She eyed Skye suspiciously. "Why?"

This was so not good, so she glared at Riona. "I don't need to answer to you. I am going to go see Anna."

"No you are not, you were going into Aiden's chambers and I want to know why."

"I don't have to answer to you." Skye repeated as she glared at the busybody, her mind whirling with what to do.

Riona beckoned to someone behind her and Skye watched as a huge monster of a man stepped forward. How she didn't see him she had no clue, but her eyes widened at his approach.

"Take her to my chambers while I figure out what to do."

Mammoth hands grabbed Skye as Riona got right in her face. "You will not ruin my plans."

Before Skye could respond, another hand covered her mouth, almost blocking her nose and air supply.

Unable to fight or make enough sound to attract attention, the beast of a man hauled her away.

In minutes, she was roughly thrown onto a chair in what she assumed was Riona's bedroom, which was actually a larger room with a number of small beds throughout.

A cloth was crammed in her mouth as soon as her abductor removed his hand.

She glared at the giant while he secured her hands to the back of the chair just before someone behind her forced a hood over her head.

Something wasn't right, but it wasn't clicking.

Skye struggled against the painfully tight bonds, which only made it worse so she concentrated on trying to use her other senses but her heart was pounding too loud in her ears from fear.

She knew she wasn't alone but she couldn't hear anyone else.

How the hell do I get into these messes? She berated herself. *This is worse than a B rated movie! No way does this shit happen to anyone else.*

Finley froze in the chair he was lounging on as Riona's guard hauled Skye into their chambers and relieved that she had not seen him before he was able to slip something over her head.

Putting a finger to his mouth to let his sister know he wanted her quiet, he dragged Riona out of the room as her man tied the girl's legs, smiling grimly at a maid that scurried by.

Closing the door behind him, he glared at Riona. "What the hell is goin on?"

"That girl was standing outside Aiden's chambers." She spat.

When Finley shook her harshly, Riona looked around and gritted her teeth before continuing in a lower voice after she cleared her throat.

"What was I supposed to do?"

Wiping a hand over his face, Finley shook his head. Looking around, he kept shaking his head, trying to think.

"I canna get into his bed with the bloody bint around! We can kill her. No one kens she be here an obviously Aiden hasna found her—"

He held up a hand to silence her and she stood there fuming while her brother thought the latest events over.

After a moment, he turned back to her, whispering furiously.

"We go back to the plan we had before she left. Have James do what we discussed an report back to me when done."

* * *

Skye couldn't believe this!

Once again, she found herself before the counsel, only this time she was in chains, the hood just now removed. There was not a friendly face assembled and Aiden was nowhere in the room.

A man with plaited grey hair and matching beard stepped forward.

"Tis her!" He accused in a raspy voice.

Turning to get a better look, she saw a man badly beaten, his face swollen grotesquely with fresh bruises, pointing at her.

She immediately felt the desire to heal him and stop the pain he must be in before it sunk in that he was accusing her of something.

"What have ye to say fer yerself?"

She turned to gaze at the elder who spoke Gaelic with such a heavy brogue she had to concentrate hard on his words.

"To what?"

"This man has accused ye o' conspirin against the Laird o' this keep."

"What?"

"Ye heard me." The man glowered.

She shook her head in confusion.

"I have conspired with no one." She insisted, silently taking back her desire to heal the jerk.

"Ross was taken prisoner an beaten almost to death. As he lay barely conscious, he heard of the plan fer ye to infiltrate the castle, assess, an report so that an attack could be planned."

With each word, Skye's eyes widened.

Riona's brother approached. What was his name? Finley?

"Ye thought to use yer bonnie looks to get what information ye could, then ye tried to sneak out when we werena lookin."

"Not true!"

He bore down on her but she refused to yield, his body brushed against hers.

"But me sister found ye at Aiden's chambers. Ye ken he would search for ye, an when he left, ye used his room to hide in."

"I was—"

"Yer a whore."

He slapped her so hard she staggered and fell, hitting her hip.

Head spinning at the force, she barely heard the elder telling Finley to stop.

She struggled to her feet, shaking her head, anger surfacing.

"You're wrong. I would never do that."

"What?" He sneered. "Spy fer yer kin, or whore?"

Her mouth opened to speak then clamped shut as she turned from him to face the elder.

Standing tall, she squared her shoulders. "I am not a spy, nor am I a whore."

Finley made a scoffing noise.

She took a deep breath as she looked in the eyes of a man who had already condemned her. "I am innocent of these accusations."

Finley grabbed her arm and forced her to face the beaten man.

"Ye call this man a liar? He suffered at the hands of men who cared little fer his life. Ross be a man of this village, why would he lie?"

Shaking her head, she answered. "I do not know, but I stand by my innocence."

"Then ye stand alone." Finley hissed in her face.

"Enough. Get the man to a healer an send the wench to the doogun."

Skye's mouth dropped open in shock but nothing came out as another man grabbed her roughly by the arm and led her away.

Thrown back into the room that still gave her nightmares, Skye jumped in fear when the bars slammed shut.

Not again!

She frantically searched the room while she had light from the torch, knowing the emptiness would change as soon as the two men who had brought her here left with her only source of illumination.

Skye wanted to scream her innocence but to what use? They would only throw her inability to answer questions from her interrogation in her face.

Instead, she made her way to the flimsy cot against the far wall, wanting her body off the floor and hoping it would help to keep the rats away.

This was not good.

Not good at all.

It did not take long before her ears picked up the sounds of scurrying pests.

Her skinned crawled as goose bumps covered her body. She felt the rags under her pull and knew they were using it climb up.

Shrieking, Skye scrambled to shake them off and pull the cloth up and away, then she wrapped the filthy things around her hands and arms so she could sweep them off when they found another way to her.

She sat there petrified, barely dosing for short periods.

Dreams of things crawling on her woke her up with a jerk.

It took her mind, clogged with fear, time to sort out the fact that there *were* things crawling on her and they must be coming from the bedding.

Desperately trying to get the tattered rags off, she brushed frantically at herself. Whimpering as she scrambled off the cot and tearing the fabric from her as she backed away, her mind a mass of numbed horror.

When the bars touched her back, she cried out and jumped, losing the battle to keep back the tears.

Tense and unable to squeeze her eyes shut to stop the tears for fear that they would jump on her if she wasn't watching, Skye clenched and unclenched her fists trying to think as she quickly brushed the tears from her eyes.

"I can't do this again. I can't." Staring into nothing, she kept whispering, scratching at the fleabites. "I can't, I can't."

Her head shot up when she heard the scurrying of the rats.

"Oh, God, please, please, please."

Hours passed without anyone coming for her. She was shivering from terror and cold, huddled in the corner she'd inched her way to, incapable of being able to comprehend if the things crawling on her were real or not, she would frantically brush at her flesh, sobbing quietly.

"Skye?"

Starting at the whispered word, her head swung around, eyes wide, and her breath caught in her throat.

"Skye? Be ye there?"

The light had her heart beating again and she hurried over to the bars. "Anna!"

"Och, Skye! Look at ye."

Blushing furiously at the sight she must present, she looked away.

"I will get ye out of there."

A sob caught in her throat and she swallowed, shaking her head at the girl. "You can't. They believe I'm a spy."

"But yer no!"

Skye smiled, brushing away a tear with a jerky movement of her hand. "Thank you for believing in me."

"I do, an when Aiden an Collin come back they will too!" Anna whispered furiously.

"The baby. How's the baby?"

Anna touched her stomach and smiled. "The bairn be fine. I doona ken what ye did, but I feel like there be reel hope now."

"Anna, you need to stay in bed."

"But ye healed me."

Skye's heart leapt to her throat as thoughts of burning at the stake and Anna truly thinking all was well now.

"Listen to me, Anna. I did not heal you. You need to stay in bed."

"But there be no more pain nor spottin! Ye did it, Skye! An tis another reason why I will get ye out of here."

"Anna—"

"What be ye doin here, Lady Anna?"

They both turned to see Finley approaching from the end of the passage.

"Tis an outrage, imprisonin Skye this way!"

Finley patted Anna's arm solemnly. "Tis difficult, I ken, but the counsel has heard information that has led them to make this decision, an we must abide by it."

He tried to lead her away but she resisted.

"I wilna leave her here alone. Aiden wouldna abide this!"

"Lass, doona stress yerself an the babe this way."

Fearful for the baby, Skye encouraged Anna to leave. "Please, Anna, it's alright."

"Tis no!"

"Anna, you need to calm down for me, for the baby, and get back to bed." Skye whispered, unable to stop the tremors.

Anna wrestled her arm away from Finley.

"Please. You really do need to take it easy. It is *not* alright to be up and about."

Anna looked at Skye and frowned.

"Alright. I will go." She glared at Finley, her words spoken venomously. "But when Aiden an me husband return they will be livid."

Finley walked beside Anna, ensuring she didn't return.

Sinking to the floor, Skye was grateful they left Anna's torch in the wall sconce so, for a little while at least, there was enough light to keep the rats at bay—hopefully.

Resting her head on her bent knees, she could not stop the shaking that continued to rack her body.

Who knew how much time had passed without rest?

The magic she used to return to the keep combined with her body's healing from the bedbugs, the lack of sleep, and stress was wearing her down.

She could not contact Sarah through the flame because leaving here without being able to save Anna's baby was out of the question.

If she had been thinking clearly, and if Finley had not shown up, she could have taken care of that and talked with Sarah about getting her the hell out of here.

Looking back at the time she and Aiden had spent in the shed took her hopes away.

She should have stayed put, bottom line.

Skye laughed as every one of her actions made her look as if she was the very thing she was being accused of—again.

How she had run away to be found by Aiden, then having sex with him only to disappear when his back was turned, and finally showing back at the keep.

It didn't take any stretch of the imagination to put two and two together and equal spy and whore no matter what century a person found themselves.

What if she had been honest?

Anna seemed to be very happy with the idea that Skye had healed her, even though she hadn't had the chance to figure out a permanent solution to her pregnancy. But Anna was young, probably still fanciful. Aiden believed she had been trying to help, but he had no idea to what extent she really could help.

What if he did?

She stopped herself. What ifs weren't going to help her now. She didn't even know if the truth would.

Exhausted, she fell into a fitful sleep.

Dreams of rats and huge bed bugs climbing her legs turned into reality and she woke, choking on a scream as she tore at her clothing, brushing off the rodents as she scrambled to her feet.

The torch had sputtered out, leaving her in complete darkness once again.

Kicking her feet to keep them from attacking again, Skye pressed her hand against her mouth to stop herself from bawling like a baby, or crying out and having any one hear her and laugh at her weakness.

Damn them all to hell.

Then she snorted.

She was already there.

Something nibbled on her shoe and she whimpered as she kicked, losing her slipper.

Skye had no idea how long she had been in the cell, if it was day or night, or if anyone cared that she was dying in here.

Her stomach had stopped growling from hunger ages ago and her feet were going numb with the effort to stand.

When her head started spinning, Skye she knew it wouldn't be long before nothing mattered.

Her hands were too heavy to lift, not that they could do anything with how hard they were shaking. Even her knees gave up their support and she barely made a sound as she slid down the wall, her last thought was how terrible it was that she wasn't going to be with her sister when she lost her baby and her husband.

*   *   *

Shaken roughly awake, Skye squinted, unable to lift a hand to shield her eyes from the light.

"Keir?" She croaked.

"The Laird sent me fer ye."

He hauled her up and she stumbled, bumping into the wall behind her. She would have slipped down if he hadn't picked her up and carried her.

It wasn't until she felt her powers overriding the 'wall' she had in place to keep from drawing on another's strength that she started fighting his hold.

"Let me down. You have to let me down."

She could feel herself getting stronger and when Keir stumbled the second time, she was able to disengage herself from him and they both stood still, Keir shaking his head, wondering at his sudden weakness and her shaking at what her powers had begun to do.

"I can walk. J-just tell me where you want me to go."

Keir straightened and stared at her, his blank eyes telling her he knew of the accusations and believed them.

"'Tis Anna. She ran out to greet us on our arrival. Her excitement caused me horse to rear—"

"The baby!" Skye whirled around, cursing herself when she stumbled to her knees as her equilibrium went off kilter.

Picking herself up before Keir could reach her, Skye raced down the hall and up the stairs as fast as her unsteady feet would allow, grateful for the bit of strength she had gotten from Keir who was following close behind, grudgingly wishing it had been more.

As they neared Anna's bedroom, she could hear the girl crying out her name.

She was about to rush to her side when her arm was grabbed forcefully and she was wrenched around, falling against a hard chest before looking into Aiden's cold eyes.

"For some reason, Anna thinks ye can save her an the bairn." Ignoring the way his gut twisted at her appearance Aiden glared down at her. "If she dies so do ye."

Skye tried to swallow past the lump in her throat and nodded, afraid he wouldn't let go soon enough as more strength flowed slowly into her.

Eyes narrowed, he searched her face making sure she understood before releasing her.

She went to Anna and tried to calm her down. "I'm here, Anna, I'm here."

The girl reached for her, blood on her forehead and skirt. "Please, Skye. The bairn—"

"I know, baby. It's going to be all right. I promise."

Thankful for what little strength she had gotten from Kier and Aiden, Skye knew it helped in keeping her from depleting Anna, but she still needed for the girl to let go.

Looking at Collin's dead stare and bloody clothes did nothing to alleviate the way her heart pounded.

"You must get on the bed. Cradle her head in your lap." She instructed as she tried to disengage the death hold Anna had on her arm, glaring at the midwife who was howling uncontrollably, barely smiling when Elizabeth shoved the woman into the hands of someone else.

"Get everyone out of here."

She turned her full attention to Anna, no longer caring about anything else.

She was going to save her family and Anna's baby.

"Listen to me, Anna. I need my hands free."

When the girl didn't respond, Skye leaned closer and reached over with her free hand to touch her cheek, sending calming thoughts, trying desperately to not take Anna's strength as the girl held tight.

"I need my hands free, Anna." She said calmly in Gaelic. "So I can do what I did last time, remember?"

"She needs her hands to help the babe, *leanabh.* Let go." Collin gently removed her hands from Skye's arms.

When released, Skye took a step further down only to have her arm clutched frantically.

"Doona leave me!" Anna cried.

"I'm not going to leave you, Anna, I am going to save the baby, remember? I made a promise." She assured her as Collin stepped between, talking smoothly to his wife his eyes bearing down on Skye silently.

She glared back defiantly. "And I plan on keeping that promise."

"I will keep me promise as well." Aiden's threat came from behind her, just before he stepped up to her side.

Pausing to take a calming breath before returning Aiden's hard stare, she spoke calmly.

"Unless you need to make good on your threat, heed this warning: Do not touch me. If you believe nothing else from me, believe that it will do you more harm than good to touch me."

He raised a mocking eyebrow then looked at his mother when she returned her attention back to Anna. When his mother nodded her belief in the girl's words, both eyebrows rose.

Centering herself at the swollen belly and preparing for what she had to do, Skye instructed Collin on what his responsibilities were as he climbed on the bed and cradled his wife's head in his lap.

"I'm not strong enough to keep her calm and take care of the baby so I need you to hold her, comfort her, tell her you love her," She looked up as she gathered her powers, feeling the warmth building along her trembling arms and centering it into her hands. "and don't stop."

Ignoring his questioning gaze, she locked her knees against the wobbling and placed her hands on the belly in front of her.

Skye concentrated, her eyes loosing focus as she followed her energy into the girl's body and directly to the womb. Her powers swirled in a kaleidoscope of colors, settling into place and shifting into the hues that would tell her where to look.

Knowing this took precious time, she drifted to the baby and directed some of her energy there when she noticed his feeble heartbeat.

Hoping to get him to respond, Skye surrounded him in colors, relieved when she saw him twitch.

Swirling muted colors around the baby too keep him from becoming frightened, she continued to fill his frail body with strength.

Seeing life enter the little form, she smiled and shifted her attention to the shades around the womb.

Searching as rapidly as possible, knowing she wasn't as strong as she should be to do what she needed, but also knowing failing wasn't an option.

Finally, at the base of the womb, she noticed a thinning of the membrane. In the center of it was a tear, either caused by the accident or perhaps grown worse during the pregnancy.

"Found it."

"Found what?" Aiden and Collin asked simultaneously.

They looked at each other in confusion having seen no movement from Skye since the moment she had closed her eyes some time ago.

"She be savin me bairn." Anna spoke weakly, her face still drained of color, the wound on her forehead prominent and awful looking against the pale skin.

Aiden looked across at his mother who stood on the other side of the bed but her eyes were on what Skye was doing, her face full of wonder.

His mother had encouraged him to have Skye brought up even after he informed her of what had transpired with the counsel, something he had disbelievingly listened to as they rushed his sister to her.

Aiden had not wanted to hear his mother's anger over being unable to attend the interrogation. If it had not been for the fact Anna would not calm down, the bleeding wouldn't stop, and he was as desperate as Collin was for his sister's safety, he would never have agreed to release Skye from a prison he knew she abhorred.

A fool.

That's what Skye had made him.

He had allowed her to go without answers to basic questions and his reward was a woman willing to hand over her virginity so she could destroy his people.

That was not going to happen now. The only thing keeping his hands from wringing her neck was the fact that Anna was finally calm.

Aiden took in her appearance and hated the way his stomach heaved at the sight, forcing his mind not to think of the areas of her body he could not see, knowing her clothing hid more than it reveled. She had spent more than two days in the dungeon and the scratches on her neck, torn sleeves showing clawed skin, and the grime on her fingers, which could not hide the jagged wounds from the rats or the pinpricks of bites caused by bugs, showing every hour of her torment.

She deserved it for having conspired to attack his keep knowing innocent people would be raped and killed. Her words of innocence had been lies and he was livid at himself for believing them. He refused to acknowledge the ache in his heart as anything other than betrayal.

As time passed, he became more and more perplexed.

She was not moving.

Except for the slight trembling of her body that she'd had from the beginning, which he had equated as fear of him, she wasn't moving.

He looked at Collin crooning softly in Anna's ear as he touched her face and neck, his eyes fixated on Skye's hands looking as baffled as Aiden felt.

When he glanced up and saw his mother's brows crease, he looked back at Skye and saw beads of sweat breaking out and dripping down her face, sweat formed under her arms and back, and her body was shaking harder than when she'd started. He stepped closer but his mother's hand reaching across the bed to touch him stopped his movement.

"She was serious when she said not to touch her. I could feel that to do so would be a death sentence."

"An what is that supposed to mean?" He asked in exasperation. "She hasna moved in over an hour an yet she be grownin paler, she be drippin sweat, and looks like she be about to fall over."

"She is a healer, Aiden. She has a gift like nothing I have ever seen." She squeezed his arm. "Anna is right; she is saving the baby."

Skye repaired the split in the womb, a very meticulous and slow process.

Somehow, maybe in her first pregnancy, damage had occurred along the lining of her womb and it had never repaired enough to hold the weight of a growing baby. She could not be sure since she had only begun to take classes for midwifery after Sarah's announcement that she was pregnant and had not learned a whole hell of a lot but she knew the accident had placed a tear in the already worn womb since she had not seen it the first time she had healed the girl.

Just because she had repaired the womb didn't mean the horse hadn't caused some other damage and she wanted to ensure the baby was going to go full term but she was deteriorating fast.

Ignoring the way her heart rate became sluggish, Skye dreaded when the colors faded, feeling the pounding in her head as if from a distance.

She gave a quick search all over and saw the bruising under the tale tell colors just as the energy gave out.

Her hands slipped and her knees gave way.

"No, no yet."

They watched as Skye's hands, slick with sweat, slipped and her body wavered before going limp.

Aiden caught her, damning the consequences.

"Lemme go." She mumbled sluggishly, too weak to resist or push him away.

Feeling her strength returning, albeit slowly, Skye became terrified for Aiden whom she knew was the one holding her.

"Lemme go. You have ta lemme go." She gathered her strength and tried to push away.

Still too weak, she fell to the floor, her head spinning even as it pounded.

Tears of frustration fell. "Damn, damn, damn, damn."

Elizabeth sank beside her. "What is it, luv?"

Pushing herself up on unsteady arms, she hung her head in shame, crying softly.

"I can't do it. I'm not strong enough." She looked up, eyes still unfocused. "I'm so sorry."

"Tis fine, Skye."

"No, it's not."

"Ye did everything ye could." Elizabeth touched her shoulder.

"Stop!" She jerked away, the movement almost costing her her position. "You can't touch me."

Elizabeth looked at her hand in surprise. "I felt that."

"What did ye feel, Mother?"

Elizabeth looked up. "When I touched her, I felt myself going weak." She said in wonder.

"I'm sorry. I tried to warn you but there wasn't time to explain."

"Explain what?" Aiden demanded.

When Skye could only shake her head weakly, Elizabeth explained.

"If I have this right, Skye's weakness causes her body to draw strength from whoever touches her." She leaned down to look at Skye. "Is that what it is, luv?"

Skye felt a tear course down her cheek and nodded.

When Elizabeth motioned for Aiden to help her up, she looked at her son. "Did ye not feel the drain when ye touched her?"

"Nay, I felt nothin."

Elizabeth frowned in thought, looking down at the girl lying weakly at their feet. "Hold her hand, Aiden."

Aiden crouched to his haunches, ignoring Skye's plea to stop he took her hand, not allowing her to pull away before glancing at his mother.

"Ye feel nothing, son?"

"Nay." He shrugged.

"Skye? How do ye feel?"

Skye shook her head, feeling strength slowly seep into her limbs, knowing she was sucking it from Aiden.

Again, she tried to pull away.

"You don't understand what will happen." She looked up at him, her eyes clearing even as they pleaded with him. "Please. I can't control it when it gets this bad."

Bewildered, Aiden stared at her. "I doona ken. Control what?"

Skye desperately tried to pull away. "I wasn't strong enough. I'm not strong enough now to stop it. You have to let me go!"

"Or what, lass?"

"Or I will take all you have and leave you nothing, dammit! Don't you see? You will die! Now let me go." She fought harder.

"I doona feel weaker for the holdin of ye."

"No."

He took her by her shoulder and forced her to look at him. "Do ye ken, lass? I doona feel anythin but the chill of yer flesh."

She stared at him then. "Nothing? You really don't feel weak?"

When he shook his head, she searched his face, cautiously placing her hands on his forearms.

"But how can that be? I am feeling stronger every moment. I can't heal myself at this speed on my own."

"Ye have magic?"

He watched as her face reddened then drained of color before nodding, her eyes slipping away from his at her confession.

"I told ye."

Aiden looked beyond her shoulder at his sister.

"The baby. I need to finish." Skye insisted.

Aiden assisted her to her feet when she tried to do it on her own and then helped her to the bed.

Skye touched Anna on the shoulder.

"You had a tear in your womb but it's gone now." She assured the worried parents. "We can get into the details later."

"The bairn be fine, though?" Anna asked worriedly.

Skye patted her shoulder. "There are some bruised organs which could hinder the proper development your son needs, so I am going to take care of that, okay?"

They both nodded in astonishment. "Son?"

Smiling past her headache, Skye nodded then wiggled away from Aiden's grasp.

"I can do this on my own now, thank you."

Placing her hand above Anna's forehead and back over her belly, she clenched her teeth when Aiden put his hand on the small of her back.

"I said—"

Aiden replied quietly. "I ken what ye said."

Taking a deep breath, she forced the warmth from his hands out of her mind and concentrated on the warmth of her powers, flowing far easier than before.

She wanted to be fast about this. No matter that Aiden said he hadn't felt any drain, at some point it had to affect him but she placed the fact that this baby's life would save Doug and her sister's unborn child to the front of her thoughts.

Centering herself, she closed her eyes and followed the colors back into the womb while projecting more towards Anna's head wound.

Collin held his wife's hand, continuing to murmur encouraging words, unsure if he was doing it for himself or for her as he marveled that he was having a son.

Not hearing his own words, Collin's eyes grew round as he watched the gash on her forehead. Tilting his head so he could see under Skye's hovering hand, he watched as it gradually began to close. It was so lengthy a time that if he had not been a seasoned warrior, trained to notice things out of the ordinary, he would never have caught the progression. He watched in amazement as the flesh under came together and then the skin closed fully while the bruising slowly vanished, leaving only the blood behind.

Aiden's body froze as his hearing faded, then he felt as if he was being propelled down a narrow tunnel.

Disorientated, he shook his head until he quickly discovered it only made it worse. His eyes lost focus and caught the strangest images. Colors swirled, brightened and dimmed at will, making his vision even more muted. He tried to focus and caught hazy shades of bones and organs, things he had seen on the battlefield but not the same. Then he saw a form floating in midair, so tiny he could hold it in the palm of his hand, curled up as if sleeping. White sparkles shimmered around the form moving as it kicked or jerked.

It hit him that this was Anna's baby, and he watched in wonder.

All too soon, he found himself pulled away from the site back through the tunnel and staggered as his vision faded to black.

Locking his knees, he waited for it to clear.

"I told you it was not good to touch me."

Aiden looked up at Skye's pale face, the green of her eyes intense from the bruises forming under them. His eyes adjusted and reached for her again.

Skye stepped back, straightened her spine and ignored the shaking.

"I did what I had to do." She looked at the other three in the room before returning her attention to Anna. "You must stay in bed one full day."

"But—"

Raising her unsteady hand to stop Anna's protest, Skye continued.

"You lost a lot of blood, something I cannot replace. One full day of bed rest and then I promise you, you can get up and dance if you wish."

Collin and Elizabeth nodded firmly, stilling any further protest from Anna.

Knowing she had accomplished the impossible, Skye headed for the door.

"Where be ye goin?"

Holding on to the handle to keep her steady, she refused to look at Aiden.

"I know I am still a prisoner." She pulled on the door, scared she was going to pass out right there as her skin went clammy.

Hands went around her and she shook her head feebly.

"What be it? Why be ye so frail? I gave ye me strength."

Unable to break away, her head feeling heavy and her empty stomach about to rebel, she whispered; "I can't tell you when I ate l-last, or slept. No amount of h-healing can help that."

He lifted her face and watched as color completely drained from her lips and his heart lurched.

"I am not a spy." She whispered just before she passed out.

CHAPTER EIGHT

"Nothin makes sense." Aiden said furiously as he paced his study. "There be a man, badly beaten, statin Skye be a spy an yet she risked her own life to ensure the bairn's life. I doona ken how this makes sense."

He wished he could speak to Skye, but she'd been given laudanum to help her sleep and keep the nightmares at bay. He thought of how he held her throughout the night, how he had laid there with the fire casting a glow over them and he watched while the damaged skin from the rats and bugs had disappeared as her body repaired itself.

Collin sat with his hands clasped on his knees nodding in agreement. "Ye need to talk to the lass."

"I have tried, man. Think ye I have no?"

"Tis different this time." Collin assured him.

"How? I have the counsel elders pesterin me to make an example of the lass an questionin me authority every minute I doona!"

"She has had nothin but fear. Take her fear away an mayhap she will open up."

Aiden paused, hand to chin in thought. "Take her fear away."

"Show her she be no alone."

A smile grew, lighting his eyes for the first time in many days.

Standing tall, he chuckled. "An I have just the plan on how to do that."

＊　　＊　　＊

Skye was sitting in Aiden's huge bed eyeing the fire roaring in the hearth, dying to get a hold of Sarah, trying not to wonder who had given her a bath.

She remembered waking up before and being hand fed, believing it was Aiden.

Then she'd been given something to drink—something nasty tasting—before drifting back to sleep. Waking up to the smell of food, her mouth feeling and tasting terrible, she was in the process of devouring her plate when a maid entered, paused as she noticed Skye sitting up and quickly left, returning minutes later to clear the empty dishes.

She knew she would have company soon, probably why the maid had immediately left when she saw that she was awake and then returned.

It was not long before her thoughts were proven correct. Her eyes swung to the door as Aiden opened it and walked through.

"Tis good to see ye lookin so well, lass."

A blush stole over her face as his eyes seemed to drink her in.

"For how long?" She asked as she put her plate away, no longer hungry.

His head tilted. "For how long what?"

Refusing to acknowledge her body's response to his nearness, she cleared her throat, making a show of gathering the skins around her, uncomfortable in just a nightgown.

"For how long will I be well? As in . . . when am I going to be hung?" She shrugged. "Or b-burned."

"Why would I be doin either?"

"I have been accused of being a spy so I supposed you hung spies. And now you know I'm a witch and I assume that it's quite normal to b-burn witches."

She hated how she stuttered.

Aiden was saddened that she would not look him in the eyes but he understood and planned to change that post haste.

"Aye, Skye, ye have been accused of bein a spy an we need to talk about that. As for the other—"

Just then, the door opened and in came Elizabeth, Anna, and Collin.

Anna rushed to her bedside, set something down on the table next to her plate of food before promptly crawling over to hug her as tightly as she could with a very large belly in the way.

Skye sat there stunned, fighting back a tear as Anna cried and thanked her for saving her son. She babbled on, amazed about how Skye knew it was a boy and how active he was now.

Elizabeth chided Anna into silence as she approached the bed from the other side.

Taking the seat Aiden provided, she smiled.

"Och, lass, ye have given me something I thought never to experience again; hope. Hope that my daughter would never have to suffer the loss of another bairn. Hope that I will have a grandchild to place on my knee one day soon, and hope that there will be many more before my days end." Elizabeth didn't bother to brush the tear away that fell down her cheek. "Ye have given me the greatest gift and I wish to return the favor."

Taking Skye's hand in her own, she patted it. "Ye are not alone, child."

Skye nibbled at her lower lip, blinking rapidly to keep the tears from falling. She shook her head not understanding.

"Ye see, luv, through simple touch, I have the ability to tell truth from lies. If I concentrate hard enough I can also do so if standing near enough."

Silence filled the room as Skye stared at Elizabeth, her mouth opening in shock as her words registered.

Snapping her mouth shut, she swallowed before asking, "You are not telling me that you are a witch, are you?"

Elizabeth laughed and patted her hand again. "I suppose ye can say that."

"I make flowers grow!" Anna said excitedly.

Reaching for the item she had put down before hugging Skye, Anna held it up for her to see the simple pot filled with soil. The girl squinted and her mouth scrunched up into a cute bow and Skye gasped as a stem broke free, growing slowly, leaves popping out and forming, petals unfurling.

"Wow."

Anna held it out proudly. "See? I can do other kinds too, but flowers be me favorite."

The tears fell then, streaming down Skye's cheeks unchecked.

Elizabeth gripped her hand as Skye hiccupped.

"I thought you would be relieved, dear."

"I-I am. I th-thought . . ." She sniffed needing to wipe her nose and grateful for the hand that reached out and gave her a cloth to do so. "I th-thought I was going t-to be, to be . . ." She couldn't finish the sentence.

Anna hugged her, smoothing her hair. "Tis fine now, Skye. Ye ken better."

"That's right, luv." Elizabeth grinned. "Why, I do not believe any of us knew Aiden had a gift. We all knew his constitution was amazingly strong but we did not realize just how much until yester eve."

Taking deep breaths and wiping at the tears, Skye nodded. She began to worry her upper lip, everyone waited as her mind raced with what she was about to say next.

Aiden watched as emotions flashed across Skye's face, from relief to uncertainty and finally to determination before she spoke.

"There's more."

He straightened, waiting for his world to crash around him at her next words.

She gripped Elizabeth's hand and then turned to look into Aiden's eyes for the first time as a tear fell unchecked.

"I was afraid of so many things. I thought it didn't matter what I said or even how I said it, one way or another it wouldn't be understood any more in this time as it is in mine." Taking a deep breath, she continued. "I am from the twenty-first century."

Everyone stiffened in shock but she rushed on.

"My aunt is a witch as well and she made this ridiculous spell trying to find my soul mate but I ended up in the forest here instead."

She searched his eyes, her own pleading with him to believe her.

Taking a deep breath, she drew her next words out. "I am not a spy."

Aiden did not bother to look at his mother for confirmation, instead he nodded, his head spinning with the words *soul mate*.

"I tried to get back home, but I couldn't." Skye laughed at herself. "I suck at spells you see? The spell my sister and aunt gave me didn't work. And then they said it was probably because I had appeared in a fairy circle and needed that place to channel so that I can get back."

Aiden held up a hand as he stepped forward. "Wait."

She stuttered to a stop, her breath catching at his frown.

"Ye said yer sister an aunt '*said*'. When did they say?"

Her mouth formed an O. "Ohhh . . . well, um . . . you see . . ."

Skye told them about her sister's elemental power of fire, explaining how Sarah could do anything with or through it, even with the smallest flame from a wick. She told them of the conversation about Sarah's baby and Doug just before going to Aiden, asking to go home so she could save them.

"When I came to you in your study and you told me that I couldn't go, I was thinking of potions or spells to put the guards you placed at my door to sleep or something."

She winced when Aiden raised his eyebrow.

"I was so scared of failing my sister, I was desperate. Enough so, that I almost risked everything on the one thing I know I can't do; cast spells. I won't tell you of the times I screwed up. I just can't center myself unless I am healing." She shook her head at her failures before turning to look at Anna. "So I wandered around until I found myself in your room."

Anna clenched her hands in anger when she remarked, "Aye, Riona had been visitin when the cramps and bleedin began. She rushed out to get that hateful midwife."

"Ahhh, well that explains a few things to me." Skye smiled. "All I know is that when I saw what was happening, nothing seemed to matter. I just had to save someone and I knew I could save your baby."

She explained how she was in the process of healing Anna when someone grabbed her and pulled her away. How it had made her ill and unable to comprehend what was happening and, by the time she was feeling better, she noticed she was alone.

"I knew that there was going to be a lot of questions, none of them good. I was in the mist of too many accusations and feared I wouldn't be believed. Or worse yet; that I would, and . . . and . . ." She shrugged, unable to say it.

"So ye ran." Aiden commented.

"When the storm hit, I knew I had failed. I didn't know what direction to go in and I was growing weak. Then you found me." She hesitated, a blush rising up to cover her cheeks.

Elizabeth patted her hand before releasing it and motioned for everyone to leave the two alone.

When it was just Skye and Aiden, she looked into his face, encouraged by the openness of his eyes even as his words gave her hope.

"I set out to find ye an when the gale hit after yer disappearance there was only one thought, that ye wouldna live sech a storm. Ye were so close to the Sheppard's cabin that if it had been daylight ye woulda seen it. I brought ye inside, undressed ye, covered ye with skins but ye wouldna stop shakin an a fever was growin, so I got under the covers an took ye into me arms to warm ye."

She watched as he took the vacated chair, his body appearing relaxed and calm, accepting of her story. She twisted around to face him and tucked her legs under her in Indian fashion, unaware that the gown twisted around her body and accented her breasts.

"You held me?"

"Aye. All night."

"I thought I had been there for days because when I woke, I felt perfectly fine and here it had only been one night." Her blush grew. "You were near the fire, your skin glowing from the flames, and I forgot everything; my commitment to my family, the implications from what had happened before I ran." She searched his eyes. "I just wanted to lose myself in you."

She swallowed when his gaze darkened.

Wanting to finish her story while she had the courage, she ignored the fluttering in her belly and stood up to pace not realizing the flames highlighted her body through the thin material.

"When we made . . . had sex . . . I knew I was lost." She looked at him then quickly away as he watched her with intent. "And the second time made everything so much worse."

She didn't see him stiffen as she paced, her hands moving in the need to get the words out before she thought about what she was saying and lost her courage.

"When you were taking me back to the forest, my heart felt like it was being torn in two. I couldn't speak because my throat had closed up." She ran her hands through her curls. "God, Aiden, I didn't want to leave." She stopped in front of him. "How could I think that? How could I, even for a moment, consider not going home to save my sister and her family?"

Aiden gathered her up and placed her on his lap, holding her close and soothing his hand over her hair, unable to speak himself through the tightening in his chest.

She wrapped her hands around his neck feeling warm and safe. "When I was saying the spell, I wanted to leave you something."

"So ye left yer ring." He removed the ring from his pinky and held it out to her.

"You did hear me." She held the ring and smiled. "My sister has Mom's wedding band. This was Dad's. I had to wrap string around it to keep it from falling off."

Feeling his heart expand that she had left him such a precious piece of jewelry, he tucked her back under his chin.

"Explain to me how ye ended up here, lass?"

"It's my awful luck with spells." She shrugged as she replaced the ring on her thumb. "Instead of returning home, I ended up in your bedroom. Probably because I wasn't fully concentrating on leaving."

Aiden stiffened as his heart felt torn. She hadn't gone back, taken care of her family, and returned.

She would be leaving for real this time.

"So ye will be leavin."

"Leaving?" She pushed away from him to search his face. "Do ye—you want me to leave?"

A sharp knock sounded as she was asking her question. Knowing only something vital would be the cause, he eased her from his lap and covered her before he went to the door.

Seeing Collin and Keir standing there, he turned back to Skye.

"I will return shortly. Will ye be here?"

She watched him close the door behind him after she nodded.

Aiden stopped Collin from speaking, motioning for him to hold his information until they were away from the chambers.

They entered his study and closed the doors before Collin informed him that the man who had accused Skye of treason was dead.

"How?"

"I dunno ken, m'Laird." Keir spoke. "Angus had been askin him for details. He began to waiver in his beliefs that Skye was the one he heard speakin. But his injuries were bad an he was in an out of consciousness."

"When Angus went back to question him, he was dead." Collin interjected. "We think twas the injuries he sustained, they werena good, perhaps internally . . ."

Aiden nodded. "Skye is no to find out. If she kenned that she coulda helped the man an didna . . ."

The men nodded.

"Ye say he was doubtin Skye's guilt?"

Keir nodded sharply. "Aye, m'Laird."

"An then he dies." Aiden pondered aloud.

"Ye be thinkin there be more to it than his injuries."

Aiden nodded to Collin. "I canno be sure but I have me doubt on the cause of his death. A man doesna stand on his own two feet to accuse another, then die in his bed."

Collin frowned. "If that be true, then we have a murderer amongst us."

"The council needs to be told." Keir warned.

"Skye's safety be in jeopardy." Collin acknowledged.

Aiden gritted his teeth not liking the sudden thought of her being safer in her own time.

"Get a guard back on her an let all ken that she be under the Laird's protection. I will inform the counsel."

After Keir left, Collin approached Aiden and laid his hand on the man's shoulder.

"It may no be enough. All ken ye have a strong interest in the lass."

*   *   *

Aiden left the counsel discontented by the outcome.

Many still questioned Skye's innocence even after Lady Elizabeth was brought forth to confirm her beliefs. He knew there was a lot he'd left out that may have helped the counsel to better support him but Collin and his mother had agreed that keeping the fact that Skye was from a different time was for the best. Although his people accepted the magic in his family, a time traveler was too much to ask his kinfolk to understand.

Only three were dissatisfied with his assurances that Skye was not involved with the conspiracy to attack the keep, but all agreed they needed to keep a watch for others when he spoke of his concern on the death of Skye's accuser.

Only the fact that he and his family had been with Skye when Ross died had helped to sway many to his side.

Aiden headed up the stairs, the need to be with Skye having clawed at his gut from the moment he left her. The absence of a guard at his chamber door caused his heart to rise into his throat. He ran the rest of the way and opened the door, finding his room empty.

He should never have let someone else keep an eye on her he thought as anger swept through him causing his vision to narrow.

"M'Laird?"

He swung around and forced his ire down so he would not scare the timid maid.

"I doona have time, wench." He made to stormed past the girl when her next words stopped him cold.

"Tis about the English lass."

He returned to her. "Skye?"

The maid turned a dark shade of red as her body shook in time with her head.

Aiden cleared his face and forced his body to relax knowing the girls fear could take up precious time.

"What about her?" He forced his words to be gentle even as he wanted to throttle her.

The girl still stuttered in fear before him. "T-the guard, T-tomas, told me t-t-to wait fer ye an t-to tell ye that the lass went b-back in her own ch-chambers."

"Get the fire started." He ordered as he turned and stormed off down the hall, once again angry.

When he got to the room Skye had occupied, he dismissed the guard and threw the door open causing Skye to jump and swirl around.

Before she could say anything, he had her thrown over his shoulders and headed back to his chambers.

"Put me down! How dare you. I am not some piece of baggage you can just toss around, you—you—you jerk you!" She pounded at his back and flailed her legs until he swatted her backside hard. "Hey!"

In moments, Skye found herself on her feet, the swift motion causing her to stumble until Aiden caught her in his arms and held her tight against his chest.

"Ye doona ever go somewhere without me permission, ye ken?"

She struggled fiercely in his arms, hitting and kicking. "Let me go!"

"Do ye ken?"

Skye struggled more, but Aiden would not budge. Finally, she gave up, breathing hard as she nodded, still pissed.

"I ken." She spat out, backing away from him quickly when he released her.

Not realizing the fire cast her body in silhouette under the thin chemise, Aiden enjoyed the view as much as her fiery nature, his cock stiffening.

Hardening his stance, he crossed his arms across his chest. "I should punish ye fer the deed."

Skye's jaw dropped before she clenched her fists at her sides. "What?"

Furious that she'd been kept in the room with only supper being brought to her, Skye refused to tell him she'd also been worried that she hadn't been able to get a hold of her sister and was afraid she'd been too late.

"How dare you leave me here saying you'll be right back and then being gone for hours and you just thi-"

Slashing his hand down to stop her, he straightened.

"It doesna matter. I told ye to stay here, an then ye traipse around wearin only a nightgown." He growled.

When he re-crossed his arms, causing his shirt to stretch over his enormous biceps, outlining the muscles she remembered gripping onto, she refused to drool.

Stomping her foot in irritation, Skye waved her hand over her body. "This? It covers me from neck to ankle."

"Aye, tis showin way too much ankle." He snorted.

She looked down and back up in sarcastic amusement. "I can't help that women here are three inches shorter than me."

"Tis why I thought ye a lad when I saw ye in the glen." He nodded curtly. "That an ye be too skinny."

That stopped her tirade, her mouth dropped as she gapped at him then she snapped it shut.

"You think I am too skinny?"

"Aye. Ye need to eat more."

Aiden frowned when a smile slowly spread across her face lighting up her features. He didn't know what he'd said to cause it but he was fascinated by way her eyes sparkled like the deepest emeralds.

He lowered his arms uncertainly as she walked leisurely up to him, her smile still growing as his eyes devoured the way the outline of her body swayed seductively when she moved.

Skye felt more feminine than she had ever felt before.

Oh, she'd felt extremely feminine in his arms, but this was different, this was a sort of power in her femininity.

Her fingers touched his shirt, running up his chest before smoothing down his arms.

She brushed her breasts against him and lifted up on her toes.

Still looking up to him, she whispered, "Skinny huh?"

Aiden grunted before he gulped.

"Do you think I am sexy?" She asked even as she felt his cock twitch against her belly.

Grinning wickedly, she rocked her pelvis against the hardening length, feeling herself moisten, and her breasts begin to pebble.

The rumble deep in his throat was the only indication she had of his thoughts just before he swept her back into his arms and walked to the bed.

Tossing her into the middle, Aiden quickly removed his boots and covered her with his body, pinning her down before she could get her balance.

"Ye shouldna tease me, lass." He growled as he lifted her arms over her head.

Her nipples quickly hardened at his rough treatment and her breathing hitched as she licked her lips, eyeing him wickedly while rotating her body against his.

"Oh?" She gave him an innocent look and batted her lashes, her eyes still sparkling even as they deepened. "What happens when I tease the mighty laird of the keep?"

Having never had a woman play with him like this, he was shocked that his cock hardened at her banter.

Having this lass tempt him with looks and touch, holding her body against him, brought out the desire to conquer.

"Mayhap ye need a lesson."

Her face flushed with desire as her mind filled with wonderfully sinful thoughts.

"Yes, Aiden, a lesson." She lifted her head, took his lower lip between her teeth, and sucked on it.

He followed her as her head lowered, taking control.

Placing her hands in one of his, he cupped her breast with the other and rubbed a thumb over her distended nipple, enjoying the way her arms opened and her breast pressed harder into his palm as he captured her gasp in his mouth.

He broke the kiss, leaned down to place the covered nipple into his mouth, and suckled hard.

She whimpered at the loss of his lips but quickly cried out when his mouth latched onto her sensitive flesh.

"Oh, yes!"

She squirmed under him until a leg broke free and she arched her lower body against his thigh, frustrated that her gown hampered her need to wrap herself around him. Her need had grown since the last time he had been inside her, and the thought of him filling her consumed her with lust.

"Wait. Please stop. Wait." She cried in frustration, not realizing he had stilled as her body squirmed for more contact. "Too many clothes. I need to feel your skin against mine, dammit."

Grinning evilly down at her, he clucked his tongue. "Nay, lass. Tis a lesson I be teaching ye."

He pinched her nipple and watched her body arch in response as her mouth opened wordlessly.

He chuckled then sucked her other nipple into his mouth, his tongue laving over the thin cotton before lifting and blowing over the gown.

"Oh, God!"

The heat of his mouth followed by cold air caused Skye to press her lower body against him as she squeezed her thighs around his leg, trying to ease the growing ache in her clit.

He moved quickly, hauling her dazed body up and placed her over his lap.

"But the lesson shall come after the punishment."

Skye shrieked as he threw her over his lap, her gown brought up and bunched in his large hand as he held her in place.

"Ye shall do as yer told, lass."

Squirming, she struggled to get free, her body still heated from his previous attentions.

"Please, Aiden, not now."

A large hand smacked her bottom and she stiffened as a screech tore through her throat.

She cussed at him and fought his hold.

"Hold yer tongue, lass, or ye shall be heard. Ye dunno want an audience—or do ye?" He mused, his brogue growing deeper as his lust sharpened.

"Oh, my God." She whispered furiously. "I am so going to kill you."

Another smack to her other cheek had her biting back a yelp.

Skye gritted her teeth even as his hand smoothed over her backside before spanking her quickly on each cheek, once again soothing over the heated flesh.

Shocked at the sensual feel of his hands over her stinging flesh had her wriggling on his lap as his large fingers squeezed her plump cheeks then eased between her legs and pulled them apart.

"Ye shall keep yer legs opened for me or yer punishment willna be as pleasant."

Her ass burned from his spanking but his touch, light caresses just shy of the apex of her thighs, caused her cunt to spasm and she moaned low in her throat wondering how she could be responding to something like this.

His hand fell again with several whacks to each cheek before slowly running his fingers between the crease of her ass and over her anus, pressing lightly against the tight entrance before skimming down between her legs to the wetness soaking her outer lips.

Skye gasped at the wicked feelings beginning to consume her.

Aiden's staff strained against his breaches as Skye ground herself against him. He spanked her again and gritted his teeth as she raised her bottom to meet his hand moaning in need. She was wet and growing wetter with the punishment and Aiden was pleased at her response to his ministrations.

"I am Laird an Master of this keep an ye shall follow me directions without question. Do ye ken?"

Skye whimpered at his words, only knowing his hands on her bottom was causing her to weep with need.

He repeated the spanking of each cheek. "Do ye ken, lass?"

Skye nodded, moaning as she wriggled seductively against his lap.

"Say it aloud."

"I ken, I ken—do what you say." She rasped out.

His hand squeezed the globes of her ass before smoothing over the red marks.

"Aiden." She gasped as his fingers slipped over her wet lips before circling her clit then dipping inside her tight channel. They both heard the sound of her juices as he slowly finger fucked her.

"Yes." Skye hissed slowly as she spread her legs further, arching her backside up to give him easier access.

Taking her juices, he brought his hand back to her puckered hole and eased a finger in.

Gasping, she squirmed more, so lost in sensations that even the fear of what he was doing was forgotten.

Already knowing the answer, he still asked. "Have you ever been taken here, Skye?"

"No." She gasped, feeling his finger push gently through the tight ring.

His finger came out and slipped back to her pussy to grab more fluid and repeat the process.

"I will take ye here, lass." He whispered into her ear as he pushed through the tightness again, swirling more of her lubricant on her as he lightly stretched her. Grateful that she responded to his dark touches so eagerly. "But no this time."

He raised her up and laughed when she protested.

Making her stand, he pulled her between his thighs and latched on to her puckered nipple beneath the gown that had fallen back into place.

Her hands slipped through his hair and pressed him closer, gasping when he nipped at the sensitive peaks then pulled.

The pain that quickly turned to pleasure as he suckled hard at her breast kept Skye overwhelmed with need. Her body was one massive nerve ending and she began to shake, pressing into him, unsure if she could stand for much longer.

He pressed the small of her back into him, forcing her to hold on tighter as his mouth ravaged the other nipple with equal ferocity.

Growling in need and frustration, she went to straddle him but he caught her up and threw her on the bed.

"Nay, lass, tis I who be in control."

She tried to pull him down on top of her as she reached for his cock.

Taking her hands into one of his, he cupped her chin in his other hand and waited for her to focus on him before he spoke again.

"I be Laird an Master."

Swallowing, she nodded as she melted at his words, a calmness stealing over her limbs even as the fire raged, not understanding why.

He switched hands, still holding hers in one of his, he lowered the other to her thigh and grabbed her gown, shifting slightly as he eased forward to suckle at her covered breast and grinned against the nipple he had between his teeth as Skye use her heels to raise her body so he could pull her gown up.

His mouth nipped on the underside of her breast before following her ribcage. Easing down her body, his hand gliding along her arm, Aiden used the gown as a vice to keep her from moving.

Shifting again, he let go of her hands and lifted her gown higher, exposing her mauns to his hungry gaze.

Skye felt him breathing on her sensitive flesh and whimpered as desire clawed at her. She tried to lift herself to him but her gown kept her in place, her fingers extended and she felt the headboard and grabbed on just before her body froze as his tongue slid roughly from her opening to her clit, taking his time before flickering over the swollen nub.

"Oh, God." She hiccupped, her legs opening wider as she pleaded for more, calling his name, lost in a whirlwind of sensations.

Her hands gripped his hair, the bed, and then back up to push against the headboard so she could press harder into his mouth, loving the feel of his unshaven face scrapping against her tender thighs.

"Oh, yes." She whispered hoarsely. "Harder. Harder."

Her breath caught when one of his fingers pressed into her, stretching her entrance in sheer pleasure before adding a second.

She was going crazy and nothing mattered. Nothing but the fingers that were causing havoc on her senses and the tongue that made her blood boil as her body grew warmer under his unrelenting assault.

She knew she was begging, her voice a hoarse whisper as her head thrashed back and forth and didn't care, her only need was in the release he could provide her.

Aiden felt her body begin to quiver as she bucked against his mouth when he inserted the second finger. Her juices coating his hand as he gently twisted the two in her fluid before spreading them.

Groaning as she clamped down with her muscles, he began to pump his fingers inside her while swirling his tongue around her clit using the back of his tongue.

"Oh, Aiden. Oh, God. I'm gonna cum." She panted.

He felt her body stiffen and he swirled the back of his tongue harder over her swollen clit as he speared his fingers in harder thrusts.

Her legs spread impossibly wider as her hands gripped the headboard.

He slipped a thumb through her sweet liquid before bringing it down, back to press against the tight bud between her cheeks, and then eased the tip of his finger into her back entrance.

Crying out as molten lava gushed through her veins and gathered at her core, she felt him press against the ring of her ass, slowly eased in and she exploded. Wave after wave of liquid heat crashed over her already fevered body as she called out his name, feeling his mouth continue its assault on her sensitive clit and his fingers stretching her as she spasmed around them.

"Aiden. No more . . . no more." She begged when she could catch her breath.

His fingers slowed while his tongue gently lapped up her juices as the world came slowly back to focus. She felt him crawling up her side and she reached for him, grabbing him close as he rolled onto his back, taking her with him.

She lay on his chest, breathing heavy, feeling her body tingle in the most delicious places as her mind was taking it all in.

She closed her eyes and smiled.

"What do ye smile about?"

Rubbing herself against him before easing up and straddling his waist, still weak in his embrace, she nuzzled his neck grinning as she kissed him softly.

It took a moment for her to figure out what to say when so many expressions came to mind.

"That was better than I imagined."

"Ye've imagined that before?"

"Oh hell yes."

"How do ye ken of sech things?"

She lifted up and waggled her eyebrows, grinning at him mischievously. "*Kama sutra.*"

His eyes cleared. "The manuscript ye told me of."

She grinned again and wiggled, feeling his still hard cock pressing against her bottom.

"Ye must tell me more of this book."

Nuzzling his cheek against hers, loving the roughness of his unshaven face, Skye inhaled his scent, feeling herself clench as her desire to have him inside her took over.

"Tell you?"

Pushing herself up as she teased him with her breasts, she smiled seductively, lightly grinding her wetness over his cock.

"Why don't I show you instead?"

His staff twitched as his hands came up to cup her waist. Aiden helped push her down further so she was pressing her moist center on his shaft. He watched with hooded eyes as she rubbed against him, the smile fading as her eyes darkened.

"You drive me crazy, Aiden. I feel strong and weak when you are near." She kissed him slowly. "And when you hold me? Nothing else matters."

His grip tightened at her words and he couldn't stop the way he thrust upwards, seeking her heated depths.

She leaned into him, her breasts pressed against his chest.

"You are so large it sometimes scares me." She whispered into his ear. "But I want you so much, and it feels so good. Even when it hurts."

She pulled at his ear with her teeth as she pushed herself back up then reached to opposite sides of her body to take hold of her chemise, sliding the gown up, little by little, seductively, her hips shimmying back and forth over his painfully swollen cock.

Watching her arms lift higher, Aiden gritted his teeth as the gown climbed high enough for her breasts to fall out.

Reaching for them, he pulling them together, kneading them as the gown fell off to the side and slid to the floor, her curls cascading over her shoulder and down her back.

Smiling in anticipation, her hands went out to his shirt and she undid the ties, spreading it open and running her hands over the hard flatness of his stomach and back up, loving the way his chest hair felt between her fingers.

Slipping her hands leisurely down to his breeches as she leaned forward to kiss his stubbled chin, Skye undid his pants and tried to push them down but he didn't move.

She pouted when he grinned at her.

"Aiden." She pleaded. "Don't you want me to show you a position from the book?"

Grinning through clenched teeth, Aiden helped her remove his trousers.

Easing back down over him, she grabbed his cock in her hand.

Feeling her juices mix with his, she placed him at her entrance and watched his face as she slowly eased down, her breath catching as the head of his shaft breached her tight opening.

Bending her knees more, she smiled like a cat before rising then sinking further.

Gritting his teeth, he felt her sheath stretch as he filled her. How he kept from plunging into her he couldn't say, but the look of ecstasy on her flushed face kept his rapt attention.

"Oh, Aiden, if you only knew how good you feel inside me."

Using her thigh muscles to ease another inch of him inside, Skye then lifted, enjoying the pain-pleasure of him filling her.

In moments, she was sitting fully on him. She stilled as she clutched him and smiled in pleasure when he twitched.

Nails kneaded his flesh as she leaned into him, feeling him stretch her more. She kissed him as she rose almost to his tip then back down, purring in his ear. Using her muscles, she did it again.

"You fill me, stretch me . . . and I want more, always more." She nipped at his jaw. "I want more." She quickened the pace, moaning.

Aiden's hands cupped the globes of her ass and he took control. He eased her up then brought her down onto his cock and she cried out.

Repeating the action, he would thrust harder each time.

Overwhelmed by the sensations his movements brought, Skye fell against his chest and devoured his mouth, licking the seam of his lips before thrusting her tongue inside then pulling away to nip at his chin, down his jaw, to his ear.

"Yes." She moaned slowly when he thrust harder. "Deeper, Aiden. I need you deeper."

She squirmed, needing more.

A fine sheen of sweat formed on their skin and the smell of her nectar caused Aiden's nose to flare.

His finger dipped between her cheeks and again pressed against the tight opening while his other hand slipped up her back to the base of her neck where he grabbed her hair and pulled her face to the side.

"Remember; I shall be takin ye here too, wench." He growled low in her ear.

"Oh, God. Oh, God."

He held her tight to him as he slammed up, grinding into her as he lubricated his finger with her juices, then went back to her ass, easing his tip in.

She fought him and he removed his hand thinking he was hurting her.

"Nooo!" She cried out. "Please. Please. I'm going to cum."

She was like no other he knew. Her struggles were from her growing needs. His possession of her was her undoing. The way he eased out and pounded in was driving her wild. The sounds of his cock against her cunt made her drip with lust.

He grabbed her by the waist and stopped, being silent as she cried out her frustrations, trying to grind against him.

"Nay, lass. Hold still an listen to me."

Moaning, she shook her head as her body shook in need.

Biting her lip and pouting, she looked at Aiden.

"I be yer Laid an Master, wench. Ye will cum when I let ye. Do ye ken?"

Her heart kicked up at his command and she nodded.

"Lean back, lass. Lean back on yer hands."

He pushed her to comply and she whimpered as the air touched her heated body.

Sitting up straight, Skye felt his finger penetrate into her ass and her cunt clamped hard as she gasped.

Easing back more, she leaned on her hands feeling his cock stretch her as his finger slipped in further.

"Aiden." She pleaded. "I'm not going to be able to last."

She rocked onto him as he thrust into her. She was dripping in need and when his other hand swirled her wetness over her clit, she arched, crying out at the same time.

Using her hands and legs she pounded down on him, moaning as his fingers kept pace with her frantic thrusts.

Over and over, she plunged onto him, his fingers hard on her clit. She rode him faster, reveling in the painful pleasure as he filled her, meeting her gasping plea for more. When he eased another finger into her nether hole, she bucked against him.

"Cum fer me. Now." He quietly ordered.

"Aiden!" She cried out as she came, jerking up to sit on him, her legs spreading as she pumped through her orgasm, his fingers deep inside her ass while his thumb brushed over her clit.

Feeling him swell even more as he came with her, she sobbed as waves of heat crashed through her.

Holding her breath as she felt everything at once, reveling in it.

As her convulsions eased, he removed his fingers and pulled her down, holding her close to him, his heartbeat racing in time with hers.

As their breathing slowed, he felt her smiling against his chest as she squeezed him.

"That was wonderful!" She shook her head and he could feel her grin widening before she pushed up a little to look in his eyes. "It feels like it gets better every time."

Smiling in admiration at her openness, Aiden tucked a lock of her hair behind an ear as his heart expanded at her wondrous look, knowing he had been her first and she knew pleasure in it.

Propping her chin on the palms of her hands over his chest, she frowned in thought. "Does it feel like this with everyone?"

Seeing his jaw clench and a glower darken his features, she lifted herself up and frowned. "What?"

Aiden growled slowly. "There will be no others, ye ken?"

Shaking her head, she grinned. "That's not what I meant."

When his features didn't clear, she kissed his chin and explained what she was thinking.

"You have, obviously, had experience with sex, so I am wondering if it is as good with me as it was with the others. Does it depend on the person?"

She perked, her mind whirling with thoughts. "How do you know if it's gonna be good or not? Or, what if they aren't into something you want to do? Like that spanking! I had no idea—"

Gasping as he flipped them to tower over her and disappointed his cock slipped out at the exchange, she placed her hands over his broad chest, her mind going blank over the feel of strength under her fingertips. She smoothed her hands over him in awe of his masculinity as her mouth watered for more.

"Do ye speak of sech things with others?"

Engrossed in how his nipples hardened as she grazed her nails over them, she answered distractedly.

"I tried talking to Sarah about this, but she was as clueless as me, having kept her virginity for her husband." She huffed then grinned as she watched goose bumps cover his tanned skin.

"After she got married, she refused to tell me anything. Damn puritan." She pouted up at him as her eyes sparkled with laughter.

Capturing her hands in his, he forced her to look at him.

Ignoring her disappointment at not being able to touch him, Aiden shook his head at her.

"Proper women doona discuss sech private matters."

Her features cleared and a curious look settled over her face. "But why, Aiden? If we don't talk about it then how are we to learn? How can it be pleasurable for you if we don't know anything?"

She squirmed under him, feeling wanton as his cock grew harder against her thigh and he held her firmly down with so little effort.

Licking her lips and feeling anything but innocent, she batted her lashes up at him. "You did enjoy it, didn't you?"

He growled but didn't answer.

Lifting slightly to brush her breasts against his chest, she smiled. "What did you enjoy best?"

Her nipples grew hard and her pussy clenched at the look on his face. She rubbed herself against his thigh, need already beginning to claw at her as she remembered what he had said and done to her.

"What else do you want to do to me?"

"Ye sorely tempt me, lass." He growled.

"I want to tempt you. I want you to feel what I feel."

"What do ye feel?"

She stopped moving and looked at him.

"You touch me; you look at me and everything inside me heats up and I feel like I'm burning. My thoughts scatter and all I can do is *feel*. The way you hold me, the way you touch me, the things you say. I can even feel the way you look at me. And I want more, Aiden. it's not enough, never en-"

195

His lips crushed hers and she moaned, mouth opening willingly to his demands, arching to feel him against her.

A pounding on the door stopped them, even their breathing.

"What be it?" Aiden called about angrily.

"Reivers, m'Laird. They've attacked old Donally an slaughtered his sheep."

"Comin!" Aiden called out as he kept his gaze on hers. "I be sorry lass—"

"Nonsense. This is important."

He looked into her eyes, searching for something.

Clenching his jaw, he leaned in to kiss her hard before easing off the bed and grabbing his clothing.

"Ye will stay in the keep. I would prefer ye to bide here but won't ask it of ye since I ken no of how long I shall be gone."

❦

CHAPTER NINE

Enjoying the way his muscles rippled as he dressed, Skye sighed in pleasure after he closed the door behind him.

Shaking her head to clear her lustful thoughts, she looked around the room, desperately needing clothes and finding nothing but her dress crumpled on the floor.

Sighing wistfully, she got off the bed and put her nightgown on before throwing a couple logs into the dwindling fire.

Stoking the flames to life, she replaced the poker and sank down.

Guessing it was near morning where her sister was, she concentrated hard for several long minutes, trying to keep her inability to help Aiden out of her mind.

"Come on, Sarah, please answer me."

"I'm here, Skye."

"Sarah! Are you all right? I have been scared to death!"

"It wasn't very fun over here either. I had to call 9-1-1 when Doug passed out."

"His heart?"

Sarah nodded. "Then they put me on a monitor and you can guess what they found."

It was Skye's turn to nod.

"But everything's all right, right? I mean, I saved the baby."

"We figured you had. Talk about in the nick of time though." Sarah looked behind her sister. "That's a big bed."

"Yeah, yeah." She brushed her off, blushing. "So why haven't I heard from you?"

"They kept us in the hospital to make sure neither Doug or the baby had a relapse." She waved her hand in frustration. "Not like I could tell them what was going on or light a candle in the hospital."

Skye let out a sigh of relief. "Well, that makes sense then, but it wasn't fun and I don't relish the thought of going through that again."

Sarah laughed just before her eyes widened and she looked over her sister's shoulder. "Ut, oh."

Skye turned and saw Aiden paused at the doorway.

She stood as he took a step inside the room and closed the door behind him. Biting her lip, Skye kept silent, not knowing how Aiden was going to react to what he was seeing.

Stepping slowly, unable to take his eyes off the figure in the flames, he made his way next to Skye.

No one spoke for a long moment, Skye's heart racing.

"Yer sister?" Aiden asked making out the familiar features.

"Yes." Skye answered softly.

"Tell me this is not a bad thing, Skye."

Skye looked from her sister to Aiden and worried her lower lip.

How Aiden stayed in place as the flames wavered with spoken words he did not know but his eyes widened. Then he gritted his teeth, remembering why he returned.

"I be pleased to meet ye an wish for a more proper time for introductions. However, I require yer sisters' attentions elsewhere." He turned his attention to Skye. "They be bringin Donally in from the fields. Tis no good, lass."

Skye nodded her understanding and turned to the flames.

"It's alright Sarah, I told them everything and it's alright. I'll get you up to speed but right now I need to go."

"Of course you do. Thank you for calming my fears too. I will see you later."

Skye nodded and headed for the door, stopping when Aiden took her arm.

"What?"

Aiden glared. "Ye will no be goin out in that."

"It's not like I have anything else."

When he went to his closet, Skye looked at Sarah in the flames and rolled her eyes.

"Are you sure you're going to be alright, Skye?"

"Of course I am. Don't worry about me." Skye smiled gently.

"Good, then call me later. I be headin back to bed." She said in her best Scottish accent before the flames engulfed her features and she disappeared.

"Here ye go. This will cover ye for now." Aiden placed a heavy cape over her shoulders and looked into the fire.

"She went to bed." Skye explained.

Nodding, he led her out the door.

"I doona want ye to heal the Sheppard completely, just enough to ensure his life, like ye did to Seelie."

When she looked at him questioningly, he stopped and took her by her shoulders.

"I will no have yer health risked. We will take this slow. Ye ken?"

"But as long as you are there . . ."

"I will no be there long enough. We be headin out to find the Reivers. I came to get ye while me men be gatherin."

Skye's heart leapt to her throat but kept her fears to herself, knowing he couldn't stay when his people were being threatened.

"You will stay safe."

Aiden smiled at the concern she tried so hard to hide and the catch in her voice as she demanded his safety.

*   *   *

Elizabeth spoke softly as they headed to her chambers after Skye was finished with the injured man.

"Poor, Donally. He came here from Ireland with his wife, May, when her family wouldn't accept their marriage."

"I liked her. She was very calm even with the sight before her."

It had not been pretty. Donally had been beaten rather harshly and it had been difficult to tell where the most damage was because of all the blood but Elizabeth had given her privacy to heal the man and she had done a rather good job ensuring his survival.

Afterwards, they had helped May clean him and make him comfortable, letting her know they would be back to check on his progress and for Skye to do some more healing.

"They are good people and did not deserve this." Elizabeth said just before Skye stopped them at the base of the stairs.

"What is it, child?"

Elizabeth turned to look over her shoulder as Skye passed her to go into Aiden's study. She watched as Skye knelt at the fireplace before the chained Seelie.

"Can you close the door for me, Elizabeth?" Skye asked, not really paying attention. "Okay, girl, time for us to finish this."

Elizabeth did as asked then watched quietly as the girl laid her hands on the animal's head.

Twenty minutes later, Elizabeth ushered Skye into her chambers and sat her at a chair for her to recuperate.

Anna was helping set a table with food as two maids quickly worked to get everything in order before leaving them alone.

Elizabeth smiled as the girls' left and walked over to the bed.

"Here we go." She pulled up a gown and held it out to Skye. "If you feel up to it, let us get you properly dressed before sitting down to break our fast, shall we?"

Decently clothed and feeling relaxed, they finally sat down to eat.

"I be very curious, Skye. Ye simply must tell us about where ye come from."

"Aye, if tis not too much trouble, I am also intrigued with the future and what it holds."

Everyone was trying hard not to think about what their men were facing and she wanted to help keep their minds, as well as hers, away from what could be happening.

"A lot has happened in six hundred years."

"Six hundred years." Anna whispered in amazement.

Chewing her food slowly, Skye thought about what she could say without shocking them.

"Plumbing!"

At their looks of confusion, she laughed and told them what she knew about indoor and outdoor plumbing, specifically about toilets and bathtubs.

"I never worked with any of that stuff so can't tell you much about how it's done but it sure is nice to have running hot water where no one has to haul buckets around. Just a twist of a faucet and there it is."

"Water goes through a pipe anywhere in a home?"

Skye nodded as she ate, trying not to grin at their look of wonder.

"Hot water just comes right out of a faucet, simply by turning a handle?"

"Pretty much." Taking a mouthful, she listened as they went back and forth over the possibilities.

"That be amazin!" Anna breathed.

"You think that's amazing, wait until I tell you about the wonders of refrigeration."

She had done it; their worried faces transformed in wonder over future technology.

Trying to answer their numerous questions on washing machines and dryers, they froze in fear when a knock came at the door and Riona entered.

"I be wonderin where everyone be hidin." She said as if offended at not being invited.

Relieved that it wasn't a messenger with bad news, the women visibly relaxed.

"Sorry, Riona. Anna was tired of being in her own chambers so we moved our morning repast to mine." Elizabeth smiled gently at the woman as she stood. "But I am most thankful for yer presence since it reminds me I have been negligent in taking care of the keep."

Looking at the newcomer, Skye couldn't help but feel angry and cautious. She was forgetting something about this girl. Unable to put her finger on it, Skye knew it went beyond the fact that her goon of a bodyguard had hauled her off and treated her like a criminal.

Riona watched as the older woman left, plastered a smile on her face, turned back to the other two, and sighed.

"I be hopin to have some company for raspberry pickin." She said as she took the vacated chair. "Do ye think it safe fer ye to go?"

"Raspberries?" Skye asked, leaning forward in interest.

"Aye, tis the season for them." Anna nodded enthusiastically. "I love raspberries an have missed their taste."

"Raspberry leaf tea is actually very good during ones pregnancy and can make the labor and delivery easier." Skye grinned at the soulful look the girl gave. "If we can get some, I could make you the tea daily to help."

"Ohhhh, raspberry tea sounds lovely." Anna sighed, closing her eyes and leaning back.

"Then we shall go berry pickin." Riona said clapping her hands and rising.

Unsure if Skye really wanted to spend her time in Riona's company, Aiden's command came to her.

"I'm sorry but I can't go."

"Why ever no?" Anna asked, not wanting to be alone with Riona.

"Aiden said I was not to leave the keep."

"Oh, poo. I want raspberries so much, ye canna ken me desire now that Riona brought it up, an ye must go with us."

Skye could see the begging in Anna's eyes to not be left with Riona and winked.

"When Aiden returns we can go."

Anna slumped in her chair. "Twill be rainin an then we willna be able to."

"Then why can't we send others out to get some?"

"I have been cooped up in this here keep forever an ye want me to send someone else to go instead?" Anna actually pouted.

"Alright, alright." Laughing, Skye held up her hands in defeat. "I give up. Let's go berry picking."

With Anna chatting excitedly, neither of them saw Riona nod to a barely discernible figure hiding in the shadows as they filed out of the room and down the stairs.

Skye was perplexed as to why there were no guards following her. For some reason that did not comfort her and she began to lag behind.

"Can we bring Seelie?" Skye asked as they walked past the study's door.

Anna frowned in thought. "I doona have the keys to unchain her, only Aiden does."

Riona waited impatiently at the door. "We need to hurry, I doona want it to rain before we get there."

Once they were outside, Anna breathed deep and twirled, arms outstretched.

"This be woooonerful!"

Walking out the door, Skye felt her mood lighten a bit at Anna's carefree laughter.

As Riona fetched buckets, Brian came running up to them.

"Are ye here to play with us, Skye?" He asked hopefully.

"Sorry, Brian, us girls are going raspberry picking." She grinned down at the boy.

He frowned and pursed his lips. "Berry picking? That be fer lasses."

Anna and Skye laughed.

Scuffing the toe of his shoe, he grumbled. "Well, mayhap I should go—just to make sure ye doona get wounded or nut'n."

"Nay, tis just us goin." Riona groused as she returned.

Both Skye and Anna frowned at Riona before turning back to the boy.

"Sorry, hun, maybe next time." Skye smiled.

Brian sulked and continued to scuff his toe into the dirt.

Leaning in, she smiled wider. "Can you do me a favor though, Brian? It is most important."

Puffing out his chest, he nodded vigorously. "Aye, Skye, I can do that!"

"Will you find one of the warriors—any one—and tell them what we are doing?"

Anna called out to Skye and she waved to her before looking back at the boy.

"Sure, but that doesna sound very import'nt to me."

"It is, Brian."

She hurried away glancing over her shoulder to see him looking around before heading off to the training fields.

Catching up to the other two, she slowed her steps.

"Maybe we should have a guard accompanying us?"

Only Skye seemed to notice Riona stumble a bit at her suggestion as Anna waved off her suggestion.

"I am no gonna wait around for someone to tell me I must go back to bed because they dunno ken I be fine." She sighed in frustration. "Do ye ken how long I have been unable to just come outside?"

Damn, but Anna was working hard on her guilty nerve.

They walked past the guards at the gate, Anna waving happily up to them as Skye felt even more wary. Looking behind her, she watched the normal hustle and bustle of the community then looked up at the guards who eyed them as they walked under the arches.

Every step made Skye feel even more apprehensive.

"Anna, I made a promise to your brother and I am not feeling good about breaking it."

Anna huffed, turned on Skye, placed her hands on her hips, and pouted.

"I am no gonna return. If ye be so worried then mayhap ye should go back, I will get raspberries an leaves for tea."

At her friend's concerned look, Anna grinned, took her arm, and dragged her along.

"Och, Aiden an Collin overreact to the simplest of things. Tis the way of men folk. What can happen to us when we will be under the watchful gaze of the tower guards?"

Skye looked back up to the guards still unsure.

"I don't know, Anna."

They arrived at the raspberry bushes in a short enough time but Skye was not liking how far they were from the main gate so she picked the berries as fast as possible, grabbing some branches with leaves as well for the tea.

A shout in the distance attracted their attentions. They all looked up to see a rider approaching, Brian leaning to the side behind the man controlling the horse waving and smiling widely.

Feeling relieved, Skye put down her basket to greet the newcomers when chaos erupted.

Horrified, she watched as the man fell, blood spurting from his neck.

Skye froze in stunned disbelief before she was in motion, racing towards them as the soldier hit the ground, Brian leaping off to kneel at his side.

She fell to her knees beside him and saw the arrow sticking from his wound. Not thinking past the immediate needs, she reached for his neck as she told Brian to pull the shaft slowly from the wound, hoping it wasn't barbed.

Once satisfied he was doing as told, her healing powers worked from the inside to close off the sliced veins and stop the flow of blood.

It wasn't until she was roughly yanked away that Skye heard the screams.

Equilibrium lost, her stomach pitched from the disconnection and she heaved her breakfast before someone shoved a handful of grass over her mouth and placed something foul smelling over her head before she lost consciousness.

CHAPTER TEN

"I hear tell, the one heavy with child comes from a line of gifted. Be that truth?"

Riona waved her hand dismissively. "I have never seen anything from her or her kin."

"Hmmm. If it be rumors only then perhaps t'would be better to exchange her for me brother."

"What?" She screeched.

"Me brother was taken in the last raid, I need to send a missive for a trade."

Riona glared at the filthy man in front of her. "I do not care who was captured, my brother paid ye well. *I* shall be returned."

The man leaned forward in his chair, the wood creaking under his skinny form.

"Yer brother still owes me." He leered, showing rotting teeth. "Although, I would be most willing to negotiate other means o' payment."

Making a face, she curled her lip in disgust at the filthy Englishman.

"Ye shall trade me for this person of yours that was foolishly captured. Take the tall girl to the mats." She straightened at the thought, her eyes lighting. "Aye, take her. Tis a good idea."

"That I might also do, but tis flaxen haired gurls that make these balls burst." He practically drooled as he cupped himself lewdly.

Riona glowered at the little man. "I am to wed the laird of those lands ye so badly want to be able to pass without persecution, Will. If I am despoiled I shant be able to wed that . . . that churl and then what? We both loose."

The man sneered at Riona.

She waved her hand in dismissal. "Take the other girl and be happy."

"God's teeth, ye are arrogant." Will raised a brow as he leaned back, his eyes taking in her form. "Ye are not even fond o' him. What makes ye think he is affectionate o' ye, an enough to marry ye at that?"

"Tis none of your concern." She looked at him from over her nose. "Just know I will be his wife once that wench is removed forever from his sight."

The man's eyebrows lowered in anger as he rose from his chair.

"What *is* my concern is your lack of respect for me and the unstable position ye be in. I think ye might be needin a lesson."

* * *

Quiet weeping woke Skye from her unconscious state. Moving caused her head to ache and she quickly spent a moment to rid herself of the pain as her thoughts turned to what happened before looking around and seeing herself and Anna in an open pen.

"I be so sorry for insistin we pick berries."

Skye turned around and saw a disheveled Anna curled up against the trunk of a tree, tears streaking through her dirty face.

Making her way quickly to the girl, Skye knelt beside her to search for injuries.

"How are you? The baby?"

"I be so sorry. I should have listened to ye." She swiped a tear away, smudging the dirt across her cheek. "Can ye forgive me?"

Taking the younger woman's face in her hands, she looked into the girl's eyes.

"There is nothing to forgive, and if there was, I would always forgive you. But this is not your fault." She stressed each word. "Now, how is the baby?"

Anna smoothed a grimy hand over her covered belly and smiled. "He has been quite busy lettin me ken he be in there and just as unhappy over me decision."

Sighing while giving a quick breath of relief, she smiled and lowered her hands to the girl's shoulders.

"Good. That's very good."

Anna's voice lowered to a whisper as Skye looked over her shoulder and around the camp.

"I have spoken with the man who captured us. He kens who we be. He be talkin to Riona now."

Scooting around, Skye sat next to Anna and placed a comforting hand on her arm.

"What did he say?"

"Once he found out who I was, he asked about me brother's keep." Anna shrugged, touching her face where Skye saw the bruise under the grime. "He was no too happy with me lack of answers."

"Oh, my God, Anna!" Skye whispered furiously as she touched the girl's cheek.

"Nay!" The girl took her hand and lowered it. "He kens the bruise. For it to be gone now would no be a good thin, I be thinkin."

Skye growled at the truth of the girl's words.

"Listen to me." Anna said, linking fingers with Skye. "I told him ye were a relative of me mother, but I dunno ken what Riona might be sayin since I had no the time to talk to her about me deception."

Skye closed her eyes and nodded while rubbing her forehead. "Do you know if the man whom Brian was riding out with is okay?"

"I doona. Everythin happened so suddenly." She squeezed her hand. "Twill be all right; Collin an Aiden will be here soon."

Skye refused to say anything, knowing she was just trying to bolster their courage, even as they shook in fear.

A scream had them jerking their heads towards a tent across the fire.

"Riona be in there." Anna whispered squeezing Skye's fingers harder.

There was a shout and two men standing nearby quickly ran to the tent and entered.

In a short time, they were dragging a sobbing Riona out.

Anna and Skye watched as she was hauled to their cage and carelessly thrown in. The force bringing Riona to her hands and knees.

When Skye tried to help, Riona glared at her before brushing away her hand and going to another corner.

* * *

"One of the farmers brought this, m'Laird." Keir said as he held out a folded sheet of paper to Aiden.

Collin stopped his pacing and turned to the tousled man holding the missive knowing this was what they had waited for and dreaded.

"Tis a ransom. In exchange for the man we captured, they will give us one of the lasses." Aiden said after a brief scan.

"Only one?" Collin asked.

Aiden nodded. "Aye. Only one."

"*Mac an donais*!." Keir cursed.

Gritting his teeth, Aiden ran his hand through already ruffled hair. "Once the exchange be made, they will negotiate the release of the other two."

They both knew the chances of the other two surviving would become unlikely once the Reivers had their man.

"If we doona meet at the designated place on time with their man," Aiden continued. "all will be killed."

Collin looked at Keir but before he could ask, the other man shook his head.

"Nay, the one they wish to trade for has no given us any information on the whereabouts of their camp. Much more *questionin* an he will be dead."

"We need that location before we do any type of trade." Aiden growled as his fist slammed onto his desk then swept the contents off in a fit of rage.

*   *   *

Anna sat next to Skye with her help after having coaxed Riona to join them. Skye grimaced at the bruises on the girl's face but kept her hands to herself.

"One of their men was taken in the raid. They be sendin a message to Aiden. One of us for him."

"Which one?" Anna asked.

"I wasna told." Riona stuttered. "I suggested they return ye since ye be so close to deliverin but this is all I got for me intentions." She touched her face and winced.

Anna scooted over as much as her swollen body would allow and tried to comfort the petite woman.

After the shock of seeing Riona bruised and beaten wore off, Skye was back to feeling wary of her and doubted everything she said.

Gritting her teeth, she looked around, trying to think of something that would help them escape.

"If we could only get a fire."

While Anna fawned over Riona, Skye glanced over their shoulders at the fire and wished they would allow them one.

Night would be falling, it was getting colder and she was worried about Anna and the baby, and she wanted the chance to get through to Sarah. Her sister could do some major damage through the fires and help in getting them out of here. Perhaps steal a horse or two while there was chaos. Anything would be better than the alternative.

"We need a fire." She looked at the two girls. "Any ideas?"

"I am no goin to ask." Riona said indignantly.

"No, that would not be a good idea, true." Skye tapped down the desire to add to the bruises, instantly feeling contrite. "I just wish we had a fire."

*   *   *

"Tis no good, Aiden. We have been over this part of the forest an there be too many places to hide. We could be ambushed."

The men were silent in their agreement.

The time had come and the barely conscience man tied to a horse was testimony to how hard they had tried to wean information from him to help in their endeavor and they feared his current condition would cause harm to the female captives.

Aiden held up his hand to stop the progression and turned to Keir. "Ye go alone from here."

Nodding in silence, Keir took the reins of the prisoner's horse and eased passed the others, not looking back as he disappeared into the dense woods.

"I doona have a good feelin about this."

"Neither do I." Aiden replied, never taking his eyes from the spot Rory had been seen last and hoping the man returned with information to the enemies hiding place.

* * *

Body shaking in barely controlled fear, Skye rubbed her sore nipple.

"I swear that woman smirked before they took her away." Skye muttered, trying to ignore the image of the man stripping her with his eyes.

They had huddled together throughout the night, Skye had done what she could to keep Anna warm without causing Riona to know she was using her gift and in the morning a man had come into their pen and hauled Riona out by her hair, but not before twisting Skye's breast hard and saying he'd be back.

"Anna?" Skye asked while looking toward the area the Reivers had left.

"Aye?" Came the dejected response.

"Is Riona English?"

"Nay. She an her brother hail from the lowlands."

There was a moment of silence as Skye mulled over her thoughts.

"I think they are English." She turned to her friend, mouth pursed in thought.

"Why do ye think so?"

"Remember when I said Riona was outside your brother's bedroom when I cast that spell?"

"Aye."

"Something has been bugging me about her ever since and I remember it now. When she spoke to me, she spoke in English and there wasn't a Scottish brogue."

"That makes no sense. Why would she lie?"

"I don't know."

More silence.

Anna sighed heavily. "Ye ken that we won't live for much longer, do ye no? They will have their fun with us an then we will be killed."

Ignoring the bruised nipple, Skye sank down next to the dejected girl and wrapped her arms around her.

"No, Anna, I do not ken."

Anna smiled ruefully. "I make flowers grow an ye heal, how is that goin to help us?"

"I can do more than heal, just get them close enough to touch and leave the rest to me. Besides you said you can make anything grow, not just flowers."

"So?"

"Can you make the roots from that tree trunk grow, or maybe even the branches?"

"Aye, but to what end?"

"I don't know, maybe nothing, maybe everything. But always good to know the extent of what we have at our disposal and what we don't."

"I suppose."

Still scared to death, she looked determinedly at her friend as a tear rolled down the girl's cheek.

"We will not go down without a fight."

*　　*　　*

"Twas horrible!" Riona cried into Aiden's chest, clinging to him as her tears wet his tunic.

"Do ye ken where ye were, lass?" Collin asked in barely controlled irritation.

"Nay, they kept us hooded. Twas no till we reached the camp did they remove the blindfolds."

"What of Anna an Skye?"

Riona looked up at the hard face of the man she held onto and her lower lip trembled.

"Anna be fine, I warned them of yer fierceness if crossed. I doona think they will harm her because she be yer sister."

Before Aiden could ask about Skye, she went back to wailing, her head pressed against his upper body.

"Poor Anna, what an awful experience an she was only thoughtful of others. I told her I be ruined, that men would turn from me in disgust thinkin I had been . . . been . . . raped." She whispered the last word in dismay then looked up, eyes red and pleading. "What am I to do, Aiden?"

Aiden clenched his teeth and took the woman by the arms, trying hard to keep his calm.

"What of Skye?" He repeated slowly.

When all she did was burrow deeper, he pried the girl's clutching hands from his arms and held her away, repeating his question.

Once again, her lips quivered.

"All she could think about was gettin me to ask those brutal men for a fire. Me!" She shivered and more tears coursed down her mottled cheeks. "As if what they did to me just from askin for Anna to be released instead of me was no enough."

Aiden looked over at Finley who was pacing as if in deep thought.

Heaving a frustrated sigh, he placed her in the arms of her brother as he passed by and went behind the safety of his desk, his brows furrowed in contemplation.

They tried to get Riona to talk as soon as she returned with Keir but all she'd done was insist she be taken away posthaste, stating she was too fearful of being recaptured without the protection of his stronghold surrounding her.

They wasted a lot of time returning to the keep and now, even with her inside the safety of the gates, she was useless.

"Ye saw nothin to help us before it be too late?"

Riona looked like she was trying to think even as more tears fell but in the end, all she did was shake her head.

Aggravated at his inability to save Skye and his sister, Aiden braced his hands on the desk in front of him and lowered his head.

"Come, sister, think hard."

Finley knew Riona's antics were going to cost them a valuable foothold. Aiden gravitated towards strong-willed women not whimpering fools like Riona was behaving, and they had discussed this. She was destroying everything they had worked for with her caterwauling. He shook her firmly, his back to the men so they could not see as he glared at her meaningfully.

Riona scowled back at her brother before she realized what he was silently telling her to do.

"Wait." She frowned angrily at Finley before she widened her eyes and stepped around him to slip back to Aiden's side. "I do remember somethin."

"Aye?"

She batted her eyes and clasped his arm. "It might be nothin, mind ye."

"What be it, woman?" Collen and Aiden growled as one.

Riona pouted and her lower lip trembled.

Aiden straightened and took a deep breath before patting her hand encouragingly.

"What do ye remember, Riona?"

"Well." She drew out the word and bit her lip in deep thought. "There was a path, well-worn mind ye, which the rogue's took often, returnin with buckets of water."

When Aiden stared at her without saying anything, she sighed and pouted. "I told ye it might no be anythin."

Aiden looked over at Collin. "A stream?"

"Or an underground pool." He shrugged in thought. "It could be many places. I will get with me men an look over the charts ye have."

*   *   *

Skye and Anna stood with clasped hands as the setting sun illuminated the raiders' return.

The leader's face was flushed with fury as he looked at them while holding a badly beaten man.

Both of them knew it was not a good sign.

They watched as they carried the injured man into a tent, the leader following, casting one last fierce look their way before ducking under the flap.

Squeezing each other's hands, they both weakly smiled encouragement to the other.

Sometime later, there came a commotion from the direction the group had arrived. Several men came through on horses while dragging another on foot behind with a rope. The rain from earlier making the captured man's footing difficult at the pace the men had kept, mud spattered his body from when he'd probably been dragged earlier.

One of the men jumped off his horse and ran to the tent, calling out for their leader.

They watched him storm out and approach the captive, punching him in mid stride.

The man fell to his knees shaking his head.

Will grabbed his hair in a fist and another punch brought blood bursting from his nose.

"Tie him up. Ye two; grab the wenches and bring them here." The flickering flames casting his face in an evil glow as he glanced their way. "I want them to watch him die."

Two men approached with vicious looks on their faces and entered their small space.

Anna and Skye backed up in fear, not getting far before their hands were yanked before them and cruelly tied, a brutal pinch to their breasts causing whimpered shrieks as the men dragged them from their confinement, trembling in terror.

Slamming a pitchfork into the dry ground, the men lashed their bound hands around it.

Will grabbed Anna's chin tightly. "Watch what happens to my enemies."

He grinned maniacally before turning away.

Skye had a difficult time looking at the imprisoned man. Even with bruises swelling his face and wrists bleeding from chains, he stood tall and defiant. If only she could help, but there were too many of them and with Anna pregnant and unsure of her abilities it would only end in disaster.

Pulling a stick from the fire, the leader eyed it with a devilish look before turning to the bound man.

As Skye's heart leapt to her throat, the man jabbed the branch into the captured man's neck and pulled it back when the hostage fell to his knees.

The girls struggled to break free, Anna begging for mercy while Skye cried out for him to stop.

Jerking the prisoner to his feet, Will repeatedly jabbed him in his chest.

Skye was weeping, trying to break free from her bindings, her face swung over her shoulder to look into the fire, her mind ready to scream for her sister when her head was wrenched back around by the hair.

A fist smashed into her face causing her knees to buckle and her vision to recede. She grabbed onto the handle of the pitchfork and struggled to stand as she was hauled up by her hair.

Her vision slowly cleared and she found herself looking into the leader's face while Anna wept next to her, unable to help.

"I told ye to watch." The man snarled as spit flew from his mouth.

He stared at her hard making sure she understood his meaning before turning back to continue torturing the hostage.

They clutched each other's fingers, watching through blurred eyes as the man was tortured, cringing when he began to scream as the pain became too much.

Anna threw up when they cut his tongue from his mouth as Skye sunk to her knees, her head crowded with the horrors they were forced to witness.

A lifetime later, they were released, Skye had long ago ran out of tears, her mind and body numb to the rough handling of the raiders as she was made to stand.

She had only one thought going through her head over the last hours.

She jerked her arm away as she looked over her shoulder at the murderer. "Be thankful I will not take so long to kill you."

When pushed back into their cage, Skye stumbled, hearing the persecutor's laughter following behind her.

They fell against the trunk, wrapping their arms around each other, weeping softly as Skye focused on the baby, making sure there had been no harm caused by the stress of the last few hours.

"His name was Rory." Anna hiccupped through her tears.

Skye nodded and tried to comfort her friend.

"Rory was a brave man."

Overcome by exhaustion, they fell asleep holding the other, their minds having suffered through too much.

Abruptly woken sometime later, Anna screeched and hit Will when he snatched Skye from her side.

"It's okay, Anna, stop it, you must think of the baby."

The man backhanded the pregnant girl causing her to fall on her hip, and then he threw back his head and roared.

"Do not be jealous me fair-haired gurl, ye be next once I have exhausted me lusts on this fine piece of flesh. Then me men shall have at her and ye will be mine."

He eyed Anna with hatred. "Tis the least ye owe me for what yer brother did to me own kin."

He tossed the struggling Skye over his boney shoulder and passed through the gates as another man locked it behind him.

Thrown to the ground, Skye lost her breath as her body slammed against a crate.

Before she could take a breath, he fell on top of her, his hands ripping at her clothes and groping her flesh.

Fear overwhelmed Skye and she lashed out, cursing him. A fist connected aimlessly at his shoulder before Will grabbed her wrists and slammed them down with brutal force above her head.

"I like a good fight, wench, but there be things that need doin soon so this first time we will be skippin the fun and tyin yer arse up."

As he moved to get a better hold, she hauled off and slapped him feeling the cold course into her hand as she brought forth her powers.

He pushed her away with such force that she fell, her head hitting a container filled with water.

"Bloody bitch. That will be returned thrice-fold." He snarled, rubbing his jaw.

Head spinning, Skye was unable to fight back as he grabbed her violently by the hair and dragged her to the center pole before binding her to it.

*   *   *

Collin looked up from the charts a group of them had been going over and frowned at his brother-by-marriage. "What be it? Ye be too distracted."

"I ken there be somethin I be overlookin. Somethin Riona said."

Finley had removed his protesting sister from the study once they found she had no more information to give them.

"Och, I dunno trust that woman."

"Neither do I but—"

Just then, two men came in and paused at the doorway.

"What be it?" Aiden asked over the girl's bawling.

"'Tis Rory."

"He be back?"

The men nodded, not looking too pleased to continue.

"What be it?" Aiden repeated.

"He be dead, m'Laird."

Silence reined as hope of finding the girls were destroyed and a valuable man lost.

"What else?" Collin asked as the man looked as if he had more to say.

Heaving a sigh, he held out something in each hand. "These were found tied to Rory's hair."

Aiden picked up the ring he had returned to Skye while Collin held the necklace he had given his wife at Yule during last winter solstice.

Aiden growled.

Taking a goblet from his desk, he threw it violently into the hearth and watched the flames engulf the vessel.

Long moments of silence followed as he became lost in thought.

"Out. All of ye, except Collin, out!

Aiden stopped one of the guards without taking his gaze from the flames. "Bring me mother an ensure I be no disturbed!"

"Aye, m'Laird!"

When the door closed, Collin approached his friend. "What be ye thinkin?"

"Flames, Collin." He looked at the man as if that explained it all. "Skye wanted a fire, an do ye ken the why of that?"

When the man shook his head in confusion, Aiden broke out into a grin.

"I once walked in on Skye talkin to her sister—through the flames—in me chambers."

Aiden missed Collin's shocked look as Elizabeth entered quickly, the door shut discreetly behind her.

"What is it, Aiden?"

"We need to contact Skye's sister. If she has the power to appear in the flames in this time to her sister then maybe we can get her to do so with us."

"I ken yer meanin." Collin said excitedly.

"Aye." Elizabeth agreed as she went back to the study door, opened it, and spoke to the guard while Aiden drew a chair closer to the hearth.

Collin crouched next to Aiden. "She can be yer eyes an bring ye to them."

"If her powers be so great, ye need to ensure she won't take vengeance till we can get to the women."

Elizabeth nodded as she waited for the sentry's return. When he handed her a pouch, she smiled her thanks and returned to the fire Collin had added logs to as the door closed behind her.

Sitting in the chair, she opened the sack.

"Skye and her sister have a natural link, making it easier for them to connect, but I have some hex knowledge of me own." She grinned.

*   *   *

"Stop, ye bastard!" Anna screamed as she crashed through the flap of the tent, the man fast on her heels grabbing her around the neck and stopping her in her tracks but not stopping her from struggling madly against him.

"I be sorry, Will. She got out somehow and I—"

Will cut him off with a wave of his hand.

"It bothers me not, let the wench watch." He grinned maliciously. "It will give her a chance to see what comes next for her."

"Anna, wait!"

Skye knew Anna had used her gift to get out and come to her rescue but, with her tied, there was no way the girl could get her free while dealing with two men.

"Yes, Anna, wait." Will sneered. "Behave and I won't cut the brat ye have in yer belly from ye."

Skye's stomach curdled at the thought and she kicked him to take his attentions away from Anna.

"You are a coward having to tie me. It's not because you have things to do, it's because you are weak.

The man fell to a knee and backhanded her. She caught her breath and turned back to him as he tore her top in half.

"You did the same to Rory, the man you captured. You had him tied too because he would have kicked. Your. Ass."

He sneered as he grabbed her hair, clenching it at her scalp.

"What do you think your lover did to me brother?" He snickered and licked her from her jaw, over her nose, to her scalp. "So ye shall be most willing to spread yer legs for me cock."

She spit in his face and he threw back his head, roaring with laughter.

He was mad!

She struggled to get free as he untied his britches.

"It is a damn good thing you have me tied or I would keep my promise."

He ignored her as he moved to her feet, not noticing her shock as she felt something squirm through the rope around her wrists as he tore her skirt while wrenching it to the side, falling on top of her before she could do any damage with her knees.

Skye glanced at Anna and saw her centering her powers.

"I will kill you and my friend will make your man watch."

Both men howled with laugher as Skye focused on the ropes, heating them with a small flame, ignoring the burning on her wrists as they healed.

She nodded slightly to Anna so the girl knew she was ready.

Heart pounding in fear and rage, she felt the rope give as he shoved her legs apart while yanking at her undergarments.

Before the cloth ripped further, she brought her freed hands up and slipped them between the opening of his shirt.

"This is where I keep my promise."

Will's face turned to fury and Skye knew she had to let go of the panic and wrap herself in anger.

"Stay back, I'm going to teach this bitch her place." He warned his man when he made to approach.

Hands wrapped around her throat, Will slowly began to squeeze.

"Let me show you how to keep a promise. Then I will show your friend."

A chill swept through Skye and raced down her arms to her hands.

Sounds faded as her vision narrowed and she enveloped his heart in icy pain then squeezed, sending waves of energy to his limbs to keep him from moving away from her.

Watching the color drain from his face and his mouth go slack, she smiled, following his body with her own as he fell to the side.

"Lesson learned." She whispered to his still face.

Her hearing was returning when she heard a struggle next to her and chaos outside.

Oh no, they'd been discovered!

Shoving aside her fright, Skye concentrated on the immediate danger from the other man as she scrambled to her feet, almost losing her footing when he fell into her as Anna struggled with him.

She watched as a root came up from the ground, wrapping around his ankle and causing his imbalance as the earth around it made the soil uneven.

Her hands gripped his face and held on as he attempted to right himself, his hands going over her own trying to remove them.

"Let go of him, Anna, but do something to hold him still!"

"Och, he be goin down!" Anna cried out as the root slipped around his other ankle too.

As soon as the girl stepped back, Skye fell to her knees with the man and focused on his brain, the ice burning its way inside. With his brain no longer able to control his movements, his hands fell limply to his sides as he screamed in pain. His screams turned to gurgles as blood poured from his eyes, ears, nose and mouth and then he went limp.

Vision clearing, Skye stared at the man in numbed shock, her body beginning to tremble.

Raising her shaky hands, she looked at them and the blood in shock.

"Skye!"

Whipping her head around, she stared unseeingly at the voice that called her name.

"Aiden?"

The chaos outside filtered into her dazed brain but his movement brought even more fear and she backed away when he rushed to her.

"Don't touch me!"

"Tis alright—"

She scrambled to her feet covering the material of her torn dress to her chest as she tucked her bloody hands under her armpits and shook her head, still feeling the cold inside her.

"You can't touch me."

His look of distress was nearly her undoing but when he took another step with his hands raised, she barked at him.

"No!"

She barely took in the fact that Collin was holding Anna in his arms.

Somewhere in the back of her mind, Skye knew she was no longer responsible for the girl's safety and she felt a moment of intense relief before her eyes followed in a downward motion to the two men dead on the ground.

"I killed them." She whispered in shock. "I killed them."

"Tis alright." Aiden repeated.

"I *wanted* to kill them." She looked back at Aiden, barely hearing his calm voice. "I can still feel it in me."

Understanding dawned and he took another step causing her to flee but Aiden was quicker and wrapped his arms around her, enveloping her into his body and holding tight as she struggled to break free.

At the feel of his touch, her hands clutched together between her breasts as fear clawed at her chest.

"You have to let go! Oh, my God, please, let go!"

Aiden held tight, his heart pounding hard against his chest at the horrors Skye had gone through.

If they had only arrived sooner, the trauma these girls went through could have been avoided but it had taken a long time of concentration and chanting before his mother had gotten through to Skye's sister.

It had only been a matter of moments before Sarah had found the encampment while the women had slept. Unable to wake Skye, she had gone back to Aiden and they had formed a way for her to lead him and his men to the campsite. With Sarah's ability to cause pandemonium with the fires burning, his men were able to slip in and battle the Reivers as he and Collin searched for their women.

Sileas and Seelie had immediately caught the girls' scent and had led them to a tent.

When they stood outside the tent flaps, Aiden and Collin had paused to assess the situation and to listen for a moment, sweat running down their bodies at the restraint of not barging in.

They heard a scuffle and some cries and Aiden looked at his friend while adjusting his grip on his sword then entered, slashing the fabric opening in one swipe, Collin right behind him.

Standing in stunned silence, they watched as Skye fell to her knees, her hands wrapped around a man gurgling in his own blood as more poured from every cavity.

"Tis alright." He repeated firmly as he turned her around, quickly enfolding her back into his embrace.

Warmth invaded her limbs and her struggling subsided. She raised her face to look at him.

"I be fine, *leanabh*." He calmly reassured her, relaxing his hold slightly.

She tried to smile but her lips began to tremble. Tears formed and streamed unchecked as she buried her face into the crook of his arm, her hands breaking free from the tight fists to wrap around his waist.

His heart splintered when she broke down and began to sob, her body racked with tremors.

"Tis alright, *mo ghaol.* I be here now an will allow nothin to happen to ye."

CHAPTER ELEVEN

They took the girls to separate areas of a stream near their camp, heated the water and cleaned them in private while guards stood watch further away.

Tenderly, Aiden cleaned the dirt and grime from Skye's body, his face a mask of granite unless she looked at him then his features softened and his lips would brush across her forehead.

After pulling one of his woolen shirts over her shivering body, Aiden brushed the dried mud from the cloth before he gently put Skye's torn bodice back over her head, wishing he had brought something for her to wear so she would not have this to remind her of the ordeal she had gone through.

Placing a chaste kiss on her cheek, he rolled up the sleeves so she could have her hands free.

When he was done, Aiden stood with her arms in his hands looking down on her bent head, concerned when she still had not said anything.

Quietly sighing, he removed a ring from his finger and held it out to her.

Skye looked at the band in silence, unmoving for a long time before taking it with both hands. Pressing her lips against it, she leaned into Aiden's chest and cried softly while he held her, smoothing a hand over her wet locks and gritting his teeth at the horror he knew she had endured.

At the encouragement of Anna, who wanted to be as far away as possible from where they had been captured, they had ridden as long as possible with breaks throughout the day until it became late and needed to stop for the night.

Now they sat before a fire, the sun making its final journey behind the hills as Aiden held Skye on his lap.

"I hope Sarah is okay. She's so close to having her baby and I can imagine how much effort she put into helping you." Skye whispered, staring into the flames.

Aiden closed his eyes briefly in gratitude that Skye had finally spoken and nuzzled his jaw into her hair and, for the second time, calmly told her what he knew.

"Yer *piuthar-màthar* made it very clear that yer sister would be closely watched an, as soon as her part was done, she would be in bed an she would check on ye on the morrow."

"Sounds like Aunt Gladys." She looked up at the tent beyond the flames. "I hope someone will get me if Anna needs me. I worry about her and the baby after what she's been through."

"What of yer needs, *mo ghaol*? What do ye need?"

He waited patiently for an answer, when one didn't seem to come, he rested his jaw on top of her head and remained quiet thinking she had gone back inside herself.

"You."

He frowned wondering if he had heard her correctly. "What did ye say, lass?"

"You asked what I needed." She said almost absently. "I need you. I need what you are doing right now; letting me get through what has happened without overwhelming me with questions. I need your warmth to keep the cold away."

She turned in his arms and tucked her side against his stomach, her arms looping around his waist, legs curled up and her head resting against his shoulder.

More time passed in silence.

If it hadn't been for her hold around his waist Aiden would have thought she'd fallen asleep.

"I keep thinking about Rory."

Aiden said nothing. He knew telling her to not think about it was irrational so he waited.

"We were bound to a stake and forced to watch everything. I wanted so badly to do something—anything—to take away his pain. The things they did to him." She shuddered at the memories. "It's why I never watch horror movies. Why would anyone desire to do things so . . . so . . . vicious?"

Not understanding everything she was saying, he knew enough of what she spoke, having seen the results of what had happened to Rory prior to the man's burial. He had also done many of the same things to the Reivers man when trying to extract information from him.

Aiden hated that she had to go through this but knew it was essential for the real healing could begin so he remained silent as she sorted through the events.

"I was so conflicted. I needed so badly to heal him but I knew if I did, it would only prolong his pain and that man, that little weasel of a man, would have enjoyed torturing him more. He was mad, insane." She buried in closer, her voice breaking. "So I did nothing."

"That be the smartest thin for ye to do, lass. As ye said, it would have only prolonged his pain an it would have made it worse for ye an Anna had he but kenned of yer magic."

He held her closer, his brogue deepening with emotions. "We be very thankful ye dinna do anythin."

She turned again and came to her knees, taking his face into her hands. "I need you to take me away. Somewhere where no one can see or hear us, and I need you to take these images from my head—if only for a little while."

Their eyes searched each other's for a moment until she spoke again. "Please."

He came to his feet, draping the skins they sat on over his shoulders before pulling her up with him and scooping her into his powerful arms.

Aiden whistled low for his hounds to follow then took her deeper into the forest.

He sat her on her feet gently while looking into her eyes, the animals curling at the base of a tree not far away.

When she stood on her toes and kissed him softly on the lips, he took the skins, laid them out on the forest floor, then took her by the hand and brought her closer to him.

Holding her in his arms, hands at her waist, thumbs caressing the shirt he had put under her torn gown, he kissed the top of her head.

Skye's hands slipped back to cup his cheeks and she lifted her face to kiss him.

"I love how you smell, like wood and leather." She inhaled deeply. "Like something that comes from my darkest fantasies."

When she looked up at him, he found a sparkle in her eyes where last there had been a dull stare, and his cock hardened at the smile that tilted from the corner of her mouth.

He eased the shirt from her body then cupped the bared breasts before him.

Refusing to think of why the gown was torn, he lowered his head and suckled at the puckered nipple, warming it with his breath and watching as it pebbled.

Her hands were still about his face and she arched her body to get closer, her head thrown back as his teeth traced her sensitive flesh.

With one hand holding the small of her back, he removed the tattered gown from her shoulders.

When she tried to help, he took the fabric and bound her hands behind her back before gently easing her to the furs, ensuring her comfort before kissing her shoulders and over her neck to where he gently lapped at the steadily increasing pulse before heading to the mounds thrust before him.

Skye whimpered at his gentle caresses, trying to free her hands to pull him tighter so his body would press against hers and whimpered when she wasn't able to.

"Aiden." She moaned in frustration when his tongue laved circles around her puckered nipples.

"Aye, lass?"

"You know what I need."

He chuckled around the underside of her breast, blowing lightly over the fevered flesh.

"Nay, methinks ye should tell me."

When Aiden grabbed her skirts, he grinned as she pressed with her heels and shoulders to lift up so he could pull her dress up with ease. When he placed a leg between hers and pushed her thighs open, she smiled in pleasure.

She was wet with need.

The way her body writhed under him, how her scent enveloped him and the light keening sounds she made letting him know she needed more, had his vision narrowed to red.

His cock strained and everything inside him wanted to burst out, to conquer and control, to take and plunder. Everything felt raw and animalistic and still he fought for control. He wanted to give her gentleness instead of the harshness she had been forced to endure.

She wiggled, trying to get out of his grasp. "You need to let my hands go, Aiden."

He lifted his head and brought his body up so he could smile wickedly down at her.

"I do, aye? I be no so sure of that, lass."

"I am sure of it, Aiden." She protested. "I want to feel you. I have to touch you."

She stopped her struggles and looked him square in the eyes. "That's what I need."

He sighed heavily as if in thought.

"Pleeeease." She begged prettily.

"Och, lass, I do so enjoy the way ye beg." He grinned wickedly before easing her hands from behind her back.

Hands free, she slipped them under his loose shirt and dragged the cloth up as her nails skipped over his flesh, feeling the goose bumps from her touch.

Pressing her pelvis against his thigh, he allowed her to push the fabric over his head and traced the hard naked skin, seeing with her hands what the darkening sky kept from her eyes.

The nails traveling down his ribcage while she rubbed her pussy teasingly against his leg was almost more than he could take.

"Ye need to remove yer braise, lass." He grunted.

"Nay, Aiden; *Ye* need to remove me braise."

Aiden looked into her face and saw the saucy glint from the dying light.

"Ye donna ken what ye do to me." He growled.

"Ah, but I do."

Rising up, he placed both knees between her legs before he gripped her undergarments. Watching her face, he tore them from her body, gritting his teeth as she gasped and opened her legs wider. Her scent invaded his nostrils and he removed his leather trews before settling between her thighs to rub his cock in her wetness.

"Oh, yes." She shifted trying to slide him into her. "Inside. Fill me."

Refusing to lose himself to her wishes, he gripped her thighs and eased them up and out while he kissed his way down her stomach, placing her knees over his shoulders to bury his tongue deep into her wet pussy.

She threw back her head and cried out as her knees stretched further and her heels pressed into his back to bring him unconsciously closer.

Two fingers slicked over her opening, coated in her juices they eased inside her and pressed down.

"Oh, God! Oh, God!"

When more of her nectar flowed from her damp pussy, he brought his wet fingers back between her cheeks and swirled around her tight hole. Pressing the flat of his tongue against her clit, he eased a finger through the puckered opening and she cried out again.

"Relax for me, *mo ghaol,* an I promise to make this pleasurable for ye."

Skye's body was a whirlwind of pleasure. Already feeling the need to explode, she tried hard to relax as she took a deep breath to steady herself.

Sweet juices flowed from her pussy and he used it to coat her ass even further then slipped a finger in, feeling the ring grip it before she took an uneven breath and relaxed.

He slid it in slowly to his first knuckle while distracting her with his mouth.

"One more, *leanabh*."

She groaned, every nerve ending coming alive where his fingers and tongue teased, and when he eased another coated finger inside she exploded with pleasure.

So sudden was her climax, her breathe stopped and then her hands flew to her mouth as she screamed, her body arching as a tidal wave of electricity shot through her and centered back to his tongue and fingers.

"Oh! Oh, please no more! Oh, my God, please. Too much." She gasped through rapid breaths, her limbs shaking.

"Nay, lass, tis only the beginnin."

He kept his fingers inside her and stretched her further as he worked them slowly open then closed, his tongue had stopped the torturous play on her clit that helped her through the sudden climax and now it lapped at the juices flowing from her.

She moaned as her body sank to the furs beneath her. "Please."

"Ye shall feel me cock as it enters ye, lass."

"Oh, God."

"An then ye shall feel me cock as it becomes buried inside ye here."

He pushed his two fingers gently deeper into her ass and felt her tighten before relaxing her grip after taking a slow breath.

"Tis a good girl."

How those simple words made her soar, her body coming back to life as his ministrations with his tongue played once again with her clit, his fingers stretching her more.

"Come, lass, I want ye on yer hands an knees."

He helped her up and gently turned her over, pressing her shoulders down and her knees apart.

"Arch yer back so yer arse be high." He encouraged.

She blushed furiously but when the fingers of his other hand slipped inside her pussy, her body automatically did as he asked.

She pressed her face against the furs, her arms bent at the elbows so her hands were above her head.

She never felt so exposed, so embarrassed, and so wet.

"Och, lass, ye make a beautiful sight in the moonlight."

She felt him shift before his whiskered face nipped at one of her cheeks. She caught her breath at how sensitive her skin was and then wiggled against him, grinning when he licked over the mark, smiling wider when he chuckled at her response.

He took more of her juices and coated around her back entrance as he played with her clit.

"Ye ken what I will do, lass?" He slipped a finger back in before gently sliding in a second.

She felt calm, as funny as that might have sounded, this position that exposed her most private parts to his gaze made her feel free and she wanted to give herself to him this way.

"I want this too." She replied as she nodded.

He played gently with her opening, sliding in two fingers then easing them out before repeating the process, never forgetting about the swelling bud above her pussy.

He eased over her body to whisper in her ear. "We will go slow, *mo ghaol*. We have all night."

Eyes closed she moaned as his hard cock pressed against the curve of her ass, his fingers making her feel full.

"I don't know that I can wait all night, Aiden." She pressed back against him as his fingers slid out, not happy with the empty feeling it created.

"Tis no of a matter to me." He nibbled at her shoulder, down her spine and back, to her cheeks, pleased at her responses to his touch.

His cock was leaking with a need to bury itself inside her.

Taking the tip, Aiden slid it over her opening, getting it wet and smiling when she wiggled back trying to get him inside her.

He spread her pussy lips apart and rocked against her opening, slipping inside an inch.

"Aye, lass, tis what I want too."

Her cunt spasmed and she couldn't imagine how she could possibly be wetter.

Arms stretched out onto the earth's floor, Skye pushed against the leaf-covered ground to press back against him, closing her eyes as he slipped in another inch, her entrance stretching to fit around his girth.

"Oh, yes, that feels good." She moaned, swaying against him.

His hands gripped her hips, his neck arched and straining at the tight wetness of her sheath.

Refusing her pleas to bury himself inside her, he took his time easing in another inch before slipping almost all the way out.

When she cried in frustration, he pressed a thumb to her abandoned nether hole and played with the sensitive opening, enjoying the way she arched her back for him. He withdrew from her pussy then slipped back in, his thumb sliding past the tight ring at the same time and she moaned as her body began to shake.

"Relax." He soothed, leaning down to nip her shoulder blade.

In and out in a steady rhythm, his thumb buried all the way in, he pulled at her opening as he pressed his staff deeper.

Skye was awash in sensations, she spread her legs wider, craving the intense feeling of pleasure and pain from the way his cock stretched and his thumb invaded her.

"More, Aiden." She begged as the cool night air caressed her heated flesh.

Aiden removed his cock from her cunt and coated his other hand in her juices, ignoring the cry of disappointment from her at his actions but, before she could protest, he buried himself back inside and his other thumb slowly slipped into her back entrance.

When she tightened on his fingers, he told her to slacken up.

"I can't." She sobbed, squirming. "It feels too good."

He stopped moving and she cried more.

"Ye must listen to me." He commanded. "Ease up."

Whimpering in need, she took a breath and then a deeper one and let go.

When he felt her loosen around him, he began thrusting again as she relaxed more then pulled his thumbs apart and smiled as she shivered in response.

"Be ye ready?"

"Yes! Please, take me there, Aiden."

He slowly pulled his cock from her wet sheath and rested it against her opening, withdrawing his thumbs as the same time.

"We will go slowly. Do no push back against me ye ken, lass?"

"Please, Aiden, please." She wiggled her rump.

"Ye ken, lass?" He smiled but forced his voice to be firm, knowing he did not want to injure her.

"Yes, yes! Please."

He pressed against her stretched opening, easing the tip of his wet cock against the resistance, it opened to his pressure and she moaned as he slipped through the ring, not understanding how she craved more.

"Relax, *mo ghaol.*"

"I can't." She cried.

"Relax." He commanded as a finger slipped around to her clit and swirled lazily over it, the rest of his body unmoving.

"Oh, that feels soooo good." She relaxed, her arms going limp as she lifted her rump to give him better access.

He continued to play with her clit then pushed his cock in a little more, using one of his hands to open her cheek wider.

He stopped at her whimper and she pouted. "Don't stop now."

She felt impossibly stretched. The feeling became a craving for more, her body broke out in a sweat, and she pushed back against him, feeling him slide in further.

Aiden grunted. "I told ye no to do that." She squeezed around him and he groaned. "I told ye no to do that too."

Skye rose up on her hands and whimpered when she felt him slip in more at her sudden movement. The pain caused her to gasp before she turned her head to glare at him.

"You're going too slow, Aiden, please don't do this to me. I need you all the way in."

"An I will be there, lass, but ye doona ken the differences between pleasurable pain an only pain, so obey me for I shall no give to ye anything but pleasure."

Tears formed and Skye turned away before he could see them, not wanting him to think it was from sadness.

She had seen the way his neck muscles strained from his self-control and it had made her breasts ache at the picture of pure alpha dominance. She bent her elbows and eased back down arching her back so her ass lifted and she smiled as he slipped in further.

"Yes, m'Laird." She whispered, a feeling of content replacing the frustration.

He growled at her total submission to his will, his cock expanding impossibly more as his balls tightened painfully. Aiden quickly wetted his fingers and coated his cock with her cream to help ease his way further into her.

"Ye feel so tight. The way yer body be displayed like a woman who offers herself freely to the man she belongs to. Yer arse shall surely be me downfall."

He gripped the globes of her cheeks and spread them wide, watching as he sunk in more.

She whimpered at his words, feeling her moisture dripping down her thigh. The deep dominance of his voice, the total control of her body and the way his hands opened her fully to him, caused her breathing to quicken.

"I need to cum."

"Nay, lass, no yet. Soon, but no yet." His fingers played harder with her clit and her body began to shake.

"Ye have almost all of me, girl."

"More then. I want all of you inside me. Deeper, Aiden, please fuck me."

Gritting his teeth, he pushed inside her until he was fully in.

She cried out in pleasure as he slowly eased out then back in. She gasped clenching down on him, the pain more pleasurable with each stroke.

"Yesss." She sighed through gritted teeth.

Watching her reactions, he gradually gained momentum with each thrust until she was crying out, begging him to take her harder and deeper, pushing back as hard as she could to meet him every time he plunged in.

His finger pressed into her dripping cunt then slipped over her distended clit.

"Oh yes. Fuck me, Aiden, please fuck me harder."

Skye felt so swollen, so full, everything was more intense, she clamped down around his cock, feeling the burning ecstasy of him taking her.

She went to lift up and he put his hand on her shoulder blades, pressed her back down, keeping her there.

"Stay, wench." He grunted as he drove into her ass.

His dominance caused pulsing need throughout her body, she quivered, squeezing her eyes tight as tears slipped through, and she started to beg him for more.

"Please, fuck me. Please let me cum! Please!"

She pressed harder against him, feeling the pressure of his hand at her back, his cock searing through her tender ass as she felt herself soar even higher.

"I can't, please, I can't wait."

"Feel it, Skye, feel me cock bury deep inside yer arse. I am yer Master, yer Laird an I will have ye feel it. How deep I can go, how I stretch ye to fullness. Can ye feel it?"

Skye cried out, her mind and body as one, focused on the intensity building inside her at his words. His mastery turned her on even more and she cried, tears poured down her cheeks.

"Can ye feel it, wench? Can ye?" He grunted his voice sharp in its demands for an answer.

"Yes! Oh yes, Master! I feel it."

Her soul focus centered on him, at the forceful way his cock thrust inside, hurting her with such passion it became ecstasy, at his balls slapping against her pussy, his fingers swirling over her bud, and the power of his hand forcing her to remain in place.

"Then cum, *leanabh*!" He demanded as he pinched her clit.

Her breath tore from her throat in a scream as the orgasm ripped her apart, her soul exploding in brilliant darkness. She was lost in a maelstrom of sensation hardly able to hear his growl as he grabbed her hips and thrust once, again, and then emptied his hot seed deep into her.

Then everything went black as she slipped into oblivion.

* * *

The next day, they road in silence as they journeyed home, Skye falling asleep in the cradle of his arms, worn out from the endless night of lovemaking.

The silence had Aiden's mind wondering to things he did not wish to think about, things like this woman who had stolen his heart should not be made to live in a time of such upheaval.

Yes, there was peace. But for how long?

Being half-English, he had his troubles from both his parents' countrymen.

What Skye had been through was not new to his people.

Aiden glanced at his sister sitting in silence as she too leaned against her husband.

Although Anna had never witnessed anything like this before, she had grown up with it and had to help those whom had returned injured from one battle or another. His sister had been born into this world, lived her life knowing nothing else.

No one should have to go through what either of them had, but the woman in his arms had come from a world where, at least in her country, there was no turmoil, to a world where it was all they knew.

How could he keep her when he might lose her to such atrocities if away at battle?

How could he even consider asking it of her?

Last night he had taken her, waking her from sleep to plunge into her eager depths until she cried out in release only to do so again and again, and still he wanted more.

Now she lay exhausted in sleep, curled under his cloak as he berated himself for his abuse of her tender body even as he desired to have her again.

He knew what he needed to do. Once he ensured she had the right spell, Skye would return to her own time.

*   *   *

When they stopped for a meal, Skye went to Anna to ensure she and the baby were doing all right.

"The bairn be fine, Skye. Donna worry yerself about it. Collin is bein very gentle with me." She touched her friend's arm and smiled kindly. "How about ye?"

"I'm fine."

"I noticed that ye an Aiden were no about this morn."

Skye blushed causing Anna to grin. "Aye, say no more. I ken how a man can keep the nightmares away."

Shaking her head, she laughed softly. "You are incorrigible."

"Tis what makes me so bonnie."

Skye laughed outright when the girl winked at her and couldn't help but hug her.

Standing off to the side, Collin smiled encouragingly at his friend. "She is goin to be just fine."

Collin was concerned when Aiden looked away from the girls to return his best friend's gaze before turning away. Following him to the fire, he knelt next to Aiden.

"Anna said Skye believes Riona be English."

"Aye. Skye spoke to me about her concerns this morn. I was gonna speak with ye about this. I have sent Keir an another warrior ahead to keep an eye on them til we return."

"What do ye be thinkin?"

Aiden looked up from the fire. "I be thinkin that too many questions come to mind and, if that be true, too many answers."

Collin nodded his agreement.

*   *   *

It took three days of careful riding, due to Anna's condition, to make it to the castle gates and night was falling fast by the time they passed the heavy doors to the warmth of the inside.

"Water is being heated for a nice bath. Til then, ye shall sit here and have something to eat." Elizabeth said as she ushered the girls to sit before the fire in Aiden's study away from curious eyes.

The dogs made their place before the hearth next to the men who stood in silence as the women accepted mugs of hot cider before being ushered off by Elizabeth.

"I am going to get these girls out of the clothes they are wearing, get them warmed up, and then put them in a bath.

I will call ye when ye can put them to bed. And when ye return, ye'd best have a smile on yer faces or ye both shall be getting an earful from me." She whispered furiously before closing the door firmly on their surprised faces.

Collin looked expectantly at his brother-in-law. "Well?"

"Well what?"

"Ye gonna allow her to push us out like that?"

Aiden snorted and turned away.

"Now ye ken why I brought me wife here instead of keepin her in me keep when yer mother found out about this pregnancy." Collin huffed as he followed along.

They sent a messenger to have Keir meet them in the enclosed chamber off the great hall that he used when conducting private affairs of business, such as the one he intended to have soon.

When Keir entered, Aiden motioned for him to sit at the small table while Collin poured another goblet of mead before sitting down as well.

"The lass be in her chambers, her guard standin watch outside the door." Keir enjoyed the soothing liquid before continuing. "When Finley heard that some of the Reivers had escaped, he became angry. He took some of his men an went after them vowin to kill them all."

"Why does that sound strange to me?" Collin pondered.

"Because Finley isna the kind of man to act rashly nor the kind to rush into the fray." Aiden answered.

"He be the kind to stay an watch the castle." Collin snorted in agreement.

Aiden nodded and turned back to Keir. "Did anyone of our men go with Finley?"

"Aye." Keir nodded firmly, a wicked smile in place. "Me cousin, Ranald."

"Good. Have ye chatted with Riona?"

"Nay m'Laird. The guard of hers wilna allow anyone to pass."

"I bet he has orders to let ye pass." Collin snickered.

Aiden growled at the thought, running his hands through his hair in aggravation. "I doona have the patience for that woman right now."

"Tis true. Ye need to have a good night's sleep before dealin with the wench." Collin chuckled.

*   *   *

For the first time in days, her body finally stopped shaking and Skye was feeling full and warm. Even the thought of not being able to get a hold of her sister could not keep her from almost falling asleep in the large barrel.

"Och, ye had best no drown." Anna yawned as she curled up on the couch, wrapping her chemise and wrapper closer as she snuggled in after putting down her cider.

Sighing, Skye struggled tiredly to her feet, unconcerned at her nudity as she took the towel from Mairi and stepped out of the tub, holding onto the edge when she almost lost her balance.

Too weary to help, she stood staring at the flames as the maid took the towel and a nightgown was placed over her head, arms slipping through the sleeves without thought, before a heavier wrap was put around Skye's shoulders and tied with a cord about her waist.

"Come, lass, have a seat. I shall send for the men so ye can get a proper nights rest." Elizabeth's brogue warred with her English accent as her concern deepened over the girl's silence.

Idle chatter had produced little response from Skye and Elizabeth was concerned. Only Anna seemed to accept her silence without worry as she handed her one honey cake after another, insisting Glenys would not be happy if they were not all eaten.

Elizabeth saw Skye looking blankly into the flames and wrapped her arms around the younger woman.

"In the morn, ye shall come to my chambers and we shall speak to yer sister. I promise." Elizabeth assured her before guiding her to a large chair and easing her into it. "Now sit and relax, Mairi is off to find Aiden."

Skye fell asleep to Elizabeth's soft touch on her hair, soothingly combing out the tangles.

It wasn't long before the men returned, smiles plastered on their concerned faces as they entered the study, both smiles easing as they saw the women curled up and sleeping.

Silently, they gently picked them up and carried them out.

Aiden looked down on the woman in his arms as he worked on hardening his melting heart. Smudges showed under her eyes and he blamed himself for not being able to deny her or his body's needs when she came to him at night.

Knowing she needed her sleep more than he needed her body, he settled her into the bed in the small chamber that had been hers in the beginning of her stay. He kept her wrap on and tucked the furs around her body, not bothering to chastise Seelie when she took her place at the girl's feet.

Leaning over, he kissed her on the forehead, the side of her temple, her cheek, and when she sighed his name, he swallowed and stood.

Ignoring the hardness of his swelling cock, he took one final look before leaving.

Nodding to the man standing guard outside her door, he went down to his now empty study. The tub had been removed and the fire was dying. He threw in a couple of logs and got the fire to come back to life before sitting behind his desk and rubbing his face with his hands.

"I am glad you got the fire going, I was worried that I wouldn't be able to see my sister."

Aiden stiffened, his head shooting up to look around the empty room.

"Where is she?"

Standing, Aiden looked into the flames and saw the image of Sarah. Still uncomfortable with this kind of magic, he made his way around the desk and pulled a chair closer before sinking into it.

"She be in bed." He said tiredly. "Very angry with ye I might add."

"I knew she would be." The image grinned then frowned in concern. "How is she?"

He searched for the right words. "She be . . . quiet."

"My poor baby sister."

"Yer 'poor baby sister' has been very concerned over no reply from ye these past days."

"I had a baby."

The image grew clearer and Aiden saw Sarah patting and rubbing the back of a baby over her shoulder.

Before he could say anything, the baby let out a belch and his eyebrows raised as the woman cooed her happiness over the sound.

Sarah returned her attention to the flames.

"You tell Skye that I and the baby are alright, that the effort it took to do what I had to do the other day caused me to go into labor, but that the baby is perfect in every way." Her voice lowered to a whisper. "I am going to put the tyke down and get some sleep. Would you tell Skye that I am okay, that we are *all* okay and I will get a hold of her as soon as possible?"

Aiden nodded his head in amazement as the image shimmered out.

"Wait! I need a spell to send her back home."

Nothing.

"*Mac an donais!*" Aiden harshly cursed as he slammed a fist into his palm.

Slumping in the chair, he ran a hand over his features, trying to clear his head.

CHAPTER TWELVE

It was cold and dark but there had to be a light somewhere. Skye squinted, trying to focus in the gloom.

She was outside in the woods and there were noises; scratching noises.

Afraid of what it might be, she still strained to make out what the noises were.

Then someone began crying. Skye tried to find who it was but no matter how fast or where she walked, the noise never got closer. She called out asking who was crying and where they were.

"Please, I can't get to you! You have to tell me where you are!"

Something jumped on her leg and she tried to scream but nothing came out. When she tripped and fell, the clitter-clatter of tiny feet took off in all directions.

Rats!

"Please, not again." She cried as she kicked and flailed her arms trying to knock the rats off.

Skye stumbled to her knees, something heavy weighed her down and then a hand reached out to her.

"Anna!"

She held on to the woman's arms, thankful she was no longer alone when a chill raced across her spine.

"You're not pregnant anymore. Where's the baby?"

Blood started forming on the girl's stomach and tears fell from Anna's face and Skye instantly remembered the threat of Will cutting the baby from her.

"What's the matter, Anna? Where's the baby?"

Anna struggled in the darkness and all Skye could think about is if the baby died so too did Sarah's baby and husband.

"Talk to me!" She shook the girl.

Anna started screaming and tried to break free and she knew the girl blamed her for the loss of the baby.

"No! No, the baby was never taken from you! We got out before, before—"

Her memory went blank and she could not remember anything she wanted to say.

Icy cold tendrils seeped through her limps and she immediately tried to let go of Anna but she couldn't. She watched as the bleeding girl fell to her knees screaming in pain, her flesh singed under Skye's hands.

Suddenly, her grip loosened and she stumbled back into something else.

She swung around, lost her balance, and grabbed onto . . . Rory!

He held her by the upper arms, his face scorched from the torture, puss and blood oozing from numerous cuts. He was trying to say something but couldn't, he opened his mouth as a rat forced its way out.

She screamed but nothing came out. Struggling, she pushed him away and saw burnt tissue from where her hands had been.

Skye ran. There was a light ahead and she knew it came from her house.

Hurrying towards the light while holding her hands together in front of her chest, fear coursed through her veins and frost tinted her lashes. She could hardly move, it was so hard, her body feeling weighed down with burning ice.

When she finally got to the door, she saw Sarah standing behind her aunt but Aiden blocked her entrance. She stumbled to a halt, unsure of what to do.

They stared at her, frowns creasing their faces. She looked at Aiden and he shook his head in disappointment.

"I didn't mean to hurt them! Please." She begged them to understand but all they did was look at her with condemning eyes.

She turned at the scratching noise behind her and saw the men whom she had killed coming towards her, blood oozing everywhere on their bodies. One of them held a dead newborn baby callously in his hand.

Suddenly, she was looking down on the scene watching the men approach her from in front while Aiden showed his disgust just before closing the door on her.

Skye screamed at last as the dead men surrounded her, dragging her down as they tossed the dead baby onto her belly, their saliva dripping onto her face and arms.

Aiden jerked to his feet, sleep instantly vanishing as screams had him running out of his study and up the stairs.

He saw Skye's bedroom door open and crashed through, Keir standing there unsure what to do when Skye struggled out of her covering and fell onto the floor on the other side of her bed, Seelie barking from the foot of the bed after jumping down.

"Tis alright, Keir, just hold the door open fer me." Aiden reassured him as he went over to Skye and scooped her struggling body into his arms.

"No, no! Let me go!" Skye fought the arms holding her, still lost in her nightmare.

Aiden held her tighter, whispering words to her in Gaelic and English, telling her it was he and that she was going to be fine.

It wasn't until he was nearing his chambers that she relaxed, her eyes opening as she looked at him.

"It was only a nightmare?" She whispered with a hoarse voice.

"Aye, lass, twas only a bad dream." He reassured her quietly as he stepped into his own room and closed the door behind them, Seelie joining her brother at the hearth.

When he eased her to her feet, she clutched his arms and looked up to him. "But it's been days, why didn't I have a nightmare before?"

"I doona ken, lass." Aiden gritted his teeth, damming himself for thinking he needed to distance himself and place her in her own chambers.

Skye almost whimpered when she saw the same face on Aiden as in her dreams.

She pushed away, wrapping her arms around herself.

"I'm okay now." She looked away from him and his stern features. "I should go b-back to my bed."

"Ye will stay put." Aiden frowned at the way she seemed to cower.

"Bu—"

"Nay, ye will stay here." He crossed his arms not realizing just yet how it scared her.

"I—"

"Nay, Skye." His voice softened and he reached for her. "I will brook no argument over this."

He pulled her close and held her next to his chest, concerned at the way her body was shivering.

"Tis fine, lass." He smoothed his hands down her tangled hair and kissed the top of her head, frowning when his body responded to her nearness.

He settled her into his bed and removed his clothing watching her watch him and fighting his body's reaction.

Quickly slipping under the covers, Aiden curled an arm around her waist, drawing her back against his chest, thankful for her chemise and pledging to let her sleep the night without him disturbing her rest.

"I shall be here to keep ye safe."

The dream still fresh in her mind kept her jaw clenched as she lay there stiff in his arms.

She was angry and knew she had no right to be, it was all just a dream, but she could not seem to help herself. He had shut the door and let the zombies attack her. She had felt that baby drop on her belly!

Her breath caught at the memory and she shivered.

"There, lass." He soothed, hand running over her shoulder and down her arms. "Mayhap twould help ifn ye told me of yer dream. Ye be thinkin about it, might as well go over it."

Skye bit her lip, embarrassed that he would find out she was mad at him over a dream, but she was never one to keep things held in for long.

"I was in the forest and I heard scratching noises, then there was Anna and she was bleeding all over the front of her dress and she wasn't pregnant. I was trying to get her to tell me what happened but my hands got cold and I started burning her and when I let go, I found myself with Rory and he was trying to tell me something when this rat came out of his mouth."

She started shaking and Aiden turned her around and held her tight to him, her head on his chest.

The rest of the dream came out in a rush as she pushed herself to her elbows and looked at him.

"And then you shut the door in my face and let those men attack me. I kept feeling weighed down but it was when they dropped the baby on me that it felt so real."

"'Twas just a dream, *leanabh*."

He looked into her eyes, his heart hammering at her story and the horror of her capture that she was reliving.

"I know, Aiden. I do. I just remember when that man said he was going to cut the baby from—"

She couldn't continue, instead she lay back on his chest and held him tight.

It *had* felt better to share the awful experience and she laid there listening to the pounding of his heart and feeling warm as her anger at him slipped away.

"I think I ken why ye felt the pressure on yer belly." Aiden said after long moments of silence.

Skye frowned and pushed herself back up to look at him. "What?"

Aiden brushed her hair behind her ear and smiled in understanding.

"I see the faces of the men killed in me dreams. There be times that I call out in anger, rage, or fear and me wee beasties pounce on me chest when they ken this be happenin to wake me."

He pulled Skye back into his. "Seelie was in yer room, Skye. She reacted with ye as she does with me."

Aiden felt Skye tremble in his arms and his heart ached.

"What be it, lass? Why be ye cryin over that?"

Skye burst out in a laugh and pushed herself up to grin down at him. "I was laughing. The poor puppy! I probably scared the shit out of her when I woke up screaming and flailing around"

Shaking his head in amazement, Aiden looked at the girl in his bed and wondered at her ability to accept things and get over them so easily.

"What means this word 'shit'?"

Skye snickered and cuddled closer not bothering to hold back a yawn.

"Just a term I use from time to time. It doesn't mean anything."

*   *   *

Skye felt Aiden get out of bed the next day but was too exhausted for anything more than a smile when she felt his kiss on her cheek.

When the door closed behind him, one of the dogs jumped on the bed to lie against her back legs as she dozed not waking until the drapes where pulled away to let in the sun.

Moaning, Skye put a pillow over her head and readjusted herself.

"M'lady asks that ye join her in her chambers." A gruff voice filtered through the covers.

Skye twisted around and saw Mairi moving about briskly after setting down a new dress for her.

Sighing, she got out of bed, knowing the girl didn't like her much, she thought it best to keep her mouth shut.

Dressed and awake, Skye headed to Elizabeth's chambers with Seelie tagging along.

"There ye be!" Elizabeth rushed over to hug her while Anna waiting patiently for her turn. "And the gown fits so wonderfully!"

"I have never been through so many clothes in such a short time."

Skye's grin went from ear to ear and when she hugged Anna next, quickly checking on her to make sure the baby was all right.

"Och, he be kickin too much for me to be worried over him, but still, tis nice to have ye here makin sure."

Elizabeth urged them to sit as all but one maid left. She sipped tea and smiled at the aroma then looked at Skye.

"I met your sister and I must say you look very much alike."

Skye grinned then her smile faded.

"Thank you. She was supposed to contact me days ago. I am very worried."

Anna reached over and patted her hand. "I am sure she be alright, *mo caraid*."

Elizabeth nodded her agreement. "We shall try to contact her after the evening meal when there is less activity in the castle."

"Thank you."

Elizabeth nodded. "The children have missed you."

"Brian! Oh, how is he? And the man that—"

"They be well. Have no worries, luv. I can bring ye to Fergus, if ye like. I am sure Glenys would be happy to have ye see what ye can do to hurry along his healing." She winked.

"I am so glad. I didn't have much time to heal him proper and I know it was a very serious wound."

"Aye, a deadly one. But he is on the mend. Ye took care of the hard part and Glenys has been hovering over him like a mother hen, something Fergus is very happy with, I might add."

A mischievous twinkle entered the older woman's eyes as she leaned closer to share a secret. "That man has been after Glenys to wed him for a number of years but she told him she was too old to marry a stubborn man sech as he."

She leaned back smiling as she took another sip.

Anna added to the story. "Brian be his grandchild, his parents lost to illness when he was just a wee lad. If ye ask me, Glenys has been more mother to him than anyone else so it makes one wonder who the stubborn one be, does it no?"

All three women laughed as Elizabeth motioned her maid over and asked her to retrieve Brian, if the boy could be found.

They were finishing their late breakfast, since Anna had slept in as well, when Brian came in with the maid.

Skye looked at the boy and fought to control herself from crying, not understanding why she felt that emotion.

"Tha mi duilich."

"What do you have to be sorry about?" Skye asked in Gaelic.

"I be so s-sorry fer no bein able to s-save ye." The boy stuttered.

Skye shook her head and held out her arms. Brian came flying into her arms and squeezed as tears silently coursed down her face. She pressed her cheek into the boys head and hugged him tight.

"You did well." Skye assured him in Gaelic lifting him up to sit on her lap and reached for a biscuit, putting a spoonful of jam on it she handed it to him.

When he shook his head, she smiled through her tears.

"Did I not ask you to find someone and tell them where we were going?" She asked gently.

When the boy nodded, she nodded too. "And did you not do just that?"

"B-but—"

"No, Brian, there are no 'buts'. You did what I asked and you did it so fast, I am so proud of you." She squeezed him again. "And because of that, we were found."

Skye turned him so he could see her face. "Can you imagine how much longer Anna and I would have been prisoners had it not been for you?"

Still he did not take the offered sweet.

"Do you know how many boys would have just ignored me thinking it wasn't important that we were going berry picking? But not you! You listened to me when another would have gone off and played instead."

"Simon an Norman Brun laughed at me when I told them what I be doin. Said I was a bairn fer doin a girl's biddin." He looked at her and frowned. "They be big lads, too."

Skye squeezed him. "See? If it weren't for you then no one would have known what had happened to us. I am proud of you, Brain."

"I be proud of ye too, Brian." Anna and Elizabeth agreed.

The boy sat up straighter and took the biscuit making the women smile.

"*Tapadh leat.*"

"You are so very welcome."

Aiden had just left Riona's door after she had told him she was not presentable and to return when she had finished her toiletries. With Riona, one could never tell how long that would take so he decided to check in on his mother and sister.

He stood unnoticed at the entrance to the chambers, his chest swelling with pride at Skye's kindness towards the distraught boy. The sight of her holding him also brought to mind images of how their children would look on her lap.

He stiffened, silently commanding his cock to settle down before he was embarrassed.

"Aiden! What a wonderful surprise." His mother motioned him in.

Skye looked up and smiled, her heart racing at the ruggedly handsome man who entered and went over to his mother, placing a kiss on her proffered cheek.

"I see ye be entertained an doona need me company." He grinned down at his mother.

"Pashaw. I always enjoy yer presence, Son. Now, have a seat and join us."

"Actually I have been lookin for Aiden to speak privately with him in the study." Collin announced as he too entered, heading for his wife and planting a kiss on her lips, leaving her to blush as he took a pastry from the tray and winked at Skye when she laughed.

He reminded her of Doug in that moment.

"Is it—?"

"Doona worry yerself, *mo ghaol.*" Collin smiled, kissing Anna again before heading to the door.

Aiden glared at the man for winking at Skye before sobering himself and patting his mother on the shoulder.

"Another time." He kissed her cheek again and headed off with Collin but stopped at the door and spoke to Skye. "I need to speak with ye. When ye be done breakin yer fast, I wish to see ye in me study."

Skye swallowed and nodded over Brian's head, her belly doing a flip-flop at his somber features.

"That sounded serious." Anna said.

*   *   *

"I doona ken the why of it." Collin said exasperated.

"I told ye already."

"Me thinks ye be a fool." The man scowled at him. "The lass be perfectly capable of dealin with our ways."

"I will speak of this no more with ye."

"Fine, be an ass." Collin stormed off and ran into a nervous Skye. Turning back, he glowered. "Here be yer chance now."

Aiden looked up and gritted his teeth before he made a comment to the other man. He ushered Skye in and closed the doors, making Skye even more uneasy.

"Have a seat, lass."

"Is it that bad?"

"Be what bad?"

"Whatever you're going to tell me that I have to sit down for."

When Aiden didn't say anything but took his place behind his desk, Skye bit her lower lip and took a seat nearest the desk.

"I spoke with yer sister."

She jumped up. "My sister? Oh, my God! Is she okay, is the baby okay?"

Aiden raised his hand to stop her. "She be fine, so be the bairn. Have a seat an I will tell ye what I ken."

He told her of his conversation with Sarah then sat silently while she digested the news.

"I am so thankful everything is all right." Skye sighed in relief. "She had a boy?"

"If that be a 'tyke', then aye." He shrugged.

Skye laughed and relaxed. "She had her baby." She shook her head in amazement and smiled. "No wonder why we haven't heard from her, not like they could start a fire in the hospital."

"Ye need to go home, lass."

Skye laughed excitedly. "All I have to do is get a hold of her through fire. Your mother said we could try tonight when the castle isn't so busy—"

"Nay, lass, tis no what I mean."

She looked at him in confusion, her heart sinking.

"Then, what do you mean?"

"Ye need to go home."

She stared at his hardened face and the silence that went with it.

"You want me to leave."

It wasn't a question. She knew by his look, he was telling her to go.

She wanted to ask him why but her pride kicked in. She wished she had walked up sooner to find out what he and Collin had discussed.

Maybe then she would know how to fight back.

She stood and looked at him, willing him to say something, anything, and when he stared back at her unmoving, she walked to the door feeling like this was one of her cheesy romance novels where the two never said what they meant because they were too stupid to read the signs and never knew how the other felt.

That caused her to stop.

Aiden clenched his aching jaw, refusing to give in to his needs when he was doing this for her own safety.

When she got up and walked away, he watched her for a bit before lowering his head into his hands, trying to rub out the tiredness that seeped into his body.

Knowing he wasn't alone, he looked up to see her standing before him and once again hardened his features, refusing to speak for fear his desires would show.

She looked at him, feeling the blush rise from her neck to her ears and silently demanded to let go of her pride so she would not regret this for the rest of her life.

"I love you."

When he continued to stare at her, she took a deep breath and repeated it in Gaelic.

"*Tha gaol agam ort.*"

When still he did not say anything, Skye swallowed and worked hard at not crying.

"Right then." She nodded. "I just needed to tell you that before I left."

Aiden kept his face unreadable as he digested what she just said.

Even when she repeated it in his language, he still had a hard time believing it, even if his cock did not. He adjusted his position to try to ease the pain but nothing could ease the agony in his chest when his study doors closed softly behind her.

Skye pulled the doors shut hating the finality of the sound. Ignoring her battered heart as much as she did the man following her, she went to her room. It had never been large enough for a fireplace so she had placed candles in a drawer near her bed. Removing a few, she carefully placed them on the table knowing she was going against everything in her by contacting her sister to do as Aiden wished.

Running his hand through his hair, Aiden stiffened his spine.

There was no other option to ensure Skye's safety. He left the now oppressive room and went to speak to Riona.

Once allowed entrance into the guest chambers, he found Riona reclining in decadent lingerie.

Raising an eyebrow, he looked at her perfect features.

"I would have thought ye to be done by now. I can see I be wrong." He turned to leave.

"No, please, doona go." She smiled beseechingly at him. "I couldna decide what to wear an ken ye to be a busy man so, please, stay an join me fer tea."

Again, his eyebrow went up. "What of yer reputation? Would no be wise of me to stay with ye undressed."

Riona's face fell and she gracefully rose to her feet gliding towards him. When she was mere inches from way, she looked up from lowered lashes.

"What reputation? It be in shreds." A tear slipped down the curve of her porcelain skin. "I have already heard the whispers as I pass an only await the return of me brother to take me from here so I doona ruin yer happy reunion. Tis why I stay cloistered in me chambers."

She reached out a hand and lightly touched his arm.

"There shouldna be whispers about yer innocence in me keep. Ye tell me who has been sayin sech an I will ensure it stops."

Riona smiled becomingly up to him. "Ye be ever the hero, Aiden, but no even ye can stop gossip."

Aiden watched her in silence, wondering why he felt she was hiding something more than the possibility of her being English.

Riona lowered her head as if in shame.

"Since it seems I have nothin to protect any more, I want to tell ye that I have always wished to be taken in yer arms."

Both his eyebrows went up.

He always believed Riona had wanted to pursue a relationship with him, and there had been a time that he had considered it, but she always seemed untouchable. Too perfect to hold in the manner he enjoyed, and he was not a man to hold back that which he craved.

"Please, Aiden; there be no reason to deny our desires." She whispered as she undid the ties of his shirt.

Aiden returned his focus to the girl before him and purposely removed her hands.

"Be ye English?"

"Wh-what?"

"Be ye English?"

Riona stared at him in shock for a moment, then she stomped her foot as heat mottled her skin.

"I be professin me feelins fer ye an . . . an *this* is what ye do? Ye accuse me unjustly!" He arm shot out and she pointed to the door. "Out! Leave me to bury me shame alone!"

"We will talk about this, Riona—when ye be properly attired." He assured her before he stepped out the door, angry at the woman's wily ways and feeling she was hiding something.

He stopped when he saw Skye standing at the end of the hall staring in shock at him.

Gut twisting at seeing Aiden leaving Riona's room with his shirt undone, Skye valiantly straightened her spine and turned away, slipping back into her room.

Unable to focus her attention to the task of contacting her sister, she had given up and had thought to go for a walk so she could think of what was happening only to come across Aiden.

There was no way it was how it looked.

She always hated how the heroine automatically assumed the hero was cheating on her simply because it appeared that way.

Lord did it appear that way!

Thoughts of the conversation between Collin and Aiden forced its way into her head.

The lass be perfectly capable of dealing with our ways.

Now she wondered if those ways had something to do with having multiple lovers, or more than one wife.

Swallowing, she shook her head in denial even as the truth hit her.

It was common in her time for men to have more than one partner. She had heard it often enough in the college library. Hell, even the women bragged about it. She just never thought it was something she would be a part of.

Could she accept that?

No.

If it were true.

She sank onto the edge of the bed, hands clasped between her knees, she thought hard, going over every possibility.

Maybe he was just checking on Riona, making sure she was okay.

That did not explain the untied shirt.

Maybe he was questioning her about Skye having heard her speaking English.

That did not explain the untied shirt.

Maybe Riona was trying to distract him from his questioning.

That explained the untied shirt.

Was that why he looked mad too?

Maybe he had told Riona about his desires for Skye and she had stopped their lovemaking and kicked him out.

Groaning, she wiped her face with her hands trying to clear her head before her thoughts got even crazier.

Wincing when her stomach growled, she remembered she had not eaten in a while. She'd had a late breakfast and had been in her room for most the day agonizing over her feelings for Aiden, while having no luck getting a hold of Sarah.

She didn't want to go down to the hall where everyone was eating right now. If she saw Aiden, she knew she wouldn't be able to eat so she'd sit there looking like she was following him. Like some lame chick who'd been dumped and couldn't get over it so she moped around looking for any chance to see the man who had shoved her aside.

Jumping up, she began to pace, angry that her thoughts were so morbid.

This was not like her! She faced challenges head on, never concerned about how stupid she looked when she wanted to make a point, and here she was acting like an idiot.

Throwing herself backwards on the bed, she flung an arm over her eyes.

"I am such an idiot."

A knock on the door followed by her name woke her.

"Skye, dear, are you in here?"

Pushing her hair out of her face and smacking her lips, Skye looked around the darkened room surprised she had fallen asleep.

"Yes." She croaked.

The door opened wider letting in more light and Skye looked over at Elizabeth and smiled sheepishly.

"Guess I fell asleep."

"I could let ye rest longer, lass. It be up to ye ifn ye wish to try to get a hold of yer sister now or later."

"No, no." Skye scooted off the bed and stood, blowing out the candle that was on its last breath, and went to the door. "Now is good."

Elizabeth smiled warmly as she took her by the arm and led her down the hallway.

"Did ye sleep through the evening repast, luv? Is that why I did not see ye there? Be ye hungry?"

Blushing, Skye nodded. "I didn't even realize I was so tired."

"Tis expected." She smiled more and patted her hand. "Anna slept through it as well, so tis a good thing we shall have something to tide ye over.

"I also asked Anna to join us because I want her to see the magic she can use outside of her natural abilities. I hope ye do not mind."

"Of course not."

They entered Elizabeth's chambers greeted by a smiling Anna in front of a roaring fire.

"So this be all about concentration, aye?"

"Yep." Skye motioned to the flames. "Because of Sarah's abilities with fire, we are able to communicate through it, something I have never been more thankful since being here."

"Then why do ye look so sad?" Elizabeth asked.

"Ye be sad, Skye?"

Making herself grin, she rolled her eyes at them and waved their concerns away.

"I need to focus now, so interruptions need to be avoided."

No sooner had she turned back to the fire and thought of her sister than there she was.

"There you are! What perfect timing!"

"I can see people!" Anna whispered excitedly.

Elizabeth patted her daughter's leg and grinned.

"Oh! Look at the bairn!"

Skye tried to hide a smirk as she made introductions.

"From what I have been told you have met Elizabeth."

"Yes, and it is a pleasure to see you again." Sarah nodded.

"As with me."

"And this is Anna, Elizabeth's daughter. Anna, this is my sister, Sarah, and her husband, Doug. And that little one Sarah is holding is your great, great, great, so on and so forth grandson, and my nephew—to whom I haven't been properly introduced." She huffed good naturedly as Anna's pleasure went to shock.

Doug beamed with excitement. "Yes. We've decided to name him Collin."

"Why, that be me husband's name!"

Everyone laughed.

"But how do ye ken all this?" Anna wanted to know.

"I was most fortunate enough to be handed some manuscripts from my father's twin brother and am making my way through my family history, which begins with your mother."

"Oh?"

Elizabeth smiled as her eyes brimmed with tears.

"I have a journal that I have plans on passing on to ye when ye have yer first child. Twas given to me when

Aiden was born. There be many empty sheets for ye to write anything ye wish."

Anna hugged her mother then sat in thought for a moment. "So ye see the things I have yet to writ?"

"'Write,' my dear."

"Aye, 'write'."

Doug nodded slowly. "There are many things I cannot decipher because of what time has done to the pages but I am getting through it."

"Tis amazin!" Anna clapped her hands. "Collin will be so excited to meet ye!"

"It will be an honor for me to meet him as well."

Anna smoothed her hands gently over her swollen belly. "This means that this wee one will be born." She looked at her mother with joy and saw her husband at the door and threw her herself into his arms. "The bairn is gonna be fine!"

Skye sobered when she saw Aiden standing there as well and lowered her eyes as she turned away from the otherwise happy scene.

Anna pulled her husband to the hearth.

"Ye have made me most happy today." Anna beamed after introducing her husband to Sarah, Doug, and Gladys.

Taking a deep breath, Skye knew she was about to put a damper on the mood but knowing there was no other recourse, she took a deep breath before speaking.

"Well, it looks like my time here is done and since I have completed what I needed to do. It is time for me to come home."

"But ye canno, Skye, ye—"

Collin hushed her gently.

"She has a family she wishes to be with." He looked over her head into Aiden's fixed stare. "I ken how much

Jennifer France

I would miss ye if ye were to be gone from me side fer so long. Ye must ken this as well, *mo ghaol*."

Anna pouted and leaned into Collin saying nothing.

Silence fell about the room and Skye kept her eyes on the flames not seeing Elizabeth's raised eyebrow as she looked meaningfully at her son.

"Aunt Gladys, I need you to really look at that incantation you gave me so that I can make it work."

"I don't know what to tell you, m'dear." She hesitated as she looked at Sarah, shaking her head as if lost in understanding.

"Skye, we miss you so very much and want you here with us." Sarah looked at her husband.

"Why do I hear a 'but' in there somewhere?"

Doug took the baby from his wife and crooned softly as Sarah took a deep breath.

"Like Doug said; some of the writings are very hard to make out but it is very clear that you are where you belong. There are a number of areas that mention your name specifically."

"In present tense." Doug added.

Gladys eased her way to the front.

"Skye, that chant is full proof, I am sure of it. Just as I am sure mine worked the way it was meant to."

"Then it's my fault it didn't work." She shrugged, ignoring her aunt's last comment, desperately looking for answers. "I broke my concentration. All I need to do is make sure I keep my focus."

Aiden shoulders hurt from how tense they had been since he had told her to go home. He was angry with himself for his feelings of elation when he'd heard the spell worked; that she was supposed to remain in this time.

More so, he was mad at the accusatory looks he was receiving from his mother and Collin.

Did they not see that she would be safer in the future? He was also angry with himself for wanting to shake her and then take her into his arms and slake his lusts inside her willing flesh.

His body was tense with frustration and hard with need but he had to ignore it all for the sake of her wellbeing.

"I do not think it matters, *mo leanabh*. Ye were in an enchanted circle. It centers the fate of one's self with the spell. That be why ye returned here." Elizabeth took Skye's hand in hers and smiled gently. "No other words or chant shall change what be yer destiny."

The baby woke up and began to cry.

"It's past his feeding time." Sarah apologized as she took the baby back and rocked him over her shoulder. "Skye, we'll look further into the spell and see what we can do."

Nodding absently, she watched as her family faded from the flames. Unable to look at anyone, she stood.

"Well, that was quite a bit of excitement."

She looked at Elizabeth and gave a weak smile as she disengaged her hand under the pretense of grabbing something to eat, even though her throat was too dry to swallow anything.

Feeling all eyes on her she went to the door Skye pasted a smile on her stiff face before she turned to them. "Actually, it makes me rather tired, so I had best return to my room."

Refusing to look at Aiden, she skirted around him and slipped outside.

Knowing a guard followed, she rushed back to her room and closed the door quickly behind her.

Finding herself in darkness, she shivered in hopelessness as she made her way to the bed and crawled up against the wall, wrapping her hands around her knees before letting the tears fall.

A knock sounded at her door, too solid to be a woman's, and Skye's heart leapt to her throat as she lifted her eyes in the dimness to look at the door and prayed whoever was there would go away.

Wishing for a lock, she heard the handle turn as it opened and then a beam of light formed around the muscular body of the one person she really didn't want to see.

"I'd rather not have company right now, thank you."

Aiden's already heavy heart ached more seeing her sitting sadly at the head of the bed.

"Do ye have any more candles in here, lass?"

"I don't need candles." She grumbled.

Ignoring her, Aiden began rummaging through empty drawers.

Sighing loudly, she leaned over and pulled out the drawer on her nightstand before returning to her position.

Prying the remains of the last candle from its perch, Aiden inserted a fresh one and lit it with the sconce hanging on the outside wall before returning the torch to the guard and closing the door before sitting in a chair facing her.

"Ye ken the reason why ye must go, do ye no, Skye?"

"You don't need to worry about it, Aiden. I will find a way to leave. There is no need to be concerned that I will be in your way."

Gritting his teeth, Aiden stiffened his posture. "There be nothin to worry about."

"Right, so you can go now."

"Look at me, Skye."

"I don't want to."

Filled with every possible reason for her to go, he feared more about what she would think if she knew everything about him and sighed heavily.

"Ye doona ken what kind of man I be."

Clenching his jaw, he berated himself for saying the one thing he agonized over most.

Skye frowned in the silence that followed. Was he giving her a chance to prove she was strong enough to stay?

Raising her head, she looked at him in wonder.

"Have you been hiding something from me?"

He searched her face. "I would hurt ye."

"I don't believe that."

"Do ye no?" When she shook her head, he sighed. "Then ye should."

"Why do you say that?"

He stood, pushing the chair back trying to think of a way to change the topic back to the reason why he should be sending her home.

"These be hard times. That ye have found out for yerself."

There, he had done it.

"I can handle these times as long as I have you."

"I canno protect ye at all times."

"During those times, I will stay sheltered in the keep under guard of whomever you wish."

"Ye said yerself it was different in the future."

Hope flared in Skye's heart as she grabbed onto what hope she could.

"Different, yes, but I have had to protect myself when no one was there for me. You have seen what I can do."

"And what happened when ye had to." Aiden interjected.

"I coped because I have—had—you to help me. In my time who will I have?"

His gut wrenched at the thought of another man protecting her and was unable to say so aloud.

"I be a hard man." He insisted.

"I have seen nothing I couldn't handle."

"Ye doona ken, Skye."

Heart racing in hope, she swung her legs over the side of the bed and stood.

Keeping her eyes on his face, she took the few steps to stand before him.

"Then show me."

His cock strained against his trews as he looked down on her flushed face. He was teetering on the edge of showing her why she needed to return to her time.

"Ye have disobeyed me on two occasions."

"I'm sorry. I won't ever do that again."

Aiden crossed his arms and looked down on her sternly.

"I be Laird an Master, my word be law unto all who reside here."

Placing her hand on his crossed arms, she pleaded with her eyes for him to believe her. "You *are* my Laird and Master."

He softened slightly even as his balls grew painfully tight. "Ye were a virgin, lass."

"So? What does that have to do with anything?"

"Ye be innocent of the ways between a man sech as meself. No matter the book learnin ye have."

She searched his eyes, not understanding. "What ways?"

When he didn't say anything, she became worried that he would turn her away.

"Show me, Aiden."

"Nay, Skye. T'would be better that ye go home than be frightened by me, for that I could no stand."

Licking her lips, she squeezed his forearms.

"I am frightened of you letting me go. Of never being with you again, of never feeling these things that only you have made me feel."

CHAPTER THIRTEEN

H is arms broke apart so he could cup her chin and his eyes searched her face, his body demanding to take her and his mind quickly following.

"Ye shall follow me demands without question. Do as I command without hesitation. Do ye ken?"

When she nodded, he took her by the hand and led her from the room.

Her nipples tightened in desire just from the touch of his hand.

When she found out they were heading to his room, she could feel the moisture between her legs but she frowned in confusion when he drew her to the adjoining room where he let her go and pushed an armoire out of the way before pressing into a carved portion of the wall.

She watched, mouth agape, as the gargoyle image sunk into the wall and a nook appeared.

Before she could do or say anything, Aiden took her hand and led her through the opening, the candle their only source of light.

"If there was ever an invasion, this is where ye would go to hide. If ye were to follow this further down ye would eventually find yerself on the outside of the keep."

Skye's heart skipped a beat then expanded at his words. He was talking as if she would be staying.

"We, however, shall only be goin this far."

In the dim light, she could not see what he was doing but from his movements it felt like he was opening another doorway.

Aiden pulled her forward into another room before her hand was released then watched in amazement as he lit the sconces on the walls.

Soon there was enough light to see the furnishings.

Her mouth dropped open in shock and she wrapped her arms around her as she shivered involuntarily when she viewed chains hanging from the ceiling, benches that showed some with padding and others without, large crosses, and other devises Skye was sure were meant for torture, scattered about the room.

"Ye have this one chance to tell me nay, Skye."

Aiden stood at her side, watching her intently as she looked from the equipment to him.

"You are going to torture me for disobeying you?"

"Ye shall be punished, aye. But ye will no be tortured."

She looked at him and swallowed.

"Tis yer choice. Decide now. Do ye stay an accept that ye relinquish all control or do ye say nay an I return ye to yer chamber?"

Biting her lip, she took another quick look around before returning her gaze to his.

Letting her hands fall to her side, she lowered her head.

"You are my Laird and Master."

Aiden found himself inhaling after holding his breath, thankful at her trust in him.

Standing straighter, he ordered the removal of her clothes.

"All of them. Let there be no a stitch left on yer body."

Skye did as he instructed, struggling with some of the laces in the back, but finally the last garment fell to the cold floor covering the shoes and stockings she had removed first.

Keeping her hands at her side and head lowered, she fought to keep from shivering in the cold room and started when his hand touched her shoulder then smoothed down her arm to take her hand as he lifted her chin with his other.

"Ye will no hide yer face from me view. Keep yer eyes lowered, aye. Hide yer face, never."

Not bothering to wait for a response, Aiden led her to the wall near a table and reached over to pull a piece of fabric from the hook on the lower portion of the sconce and wrapped it around her wrists before raising them above her head and shackling each in hanging cuffs that kept her arms spread out.

The feel of his warm hands smoothing over her skin only alleviated some of her fear when she saw things that looked like canes, whips, and floggers, draped over the table, so she kept her eyes trained on his chest.

When his body brushed against hers, Skye gasped at the feel and inhaled his scent, closed her eyes, and allowed his smell to calm her.

As his palms eased across her flesh, she opened her eyes and watched.

His silence and stern features caused her nipples to ache surprisingly in need and when his large hands caressed her arms, she could feel the familiar roughness of his skin, remembering he was a hardened warrior who constantly proved he cared for her needs.

There was no other place she would rather be but at this man's mercy.

Her breathing hitched when he did the same to her ankles, pulling them apart and enclosing shackles that kept her legs spread after he had wrapped them in cloth.

Aiden had been unsure about her hairless body, but as he took his time skimming over the long smooth legs to the apex between them and seeing her wet lips that would have been otherwise covered, he decided he would have it no other way.

Inhaling her fragrance, he traveled up her belly to her lower back as he stood.

He had picked this area because the light from the torches clearly showed her skin tone and facial features and at that moment, he couldn't be happier at the way her eyes were dilating and her breathing began to become heavier.

"Who be yer Master?"

Skye immediately noticed the lack of 'Laird' in his question.

"You are my Master." She whispered, enjoying the closeness of his body.

The palms of his hands pressed harder as they moved over her flesh warming her. One hand rubbed against the fullness of her ass as the other speared its way through her trimmed curls as he brushed his fingertip over her clit, again liking how her woman's folds were exposed.

He watched her swallow and his hand slipped between her slit at the same time he swatted her ass.

"Oh!"

Her eyes flashed up to his in shock before she bit her lips and lowered them again, going insane as his finger had pressed further inside her when she jerked.

Another smack on the other cheek had her rocking against the finger inside her, going from a barely held back whimper to a moan.

Removing his fingers, he could not help himself when he cupped her ass and pressed her against him. When he felt her take a deep breath, he slapped her ass again then moved away from her.

Skye inhaled his scent as he pressed her against his body and was unprepared for the third blow and then the rush of cold air over her warmed skin when he stepped away.

Suddenly, she felt something strange tickling her back, like a dozen soft fingers caressing over her skin, causing goose bumps to skitter over her flesh.

"This be called a flogger an ye shall feel its lash over yer body."

Skye stiffened then felt his body against her back, the hand holding the flogger came around her front to press into her belly.

"Tell me why ye shall let me do this?"

She frowned, not understanding how he could ask her that when it dawned on her that he wanted her to hear her own answer.

"Because I trust you."

She blinked as those simple words rang with more truth than she could have thought possible and the tenseness left her body with her next breath.

"Aye, an when ye call me 'Master' of yer own free will, I will ken this an more. An when that happens, there be no goin back."

Shaking her head in confusion, she frowned when he moved away, his hands the last to leave her skin as he brushed her hair over her shoulder.

The flogger kissed her shoulders, heating her skin with each stroke. After the initial fear subsided, she could admit that it wasn't painful. It actually felt wonderful, like soft thuds as it rained down over her back and buttocks.

So began her journey of wonder.

She couldn't help the moan that escaped when he stopped and touched where he had struck her last, once again pressing into her body with his.

His leg pushed between hers forcing them apart and she wantonly pressed down on his muscled thigh, rubbing herself against him.

Placing the flogger over her shoulder, Aiden let the straps caress her breasts as his hands came up around her waist to cup her full globes and roll the hardened nipples between his fingers, causing her to arch into him and her head to fall back against his shoulder.

Making sure he watched her body reactions to each strike of the flogger, he had to grit his teeth to remain in control as his own body betrayed the pleasure he was receiving from her movements, and when he pressed against her, he watched her face flushed and mouth slightly open in a gasp of pleasure.

"That was the warm up." He whispered against her neck.

He took the flogger from her shoulder and held it over her back so the falls could tickle her body before he began again. This time, putting a little more force into the swing but not enough to cause more pain than she could handle

Watching to see when she got to the point where she didn't think she could handle another strike, he would stop and caress her flesh, kissing the spot as his hand reached around and squeezed her breast.

Awash in sensations, Skye no longer wondered how the pain could be so pleasurable, even when the falls of the flogger came around to slap her breasts or between her spread legs, whipping at her pussy.

The lash ignored no part of her body and when it fell on her backside, she pushed back and wiggled, moaning for more.

Her mind could not keep up with the increasing heat growing inside her.

Taking a deep breath, she released it slowly, letting her mind clear of all thought as her body took over.

Several times, Aiden would run his hands over her skin as if checking on her, or taking her face in his hands to make her look at him.

"Be ye alright, lass?"

"Oh yes." She breathed. "I feel . . . I feel . . ."

She couldn't think. Explaining things were too difficult. Aiden could see this and smiled, kissing the tip of her nose.

Putting the flogger down, he wrapped her body into his embrace pulling her against his chest, a hand slipping through her hair to the base of her skull, grasping the strands to pull her head slightly back as his fingers sought her folds marveling over how wet she was.

"Ye be soaked, *mo leanabh.*"

Why she melted even more when he called her his 'little one' Skye could not say, she could only feel. Her skin so responsive to his touch that her thoughts scattered and she moaned in fulfillment, leaning her head against his arm as he stroked her.

"Oh, God." She cried out when his fingers slipped inside her sensitive entrance. "Oh, yes."

Aiden ignored her whimpered protest when he withdrew his fingers and removed a small dagger from the back of his pants and placed the flat of it against her cheek as he tightened his hold on her hair.

"Do not move." Was all he whispered before turning the knife and carefully running the flat of the blade down her jaw to her throat.

Oh my God! Her mind cried out as her body shivered, desire coursing through her veins.

"What do ye feel, *leanabh?*"

"Feel?" She gasped, eyes closed to the sensations.

"Aye, what does yer mind tell ye as I press this blade against the fragileness of yer throat, knowin I hold yer life in me hands?"

Skye tried hard to listen to his words, focusing on what he was doing and how it made her feel.

"I feel possessed. Lost, needy . . . captured. And I don't understand it."

Aiden watched a tear fall from between her lashes and smiled.

"Ye doona need to ken, *leanabh*, ye need to just accept."

He gently licked the tear away then trailed the edge of his blade to her breast, following the curve to her distended nipple, careful of her heavy breathing and low whimpers.

Stopping, he moved to stand in front of her, easing the pressure of his dagger until he was steady, once again his knee pressed between her open legs, never taking his eyes from her face.

"Do ye wish me to stop?"

"No, Master!"

She stilled as soon as the words left her mouth and her eyes flashed open in surprise.

A slow smile spread across his face and Skye forgot what she had said to cause it and blinked, holding her breath at the beauty that transformed his face from intent to pure male satisfaction.

"Ye have pleased me, *leanabh*."

Suddenly, all she wanted to do was please him.

Blushing, she lowered her eyes to his lips and licked hers in need.

Gritting his teeth to keep from losing control, he eased back on the blade and pressed the handle against her mouth, his brogue thickened.

"Hold it."

When she opened her mouth, he placed it between her lips, ensuring the blade would do no damage before letting go and stepping back, his hands smoothing over her cooling flesh.

Skye watched as he unlaced his shirt, her mouth watering when his muscles rippled as he eased it from his shoulders and pulled it from pants that hugged powerful legs.

Sweat glistened from the hard angles of his body and she ached to slide her hands over the hair that lightly covered his powerful chest and press her fevered body to his.

All she could do was groan in frustration.

Aiden gripped her hips after tossing his shirt carelessly to the side, his fingers digging in before easing his hold to come up and cup her breasts, squeezing her nipples as he pressed them together.

Keeping himself from taking her was the hardest thing Aiden had ever had to do.

He released her before he forgot his purpose, removing the dagger from her mouth and placing it on the table as he slipped behind her, nestling her under his shoulder as he gripped her neck, forcing her to lean against him, he then cupped her mound and pressed her to his swollen cock.

Her eyes closed as soon as his hand encircled her throat, letting her body fall into his, not questioning the hold he had on her neck.

"To whom do ye belong?

"To you." She sighed.

He tightened his hold and bit down onto her shoulder causing her to gasp and try to move away.

"Whom do ye belong to?" He repeated quietly.

"To y-you, Master!"

"There be no goin back."

Aiden eased his grip on her neck as he plunged two fingers into her wet depths, feeling her juices cover his hand.

"Oh, God!"

Skye had no idea that every nerve ending had made its way to her pussy and the sudden invasion of his fingers made her feel like she was about to cum. The sensitivity was overwhelming.

"Please, I'm going to cum!"

"Do no cum." He demand, keeping his fingers deep inside her.

Her breathing intensified as she tried to stop herself from going over the edge, his harsh command somehow helping.

He felt her muscles gripping his fingers as she squirmed and when she settled down, he removed his hand and released her neck, smiling when she pouted at the loss of his touch.

Hands kneaded her shoulders before he released her yet again only to quickly return with the flogger.

Body on fire with a need for release, the kiss of the flogger became an added sensation to heighten her enjoyment as it traveled over her back. This time the strikes were falling harder . . . and she wanted it that way.

"Yes, Master. Please." She pleaded, unsure why and not caring.

He brought the flogger over her reddened ass, down her thighs, calves, and back up, she leaned down to press her backside up, coming to her toes. She began to shiver even as she begged for more, the falls sometimes just skimming over her wet skin, the next time thudding. Her body began to hum and she felt herself drifting into a trance like state as a tear slipped down her cheek.

She began to cry, the feelings too immense to contain.

His body suddenly enfolded her heated flesh to his. His arm wrapped around her waist in a tight grip as the other encircled her neck and she soared higher, her head feeling like cotton. His hot breath caressed her ear and she shivered, her face flushed with desire.

"Where be ye, *leanabh*?" He whispered as his thumb stroked over her rapid pulse, watching the silent tears falling from the corners of her eyes.

"I don't know, but it feels like a dream, Master."

"Aye, a dream no many can find." Aiden brushed his lips over her shoulder setting off a moan. "I ken ye be keepin yer eyes closed, but takin away the option will heighten the feelings."

He leaned over and picked up a cloth from the table, wrapping it over her still closed eyes and tied it behind her head. His cock hard against his trews, he adjusted himself trying to ease the ache knowing he would not be lasting much longer.

He also knew she was ready by the gasping in her breath and puckered nipples.

"Ye have felt the pleasure, now ye must accept the pain."

Not even his words could free her from the mists of pleasure swirling through her mind and over her body. Even the chill from the dungeon aroused her as he stepped away.

"This one has a little more sting to it, *leanabh,* but ye have been well prepared." He warned as he dangled the strands over her skin, moving it slowly back and forth.

When it stopped, she tried to brace for the impact but her body wouldn't respond.

The first swing never touched her and she shivered at the cold air whipping past, as did the next.

The third struck her shoulder blades and she gasped at the difference but her body seemed to accept the sharp tingles.

The blows came closer together and she brought her shoulder blades forward to arch her back, her head falling to her chest trying to give him more of herself.

"Yes, yes." She sobbed. "Please, Master, yes."

After touching her flesh to feel the heat, Aiden traveled the flogger over her body, repeating the same process as he had with the lighter flogger.

When her skin showed signs of red marks, he slowed to a stop before dropping the flogger on the table.

She was drowning in desire unable to stop the moans, sweat trickling down her arms and legs while moisture seeped from between her legs, no longer able to control the shivering.

As if from a distance, she heard a scraping noise and she moaned craving his touch.

Aiden pulled over a wooden piece of furniture. The seat was higher than normal in a wide V shape.

Placing it directly behind her, he removed the cuffs from her feet first, rubbing over her skin as she stood, inhaling the scent of her desires and fighting back the animal that demanded release.

Removing the shackles from her hands, he held onto her as she leaned weakly into him. He rubbed the circulation back into her limbs as she began to kiss him, rubbing her body against his in a silent plea to be taken.

When he was satisfied that she had adequately recovered, he lifted her onto the wooden chair, placing her legs over the extended pieces and securing them with a strap.

Skye knew what he was doing on some level but her overpowering need to feel him inside her was her soul focus.

"Please, Master, please fuck me." She implored as she licked his chest, breathing in the masculine smell, rubbing against him wantonly, crying out when he lifted her away from his body, her hands reaching out, seeking contact.

"Please, I need to touch you." She sobbed, crying out joyously when he pressed against her.

Not realizing he was settling her against the angled back, she opened her legs and felt them secured to whatever she was sitting on. She shook her head as he brought her arms behind her and told her not to move. She whimpered in need as she felt a strap go around her waist to her back, his groin pushing into her cunt as he bent to tie the strap around her hands.

"Please." She begged, drawing the word out, not caring how desperate she sounded. She was throbbing and she felt swollen, the aching pulsed between her legs, she needed to be filled now!

Skye squirmed, unable to withdraw the blindfold or to move and cried out in frustration.

Covered with sweat, Aiden untied the laces of his pants letting them fall to his knees as he opened the drenched folds of her lips. He grabbed onto his painfully hard cock and shoved it deep inside her.

Skye's breath caught in her throat when she felt his fingers spreading her lips and she tried to push against them as her nerve endings zinged at his touch and when he slammed into her, she exploded, tossing her head back, mouth wide and silent at the force of her orgasm.

He continued to pound into her as sweat dripped down his body, her cunt a tight glove as she contracted around him, demanding he spill his seed deep inside but he held off.

Removing the cloth from her eyes, he gripped her hair at the base of her scalp.

"Breathe, *mo ghaol*."

Skye tried to shake her head, letting him know how impossible that was when finally she gasped, crying out through the tight muscles in her throat just as another wave of molten heat raged through her.

Skye's second orgasm clenched his cock tight and Aiden roared his release, hammering faster and deeper as his balls tightened painfully.

She cried, unable to bear the intensity any longer.

Aiden took a shuddering breath before leaning in to press his mouth softly against hers.

Skye trembled as she nibbled on his lower lip, her body spasming with aftershocks as Aiden slowly glided in and out before easing from her tight channel.

Undoing her bindings, Aiden took her face into his hands and brushed away the tear that fell from her lashes with his thumb as he leaned his forehead against hers, trying to get his breathing under control.

Arms heavy with exhaustion, Skye lifted them slowly to wrap around his neck, turning her head to kiss his cheek, snuggling in as he lifted her into his arms and carried her back to his room.

Aiden placed her on the bed gently after pushing the covers out of the way, and then he went to the basin, wrung out a cloth before returning to clean her.

After he cleaned himself, he eased in next to her before covering them with the furs.

He held her tight, her head resting on his chest with a leg thrown over his upper thigh.

He looked up at the shadowed ceiling, his heart at war with his common sense.

Barely able to remain awake as his heart rate lulled her to sleep, Skye managed to say the only thought she could utter before drifting off to sleep.

"Please, don't let me go."

Aiden sighed at her quiet plea and ran his hand over her curls not trusting himself to say anything.

CHAPTER FOURTEEN

Hours later, Aiden slipped from the bed and dressed in his clan tartan. He added more logs to the fire before gathering their clothing from the dungeon, taking a moment to look at the place where Skye had given everything to him.

His heart swelled with pride and determination.

She was his. She belonged with him and for the first time in his adult life, he was going to be selfish. He had made his decision in the early morning hours before finally being able to sleep.

Returning to the room, Aiden carefully laid Skye's gown over the back of a chair before gazing down upon her sleeping face.

He was concerned that he wouldn't be back before she woke and he knew the way she was feeling last night might be the extreme opposite this day, as was wont to happen after such intense play, especially for one as untried as Skye.

Sighing softly, Aiden left determined to ensure the room was set up properly for his first day of courts since returning from the war and then he would return to check on Skye before getting back to begin the proceedings.

He would also send Keir to guard his chambers in case she needed him.

Besides Collin, Keir was the only other who would understand what Skye might go through and he didn't want any mistakes made with her care.

Satisfied with his decision, he hurried to complete his duties as clan chief.

Skye heard the door close and sighed, too tired to do anything else but stretch and turn over, burrowing under the covers smiling as she smelled his scent around her.

Her mind drifted lazily.

As her amazement over what had transpired the night before grew, the fog lessened and she frowned.

That had been the strangest event of her life.

Besides appearing in the fifteenth century.

It was like floating in space, being separate from herself. Like the effects of a drug.

And the sex! Oh Lord, that was amazing!

She hugged the covers close and grinned.

Then she frowned in confusion.

She'd gotten that way from a flogging.

Aiden had flogged her!

He'd also taken a knife and choked her as well.

Okay, not 'choke', but everything he had done was violent.

Okay, not 'violent, but . . .

But what? He hadn't physically harmed her. Mentally either. What had he done? He'd flogged her, taken a knife to her and held her throat.

And she'd gotten off on it.

Literally.

She got up, stretching the sore muscles of her body, and paced in the dim light pushing her hair out of her face in frustration.

Was he disgusted by her?

Had he used her because she'd begged and pleaded like a blithering idiot?

Stopping, she stared at the bedroom door. She needed to talk to him, hold him. She needed to find out what he was thinking.

Whirling around, Skye began pacing again.

What if he didn't want to see her?

Maybe that was why he'd slipped out before she woke up.

She went to the tapestry that covered the window and looked out at the pre-dawn sky.

Why had he left so early?

Swallowing shakily, she let the curtain fall and shivered, more from the worry that suddenly overcame her than the cold morning air.

"Stop this." She commanded herself. "You're starting to sound like an idiot."

Forcing herself to breath slowly, she began to pace again, making sure she took slow measured steps as her mind kept slipping back to Aiden and what he thought.

"So what if he left early. He's a damn Scottish Lord in the fifteenth century. It's not like they have a nine-to-five job." She huffed at herself.

Skye moved to the fire and looked at it before gritting her teeth and turning away.

"I can't talk to Sarah. I can't talk to anyone."

Who could understand anything she'd explain?

Hell, she couldn't even figure it out.

No matter how many things she had shared with her sister, she wasn't sure this was something she could talk about.

If only she could just calm down and think.

She was so damn stressed.

This wasn't like her.

She over-reacted to things yes, but she wasn't the kind of person that let things get this out of hand and it wasn't as if it was out of hand, she just felt like it.

Everything felt . . . consuming . . . and she couldn't stop thinking about Aiden.

Everything revolved around him.

Like she was stalking him in her mind.

"Oh, shit." She whispered in shock, suddenly remembering her last words to him.

Please, don't let me go.

Had he answered her?

Had he ignored her?

Skye became frantic, her thoughts scattered.

She could not stop thinking and she couldn't think about anything but him, them, and what they had done.

I have to stop this! I'm going insane here!

She grabbed her head tense with the need to relax so she could figure out what was going on.

Dropping to her knees, she hunched over, arms crossed holding onto her shoulders and began rocking as her mind continued its whirlwind of frenzied thoughts, all with a constant need to stop it.

> *Calm me down, let me think.*
> *Wrap my body in petals of pink.*
> *Ease my thoughts, free my mind.*
> *So the answers I might find.*

She hesitated over the words, trying to find the right mix to settle her racing heart and scattered thoughts, too upset to worry over making a mistake.

She kept rocking and repeating the chant. Relieved when it seemed to be working, her mind slowed down, her body relaxed.

That's when she felt something strange and looked up.

Aiden rushed up the stairs to his chambers, knowing he had little time to check on Skye and opened his door to see her in the middle of the floor, surrounded by pink flowers, her hands held out catching them as they fell out of thin air.

"*Dè a tha seo?*"

Skye turned her bemused look to Aiden and scrambled to her feet blushing as she stared at him in a formal looking kilt.

"Ummm. This is a spell gone wrong." She winced. "I told you I wasn't very good at them. It won't last long." She shrugged and gave a crooked smile. "At least it's not raining."

Images of her trying to go home whipped through his head.

"Why do ye need to cast a spell, lass?"

Suddenly shy and unsure of herself, Skye lowered her eyes and shrugged.

Believing the worst, he closed the door behind him and crossed his arms.

"Ye were tryin to go home."

"What? No!"

"Then explain what ye were doin."

Searching his chiseled face, Skye began to chew her lower lip. She had no clue what to say without him thinking her completely nuts.

"Ye will answer me now."

Swallowing hard, Skye couldn't stop the tear that slipped from her lashes.

"I was trying to stop myself from going crazy."

As soon as she said the words, the floodgates opened and she covered her face.

Aiden suddenly knew what was happening and he was beside her, gathering her up into his arms and holding her close.

"Och, *leanabh*, twill be alright."

She wrapped her arms around his stomach and held tight, shaking her head against his chest. "But I *am* goin crazy, Aiden."

"Nay, lass. This will pass."

"My mind is going in circles. I feel like I can't think of anything else but one thing."

"An what be that?"

He chuckled at her words even as he watched in amazement as the petals falling from nowhere lessened.

She looked up at him with big eyes. "You. All I can think about is you."

Smiling, he kissed her forehead. "Tis no sech a bad thing, is it, *leanabh?*"

"It's consuming." Was all she could say.

He pressed her head back onto his chest and sighed. "I should no have played with ye last night."

If he had been thinking properly, he knew he never should have played with her with such intensity knowing he had no time to help ease her from her melancholy.

"I need to leave, lass. I have duties to attend to." He took her by the shoulders and held her away from him. "I came to check on ye an to hold ye before I had to go. We have thins we need to discuss."

She looked at him and frowned not liking the possibilities.

If he would only give her an idea of what it was they were going to 'discuss'.

She raised herself on tiptoe and tilted her face to his.

Looking down on her flushed face, Aiden didn't trust himself to stop at a kiss so he inhaled her scent as he placed his lips on her forehead, then stepped away.

"I will send Keir up to keep guard on ye til I can return. All will be well."

Biting her lower lip, Skye just nodded and watched him leave.

When the door closed behind him, she let go of the breath she was holding and looked around at the petals that littered the room and went about gathering them up and tossing them into the fire.

When she was done, she made the bed and sat on the edge, her mind filled with fear that he was still going to send her home.

If only she could just figure out what he meant by, 'all will be well'.

All will be well when she was gone?

All will be well because she was staying?

She had been so lost in her whirling thoughts that she jumped to her feet when a voice came out of nowhere.

"He left ye too, aye?"

Gasping in shock, Skye stood there staring in confusion at Riona who stood at the entrance to the adjoining room.

"How did you get here?"

"From the secret passage, of course."

"Of course. And how did you know of it?"

"Aiden showed me." Riona shrugged. "I know of the dungeon too."

"You do?"

"There was a time when Aiden couldn't get enough of me, he would bring me to that room and we would do things, then we would make the most passionate love."

Riona looked about the room then returned her gaze to glare at Skye.

"I am sure you know of what I speak."

Skye mind was racing as she looked around making sure there were no more petals.

"He brought you there and . . . and . . ."

"Aye, many times."

Skye's thoughts went crazy as Riona's first words echoed in her head.

He left you too.

"He came to me earlier wanting to do it again but I told him only if he married me. He left angry."

Skye remembered seeing Aiden when he had walked out of the girl's room and hated how pieces of the puzzle seemed to be fitting together. She shook her head, trying to clear it but she found herself falling back into the whirlwind of feelings she had before Aiden came into the room.

"Why are you here now?"

"I have decided to leave. I will no longer accept being used at his will, to be thrown away when another catches his eye. Then my man told me Aiden was sending ye away and I was appalled that he was already doing to ye what he had done to me and I thought to offer ye an escort."

Riona raised an eyebrow at Skye's blank look.

"Unless ye enjoy being used with no thought to yer reputation?"

Was that what Aiden was doing to her? Using her when and how he wanted? He'd already told her she had to go home. Had he had sex with Riona while she was still captive and when he had seen that she'd been responsible for two men's deaths that she wasn't trustworthy, maybe even dangerous?

Was that why he had gone to Riona earlier?

To take her back after deciding Skye would be returned to the future?

So why last night?

Because Riona had probably turned him down, maybe even told him he had to marry her.

Men hated ultimatums.

Skye had never asked him to marry her but she had told him to keep her.

Had begged even.

And he hadn't answered her plea last night.

Why buy the cow?

"Look, I am leaving, are ye coming or not?"

Shaking her head, she tried to clear it of the confusion and fear.

Skye didn't want to leave him.

Everything in her screamed to find him and beg him to keep her.

Clenching her fists and shook her head. She had already begged and it had gotten her nowhere.

What an idiot she was.

Nodding decisively she made up her mind.

"I would appreciate an escort. But only until we get far enough away then I will go my own way."

"Fine. We will give ye food when ye decide tis time to go yer separate way."

Skye followed Riona and watched her move the armoire and push the gargoyle, just as Aiden had and she was even more convinced that she was just one more in a long line of women Aiden had taken to his bed.

Riona took a torch from the wall and went down the passageway, ignoring the entrance to the dungeon.

"How did you get to his room this way?"

"There's a connection from a few of the rooms to this passageway."

They went down a steep stairway so narrow she imagined Aiden had to go sideways.

"Did he ask you about being English?"

"He has always known I was English."

"He did?"

"Aye, but told me twould be easier to be accepted by the elders if I was Scotts. So my brother and I took on a Scottish accent."

Riona stopped and turned in the confined space, her eyes narrowed in anger.

"He said he would marry me. I believed him and would have done anything for him."

Skye was shocked at the girl's fierce look and for a moment, she thought she was speaking to a woman possessed.

She hurried to catch up to Riona as she thought of the feelings she had been battling since waking up. Maybe these consuming thoughts wouldn't pass as Aiden had assured her.

The further they went the more Skye became concerned with her decision and it occurred to her just how rashly she had been.

"Maybe I should have gotten dressed? Or put on shoes. My feet are freezing and the stones are wet."

"We cannot turn back now. We are almost at the end and need to be gone before they are finished with the tribunal. Ye can wear something of mine."

"Tribunal?"

"Aye."

When Skye felt a breeze circling through the damp air, she knew they were close to the end and she suddenly doubted everything she was doing.

"Why do we need to do this in secret? It's not like we are prisoners." She said when the ground leveled off.

"For what? So he can convince ye to stay? He does that well. I cannot tell ye how many times I have returned with the assurance that he would protect my good name only to bed me again with nothing but empty promises."

They stepped out of the tunnel and Skye shaded her eyes from the sun.

Riona turned to glare at her and Skye took a step back only to bump into something solid. She whipped her head back and saw the giant that was never far from Riona.

"Tis because of ye that he has not married me. But he will. Once ye are gone, he will follow through with his promises and this land will be rightfully returned to me."

Skye glared and swung her fist, connecting satisfactorily with the other woman's eye.

"You lied to me!"

Skye was yanked off her feet, her mouth stuffed with a smelly cloth as she was hauled away.

A fricken broken record!

That's what she felt she was on.

*   *   *

"I knocked when I had no heard any noise for some time, an there was no answer. I thought she be sleepin but I grew concerned, so I opened the door an she wasna there." Keir explained to Aiden after pulling him from listening to his tenant's complaints.

"Ye looked everywhere?"

"Aye. Her gown be laid over a chair an the armoire moved to the side. I sent two men to the entrance an came directly here."

"Ye did right." Aiden assured him.

Aiden paced, furious with himself for leaving her alone. He ran his hand through his hair not believing that she would flee in secret when she had let him know she wanted to stay. So why would she run?

Collin came rushing in. "I heard what happened. Is there someone lookin fer her?"

Keir nodded and they stood there waiting for direction from Aiden.

"Why would she run?"

"Did ye upset her?"

Had he?

"I canna say. The lass was upset last I saw her but leavin wasna somethin she be courtin."

He began pacing, speaking aloud to himself.

"Besides, she doesna need to leave when she has the power to cast a spell an . . ."

He suddenly remembered the results of her last spell.

. . . a spell gone bad . . . I told you I wasn't very good at them.

"Would she be headin fer the fairy circle again?" Keir asked.

A quick moment of thought had Aiden shaking his head. "I doona think she would have left of her own wants. Doesna feel right."

"Ye think she was taken again?"

Aiden threw up his hands and shook his head. "Besides me sister, Mother, an us, who else kenned of the passageway?"

"No one." Keir said.

Silence as each man was deep in thought.

"The midwife."

The men turned to Collin.

"The last time we were here, Anna said the midwife was with her when Reivers tried to invade the keep an they hid together in the passage."

Keir rushed out of the study. "I will send men to each of the entrances."

Aiden turned to Collin. "Find me mother an bring her here. We need Sarah's help again. I will inform the council."

* * *

"Kill her!"

"Yer brother said to wait."

"Bloody hell, I said to kill her now!"

Riona tried to take the knife from the much larger man, her face flushed with fury.

"Do not make me hurt you."

Riona stared at the man as he spoke distinctly, a hand gripping her upper arm.

Gritting her teeth, Riona jerked her arm from his grasp, fully aware it was because he allowed it.

She stormed up to Skye and sneered. "He will kill her anyway. Why wait?"

Skye stiffened and glared back at the girl.

Riona slapped Skye across the face.

Her head snapped to the side with the force, only sheer will kept her on her feet.

Slowly, Skye turned her head back, trying to get her vision to clear. "Why are you doing this?"

"He was going to marry me. Then ye come along and ye made him forget his promises to me."

Riona began to pace, her arms stiff at her sides.

"This land belonged to my father and Aiden's stole it from us. It belongs to us! Finley and me." She spat when she stopped in front of Skye. "We were left with nothing. No lands, no family to take us in. They say my father was a traitor and they allowed a Scottish usurper to take over British lands."

Skye remembered Elizabeth mentioning how her husband had gotten the land.

"Ye should not be telling her anything."

"Bah! She's going to be dead soon anyway."

*   *   *

Collin found Elizabeth and his wife exiting the older woman's chambers.

"Collin!" Anna rushed to him, her face anxious. "Doug read in the manuscripts and said that there was to be an attack through the passageways hidden in our rooms."

Wrapping his arms around his wife's body, he held her for a moment.

"We thought as much. Do ye think ye can contact Sarah in the study?" He asked of Elizabeth.

"Yes, but why?"

"Skye's missin an we think she was taken by the use of Aiden's passageway."

Elizabeth's hand went to her throat. "Oh, no! No wonder Sarah couldn't get through to Skye and came to us."

They watched as warriors slipped past them and stood guard at their chamber doors.

Collin explained to the women what they were planning as he ushered them to Aiden's study.

When they entered, Elizabeth rushed to her son's side.

"Collin explained everything." She went on to tell of her conversation with Sarah as she sat in the chair in front of the fire that Aiden had made ready for her.

"Wait." Aiden laid a hand on her shoulder to stop her as Keir brought in the midwife.

The woman threw herself at Aiden's feet begging for mercy.

"Ye best tell me that which I need to ken, an fast." Aiden demanded.

"I will!"

He knelt down and grabbed the woman by the cowl about her shoulders.

"Then begin, an doona make me ask anythin twice."

"No, no, I will not." She swallowed looking around at the stern faces.

"I be Edward Bowers' sister, Margaret."

Aiden suppressed the shock of hearing her speak without a Scottish brogue.

"So?"

Elizabeth stood and touched her son's forearm. "Edward Bowers owned this keep before yer father."

"Yes, yes! That be him." The woman nodded vigorously.

"Why be ye on this land now?"

"Finley and Riona are my nephew and niece."

"What?" The men said at once as the woman gasped.

"Please, have mercy." Margaret began to blubber, fear making her hand shake as she reached out."

Nodding at his mother who took a hold of the woman's arm, he turned his attentions back to the midwife.

"Go on."

"Edward died five years ago from a knife wound he received while in one of the many taverns he frequented after the king took this land from him. Finley swore to his father that he would reclaim what was rightfully his and sent me to seek a position that would enable me access to the castle and to report to him whatever news was of importance."

"Perhaps that be why he tried to court me." Anna pondered.

"Yes." The woman agreed. "He made arrangements to meet ye at the social ye were having. That is when he began to visit here. He sold everything they had to give them the appearance of wealth."

She turned to Aiden. "Riona was to draw ye in with her charms as well, perhaps to get ye to marry her."

Gritting his teeth, Aiden glared at the woman. "What be their plan now?"

"I do not know—I swear!" She cowered holding her hands up as if to ward off a blow. "All I know is Finley was very interested in the hidden passageways I told him about. I had to tell him! When he lost control and Anna saw him beating his horse, he took his rage out on me, any time he found out I hadn't told him even the smallest thing, even if it wasn't true, he beat me."

She curled up shivering. "I feared for my life."

Aiden steeled himself as his mother nodded, indicating the woman was telling the truth. He knew what a man could do to another man, let alone a defenseless woman, when in a fit of rage but Skye and his people's safety were at stake.

"Will he attack through the passageways?"

"I do not know. I was never allowed around when they discussed plans unless one of them said something off hand in front of me. But twould not be unlike him to try. I do know, he made friends with men of bad character and complains about needing the funds that he promised them. He believes he can take care of all his debts when he regains his inheritance."

"Has he been behind the attacks before?"

"Aye. I heard him tell his man, James, to capture one of your farmers and beat him. Riona was pleased that the farmer thought her voice was believed to be from the female everyone was accusing of being a spy."

Aiden looked over to Keir and Collin.

There was one question answered.

Finley was behind Ross' brutal beating and most probably his death when he started to question himself on who he had heard speaking.

"Where be they now?"

"I do not know. I have seen neither of them in two days."

"Confine her some place outside the castle."

"What will ye do with me? Please, have mercy."

Aiden didn't have an answer for her.

Turning to his mother after one of his men had taken the midwife away, he waited for her to confirm his thoughts.

"She tells the truth as she knows it, Son."

"Aye." Nodding curtly, he continued. "If this be eminent then have Sarah tell Skye to get to safety but to stay away from here, I doona need her to show up durin battle an have her to worry about as well."

*   *   *

Riona sauntered up to Skye with a smirk on her face. "James here saw your little perversions with Aiden last night and told me about them."

Mouth dropping, Skye blushed as shock and anger coursed through her veins.

"I always knew he was a filthy beast and ye are no better."

"And yet you want to marry him." Skye couldn't help but say.

Livid, Riona slapped her. "So I can get back what belongs to me!"

Spitting blood and forcing herself to keep her bound hands from lashing out as well, she looked back at the girl. "Then what?"

"Then he dies." She shrugged. "Finley plans on getting him drunk and placing him in my bed. I will cry rape and force him to marry me. Eventually he and his family will be killed and, because of our marriage, the lands returned to us. And it will work this time."

James snorted causing Riona to whirl around and glare at him.

"What?"

"Tis not likely to happen now."

"Ye know nothing." Riona hissed.

"Finley and I both know ye ruined any chances of marriage with that display of childish behavior when ye returned from the prison camp."

"If it were not for this whore, we would have been married by now."

James laughed outright.

Riona's face burned with red blotches as her fury took over. She stormed over to him and swung her hand.

Being faster, James caught her wrist and squeezed, his face becoming impassive as she cried out in pain, unable to do anything but drop to her knees.

More insanity, was all Skye could think as she watched, trying to break free from her bonds as they were preoccupied, wondering what she meant by 'this time'.

James leaned down, her hand still in his as he sneered at her.

"Ye were worthless but is does not matter now, Finley should be entering the castle via the passageways and taking over."

"What?" Skye gasped, forgetting about loosening the ropes.

Riona clasped her injured hand when James let her go. "Ye bastard."

James looked at Riona with disdain and walked away.

Skye watched as Riona stumbled to her feet and walked in the opposite direction as James, giving her a glare before she left the clearing.

Trying to calm her breathing, Skye knew the last time she had used the spell to get home, it had returned her to Aiden and she was resolved to try it again, even without a faery circle.

"Skye?"

Startled at the sound of her whispered name, she looked around.

"Skye!"

Blinking, she looked at the flames. "Sarah?"

313

"Yes, shhh. Keep your voice down. Are you alright?"

"Sarah! You need to get a hold of Aiden, you have to tell him that he's about to be—"

"We know."

Skye paused. "You know?"

"Doug found it in the books."

"I need to get to him, do you think the spell I tried to use to get home will work the same way?"

"All I know is Aiden told me to find you and tell you to lay low until the fighting is over so he doesn't have to worry about you."

"Dammit, Sarah." Skye whispered heatedly as she looked around.

"No, Skye, listen to me. Aiden already had it pretty much figured out before I said anything. What he doesn't know is that you bring the bad guy to him."

Sarah looked over her shoulder at her husband. "What was his name?"

Doug's reply came from the background. "Pin or Fin something or other, too hard to make out."

"Finley?" Skye asked.

"Yes! That's probably it."

Skye shook her head at Doug's excitement when she was obviously a prisoner.

"Do you know what that means?"

"Sorry, sis, yer gonna have to spell that one out for me."

"The story reads that the invaders were pretty much annihilated, but this Finley guy gets away, somehow you bring him back."

There was a low comment made and Sarah snapped. "Bring, brought, whatever." Sarah turned back to Skye. "Sorry, not getting much sleep lately."

Nodding in deep thought, Skye frowned.

"Maybe he comes here and I use the spell that brought me back to Aiden and we both appear back at the keep."

"Oh! That might be it. There is nothing saying you appear, but there are little references to witchcraft anyway."

There was a pause as they both thought about the possibilities, Skye keeping an eye out for either James or Riona.

"You need to change the wording just a bit Aunt Gladys says."

Skye groaned.

"No, listen. Take away the 'I' in the beginning and say 'us' or something so that whoever you are touching will return with you . . . hopefully. Then, at the end, instead of 'return to where I belong' make it 'to whom I belong.' Your heart will take you to Aiden."

"Oh, that's good! I can do that."

"Will you be okay?"

"I'll be fine. They don't seem intent on doing anything to me until Finley gets here so get some sleep. I'm really pushing it keeping in contact with you this long."

"Well, I'm not gonna sleep well with you imprisoned again so I'll keep an eye on you while out of site . . . Doug says we'll take turns."

"Can you help with the ropes a bit before you leave? They're too damn tight."

"Stand still"

Coming to stand closer to the flames, Skye held out her hands.

"Not too much, just enough to help me get them off when the time is right."

A flame flickered closer to her before a few embers landed on the twine, singing it loose.

Nodding her thanks, Skye looked away from the flames and began to work on the cords around her wrists.

*   *   *

Aiden and Collin's men hid in various places, waiting for an attack while the women and children were removed from the perspective battle scenes as covertly as possible.

It was early evening. About an hour before the sun was to set, it began to rain and that was when they watched the Reivers sneaking up to the main entrance of the passageways.

"I count around three score enterin the tunnel." Collin whispered.

"So did I." Keir affirmed.

Keir received a nod from Aiden and passed the information on via hand signals. The word would get to their men before the enemy could get to the end of the passageways and to the rooms they opened up to.

Aiden knew they had fewer men around the chambers but, no matter how cautious the Reivers were, they had the element of surprise on their side.

Two of the older boys were stationed on separate towers, they would ring bells to tell everyone when the fighting had begun on the inside of the keep so that their men on the outside wouldn't begin the battle too soon and alert the others with the clamor of fighting.

"I doona see Finley or his man." Collin whispered.

Aiden nodded. "Neither do I."

"Tis likely the coward be hidin til it be safe." Keir pointed out.

Aiden clenched his teeth. "Or he be the one keepin Skye prisoner."

"What do ye want us to do?" Keir asked.

Aiden struggled with that question before answering.

"Ye stay an fight. If there be anythin wrong with Skye, her sister has the power to help her. If tis truly bad, me mother will send one of the lads to me."

The plan was simple; Years ago his father had prepared for such an occasion and had flour sacks taken apart and resown flat to reach from twenty feet into the passageway to where the tunnel broke off to go to the other chambers, then a fine layer of sand and flour was poured on top. The sand would damage their vision while the flour would cause any torches used to flash, causing pandemonium.

Rope was fastened in such a way that when pulled, it would release the sand. Men, on both sides, would get those stumbling out on either end and the rest would be dealt with easily enough.

If all went well.

*　　*　　*

Skye sat huddled before the fire as the rain fell, thankful for the covering James had tossed her when he'd brought her over to the fire, wishing it would keep her warm as well as dry since she could not use her bound hands to rub her arms.

Riona had thrown a fit when they hadn't sought more reliable shelter and had stomped to the tent James erected and disappeared inside, snatching the ends closed as a final show of anger.

It had only been a few minutes since her aunt had checked on her and whispered that Doug was trying hard to read what Elizabeth had written about the invasion, but time had eroded much of the words and he wasn't very optimistic. However, he was convinced about the references to Skye showing up with Finley.

She knew they were telling her this to keep her from becoming scared over what might happen to her while in captivity but they refused to tell her anything other than the immediate future, explaining that any knowledge about what might happen could change things and not for the better.

Resolved to discuss this refusal to pass information with her sister and Doug later, Skye watched and waited, still exhausted and feeling the effects of the emotional upheaval she had experienced since waking up.

Fantasizing about having an umbrella to keep the cold rain off her, Skye was startled out of her thoughts when someone came crashing through the woods towards them, James already on his feet, sword in hand.

Finley drew his horse to a cruel stop before the fire, leaping off with angry determination.

Skye took in his disheveled appearance while ignoring the furious demands Riona screeched when the girl found out it was her brother who woke her.

It wasn't the wet and torn clothing or the blood smeared on the side of his face that made her stand but the way he kept his eyes on her as he approached.

Grabbing her upper arm, Finley yanked her roughly to him causing her to stumble and loose her balance as she crashed into his chest and clutched his shirt to keep from falling.

"Ye will be my vengeance."

She so didn't like the sound of that.

"Concentrate!"

Finley swirled around, keeping a firm hold on Skye as he glared at James.

"I am concentrating! I have been focused on nothing else since I escaped the battle those bumbling fools got us into."

James looked confused but held his tongue. Skye looked into the flames, saw her sister, and knew she was the one who spoke out.

"Ye lost?" Riona squealed. "God's blood, ye should have kept to the original plan!"

"Shut up! Ye lost any chance of that the moment ye started yer caterwauling in his study."

"I did not! I was trying to make him feel like he needed to protect me, protect my virtue. Since you couldn't get him into my bed, I had to do something!" Riona spouted as she poked him in the chest.

Softly, so as not to be heard over the angry exchange, Skye began her chant.

"Through time and distance, let us arrive
without hindrance.
To right the wrong so I may return to whom I
belong."

She was on the third repeat when she felt the queasiness begin. It was also when Finley hollered for James to take his sister out of his presence and focused back on her.

"What are ye rambling on about?" He demanded, gripping her tighter in his anger.

Skye looked up, a smirk on her face. "This is why you don't fuck with a witch."

Then she seized Riona, and because James was grabbing her, they all vanished together.

Chapter Fifteen

As soon as they appeared inside Aiden's study, Finley dragged Skye to the floor as his legs gave out.

Her ears were ringing with the piercing screams of Riona until they were suddenly cut off.

Someone pried Finley away from her and then she found herself held in a tight embrace. Taking a deep breath, she was surrounded with the smell of everything that was Aiden and gratefully gave herself over to his strength as the commotion surrounding them told her the other three were being taken prisoner, Riona protesting her innocence.

"Be ye alright, *mo leanabh*?"

"With you holding me, how could I not?"

Feeling his chest rumble with laughter, she smiled for the first time, free from her troubled thoughts.

Aiden's hands smoothed over and down her hair before cupping her chin in his hands and raising her face so he could look at her.

"How did ye do that?"

"I did the same chant as the one in the forest, with a small twist and, since the others were linked to me, they came too."

"Ye took a great risk, lass."

"Please, Aiden, please don't be mad. I couldn't handle that right now."

"Nay, lass. Neither could I." He smiled down at her.

Suddenly, there was a cry from far away and Aiden lost his smile.

"Who is that?"

"Tis Anna, the bairn be comin."

Skye twisted in Aiden's arms to look at Collin. "It's still early."

Collin nodded his face ashen.

Pushing away from Aiden, she grabbed Collin by the hand.

"Come on, we need to go."

"What? Nay, I can do nothin but wait here."

She frowned in confusion at the man. "You're kidding, right?"

"Ye must go though, ye can help them."

She lowered her brows and pursed her lips. "Yes, I can, but you are coming with me."

"Tis no me place up there."

"Bullshit. You started this. You will be there to finish it. Now come with me or I don't go at all."

Skye stood firm in her resolve of ensuring some medieval mentalities would change.

"Ye would deny Anna's safety?" Collin asked in amazement, looking from Aiden and back to Skye.

"No, Collin. But will you deny her the comfort only the man she loves can give her in one of the most stressful things she will ever go through?"

"I doona ken."

Throwing her hands up in frustration, she grabbed his hand again. "You will. Now, come with me."

They raced up the stairs, Skye saw Finley, Riona, and James being hauled around the corner to the same dungeon she'd been forced to suffer in and could not squelch the moment of satisfaction that brought her, even as she shivered with memories.

They entered Anna's bedroom right after Anna cried out again.

Skye brought Collin over to the girl and picked up her hand causing her to open her eyes and turn her head.

"Skye!" She said through a hoarse throat. Then she saw Collin and Anna began to cry harder.

Collin took his bride's hand and placed it over his heart as he scooted closer to her side.

"Twill be aright, *mo ghaol* I be here an I won't leave ye."

"Tha ghaol agam orti."

Elizabeth smiled when Anna professed her love for her husband, gave her daughter a quick hug, and slipped to the other side of the bed.

They went through another labor pain and Skye looked at Collin, worried he wasn't going to be staying on his feet for long if she didn't get started.

"Ready?"

Barely taking his eyes off his wife, Collin nodded, a drop of sweat already falling from his pale brow.

"Okay, we do the same thing we did before: You keep telling her how you feel, how proud you are and I'll do the easy part."

She winked to ease the tension as she placed her hand under the sheet and onto Anna's stomach, then held onto her friend's other hand and closed her eyes.

Centering herself, Skye felt her powers flow along her body and through her hands and followed the colors.

"Even though he is early, the baby is perfect. Anything that needs to be taken care of I can do easily enough so I am going to concentrate on the pain."

The colors vibrated as another contraction coursed through Anna's abdomen.

"Please hurry."

Skye felt the squeezing of her hand as if it was an afterthought and she sent calming waves to course through Anna's belly and out, building it like a wall or a layer, hoping it would diminish the pain from her contractions.

Either her labor had been going on for some time or her labor was going fast, because the spasms seemed to be coming one after another.

Noise became muffled as she went deep into her healing and she didn't hear when Aiden came up behind her, assuring his sister that he wasn't watching anything he shouldn't, but that he was going to make sure Skye wasn't exhausting herself.

She didn't need to hear anything to know when Aiden wrapped his hands around her waist in a gentle embrace and an easing of strain left her back and shoulders as she began to feel rejuvenated.

It was his voice in her ear gently telling her to let go that finally reached her and she eased her hands away, allowing herself to lean back into his strength and refocus on her surroundings.

The sound of a baby crying had her turning her head as Elizabeth finished cleaning the infant and placed him in the new mother's arms.

A feeling of joy filled everyone's hearts and Aiden tugged at her.

When she stepped away, Anna looked at her with concern.

"Ye said the bairn might need—"

"Don't worry, hon." Skye patted her arm then took Aiden's hand. "Nothing needs to be done now. Tomorrow is soon enough, and I won't be far away if you need me."

Hearing that made Anna relax and she nodded before turning back to the baby, smiling. "Is he no beautiful, Collin?"

"Aye, lass, as beautiful as his mother."

Elizabeth placed her hand gently on Aiden's forearm to stop them for a moment.

"I will contact yer sister for ye Skye and tell her all be well, ye get some sleep."

Blushing as Aiden nodded to his mother, they slipped out of the room, Skye willingly following in Aiden's footsteps.

They stopped only long enough to tell Keir the baby and the new mother were fine and that he would deal with the prisoners in the morning.

They entered a different chamber and before Skye could ask any questions, Aiden had her back in his arms and his mouth covering hers.

She melted instantly, moaning with need as his hand cupped her throat and his tongue thrust between her lips.

Her nipples tightened and her hands fisted into his shirt as she rose up onto the balls of her feet, demanding more.

She whimpered when he broke the kiss and sighed when his lips brushed over her cheek and forehead.

"This be me new chambers til me other one be cleaned. Tis a mess ye dunno wish to see right now, but there be no hearth for a fire, if ye rather speak with yer sister—"

"All I want is you."

"Ye—"

She placed the palm of her hands on his chest to stop him so she could continue. "But I want you forever. I can't wake up some morning to have you tell me I cannot stay."

She searched his face, her heart beating wildly with trepidation in her chest.

His large callused hands cupped her face and he kissed her nose.

"Tomorrow will be me last day without ye as me wife."

Eyes widening in wonder, she felt her mouth drop open.

"That bein, if ye will have me, *mo leanabh*."

Tears welled up and fell as her lips trembled. "You mean t-that?"

"Aye, lass, twas a decision I came to this morn but I couldna tell ye since I had to get to me duties as Laird. I didna think ye would be gone when I had the time to speak of this with ye."

Blushing, she shook her head, still confused.

"I felt lost. My head was filled with so much doubt that I believed Riona when she said you had used her and then left her when you were bored of her. I was such a fool—"

"Nay, lass, tis somethin I should have been prepared for. Ye were experiencin a normal reaction to sech a strong scene last night an I dinna take proper precautions. Next time I will make sure I take care of ye right an no play with ye when I must attend other duties."

A slow smile spread over Skye's features. "I like that 'next time' part."

"Ye do, aye?" Aiden grinned down on her beautiful face as he brushed her hair back.

"It is amazing that something like that could do so many wonderful things to me. It was like an amazing drug, the things that you did to my body and the way I felt like I was somewhere else. It was amazing." She repeated in awe.

He chuckled at the wonder in her voice.

Skye took his roughed cheek into her hands. "*Tha ghaol agam orti.*"

A gentle smile softened his rugged features and he pulled her face to his. "I will see that ye will never regret that, *leanabh.*"

Then he swung her into his arms and carried her to bed.

EPILOGUE

Skye was excited and it bubbled over to everyone else.

"Christmas in July! Isn't that exciting?"

Anna gently patted baby Dougal over her shoulder and grinned.

"Tis indeed as it must be for Aiden since tis his birthday as well, so he gets two presents."

Blushing, Skye stopped her hurried packing. "You didn't say anything to him, right?"

"Nay, but tis gettin difficult, so I be glad the day be here!"

Four months had passed since Finley and the Reivers had attempted to invade the castle.

There had been a short trial.

Skye was shocked to find out that the midwife had been a relative as well, but because she had given the information about Riona and Finely, she had been spared a hanging and was banished instead.

Her plea for Riona to go with her was heard. After the girl's locks were shorn and her shoulder had been branded with a "C" for conspirator, the two women were sent away with the threat of death if they were ever seen on Scottish lands again.

The captured Reivers and James were hung and their bodies displayed outside the keeps gates as warning, causing Skye and Anna to stay within the gates until the bodies had been removed.

Because of his position, Aiden had to petition the English crown for approval of his judgment over Finley, so he had taken the man to England with Kier and a few other men, leaving Collin and his guards behind to watch over his family.

Henry VII had been the one to grant Aiden's father the castle and surrounding lands, so his support was given and Finley had been hung—the rest Skye didn't want to think about.

Aiden had been gone just over two months and had only returned ten days ago.

The week before they left, Aiden had taken every opportunity to prove his love, showing her how he could bring her to the same pinnacle of pleasures after an intense dungeon scene and then to lightly play with her the next day to ease her from the confusing obsessive feelings such heights brought on.

Because her family kept in constant contact, Skye had been able to remain sane while separated from her new husband. Now she was overjoyed with the news she would soon be sharing with him.

When Sarah informed Skye that they would be traveling to Scotland to visit the very castle she resided in come summer, she and Skye spoke about exchanging gifts. Their aunt had said it would be a wonderful idea and believed it could be possible with the right chant if they found the exact location in both times. To keep Skye from making a mistake, they would have her place a box in the designated area and they would dig it up and replace with their own, if the spell worked, it would be transported back to their time.

Sarah, Doug, baby Collin, and Aunt Gladys had arrived in Scotland three days prior and they had finally found a location each could get to from their prospective times.

Gladys had purchased a steel box and had it lined with cowhide that she had cured in her own special concoction of juices from herbs and roots to help transport it back in time. The plan was that her sister would unearth it the next day and place their gifts inside and the chant would send it back in time for Skye to receive.

It had been difficult explaining to everyone to be careful of what they were going to give since the gifts inside might seriously erode any type of material away. Even though Sarah would receive it the next day, it was still hundreds of years in between and they weren't sure how well it would work this first time.

Try to explain that to the common person!

Feeling arms wrap around her from behind, Skye's heart soared and she whirled around to return Aiden's hug.

"Do you have it?"

Aiden smiled down on his wife's glowing face and tried hard to frown. Instead, he kissed her on the nose and handed over the small bags.

"I canna believe ye be givin pennies as a gift to yer family. They will think ye have married a pauper."

"Oh, poo. I explained it to you before so, for the third time; a penny now is serious business then."

"Aye, lass, an it disna make any more sense as it did the last two times."

"I know what my family would love, and when we all open our gifts tomorrow you shall see."

She grinned up at him, his eyes cleared, and he was lost.

"Yep, ye have me brother wrapped around yer little finger." Anna laughed.

Skye laughed and squeezed her husband before turning to the younger girl.

"You are only repeating what I told you about Collin."

"Aye, tis somethin I completely ken now that I see it with ye two."

"What does she mean?"

"She means that you love me. Lots." Skye grinned back at him.

Aiden looked at her flushed cheeks and his heart filled with emotion.

Skye had been his wife for four months and each day he wondered how it could be.

"Aye, *leanabh,* I do."

"I found it!" Elizabeth said as she entered then stopped as she caught the exchange between her son and his wife.

Smiling she slipped around them, grinning from ear to ear and placed an item in the box.

"What is it?"

"Tis a knife I had made for Gladys, so she can use it to cut her meat with."

Skye chuckled softly. There was so much to tell them.

"I think my aunt will be thrilled. I can't wait for tomorrow!"

*   *   *

Everything worked out perfectly and now they stood in front of the roaring fire in Aiden's den chatting excitedly as they opened their gifts, unconcerned over the warmth the fire brought on such a warm day.

Skye had to keep herself from going crazy as they spent so much time over the wrapping paper before she forced them to open the gifts.

They placed the wrapping paper aside, stating they wouldn't burn it until they could look more closely at in the light of day.

Aiden was shocked at the response her family had over the pennies and frowned.

"Now, now, Doug." Skye admonished. "You let them cash those pennies. I know how difficult times are with the baby and Sarah having to work part time. And I want this to be a yearly thing, so let it be."

"But—"

Before Doug could complain further, she held up a hand. "And, if you look into that little bag to your right you will see that I thought of you too."

Beaming, she watched as Doug's face lit up as coins came tumbling out onto his palm.

"There are different kinds of groats, and riders, and farthings and whatever else they are called. I don't have them all straight yet."

Gladys cleared her throat. "There's a cottage about six miles from the castle up for sale. I will be buying that with my penny."

"Buyin a cottage for a penny?"

Grinning, Skye nodded to Collin, who finally took his eyes off the Bowie knife he was given.

"I told you all, but do you ever listen? Noooooo." She smirked.

Anna was shown how to use the baby bottles as Skye placed the binky in little Dougal's mouth, but it was the snaps on the baby clothes that had Anna in wonder, causing Elizabeth to take her attention from the warmth of the matching cashmere sweater and mittens.

Aiden's silence caught her attention as he looked through a notebook given to him by Doug.

"What is it, my love?"

Aiden looked up in wonder then over to the flames.

"I want the best for my sister-in-law, as well as for my ancestry." Doug said. "It was a long hard decision to make since I don't believe that changing the future is a good thing but I learned yesterday that I can leave it in your very capable hands."

Skye frowned in confusion and looked over Aiden's shoulder at the book.

"Doug!"

There, in Aiden's hands, was page after page of Scotland's history.

Wars and their outcome, commerce, free trade, plagues, crops, and everything else that occurred over the next six hundred years.

Doug smiled and made himself comfortable in a way that told Skye they were in for a good story.

"I wasn't sure if I should do it but when I went to a local tavern yesterday and they learned my name, a man came over, about my age.

"He sat down and we talked. His name is Edward and he said he had been coming to this tavern for a long time waiting for me. He completely stuns me when he says that he is your direct descendant!"

Before anyone could digest the news, Doug continued. "He told me of a manual that was handed down to every generation of castle owners. He also said there had been a seer somewhere in their family that had written of future events ending with my coming to Scotland."

We are going to the castle to meet him and his family tomorrow night."

"Isn't this fabulous?" Skye clapped. "You need to tell us everything!"

"If all goes well maybe we can all chat?" Sarah asked.

"I would like that." Elizabeth smiled.

"Aye." Aiden agreed.

When the evening ended, Aiden took his wife's hand and led her from the room.

"What do ye have there? My birthday present?"

"Nope, that is something I am going to wait until we get into our room to give you, this is your Christmas present."

"I couldna open it with the others?"

"Ummmm, no. Not a good idea."

"Keir!" Skye called out when she saw the man walking from the kitchens. "I have something for you."

Keir approached and smiled. "What be that, lass?"

She handed over a handle and placed it properly in his hands. "Hold it like this and when you press this thing here don't let go and don't move."

"Mayhap I shouldna press that 'thing'?"

"Oh, but you have to, it's the best part." Skye looked at him with wide innocent eyes.

When Keir hesitantly nodded, she made sure Aiden stood off to the side.

As soon as he pushed the button, a blade shot out and Skye clapped her hands.

"It's called a stiletto. Isn't it the absolute coolest thing ever?"

Both Aiden and Keir stood in shock. Then they were both taking turns trying it out.

"Why did ye no get me one of those?" Aiden groused when Skye pulled him away.

Stopping on one of the steps, she smiled back at him. "Because I happen to think what I got you is better."

Quirking a brow she waited.

Grinning, Aiden lifted her up, swung her over his shoulder, and bounded up the stairs to their room, Skye protesting with laughter the entire time.

When he set her down her body slowly drifted over his until her feet hung just above the floor.

He kissed her hard, his tongue pushing past her lips to swirl with hers.

"Aiden." She gasped. "The gifts."

"They can wait."

"No, I want to give them now. I-I have to." She panted.

Groaning, he eased her to the floor and let go.

"You open this while I take care of something."

"Where be ye goin?"

"Just in the other chamber for a moment. Go ahead, open that and I will return with your birthday gift."

Skye slipped over to the alcove and opened the package she had her sister buy for her and slipped into the bright pink lingerie set with matching fluffy heels and sheer robe.

She stepped out and positioned herself, waiting for Aiden to look up from the book in his hands.

"Look at the paper." He said in awe as he gingerly ran his hands over the pages while sitting on the edge of the bed.

"It's the *Kama sutra*."

Skye had asked Sarah to find her one that was a G-rated as possible, since she wasn't sure how well he would take explicit pictures and here he was amazed over the print of it.

"Have ye ever felt the texture of these pages? The brightness of the pictures? Why there be nothin but a flat surface, as if—" He looked up and his jaw dropped.

Skye blushed and her smile deepened. "You likee?"

His mouth moved but nothing came out.

She slowly lowered her hand from above her and took slow, sensual steps toward him, her face pure seduction.

"This be me birthday gift?" He rasped out as he laid the book down beside him.

Pushing him teasingly back, Skye straddled his waist as she climbed on top of him.

"Mmmm, yes." She kissed his neck, laving with her tongue. "Do you like?"

"I like Christmas in July."

Kissing his stubbled jaw, Skye smiled wickedly. "But I already have your Christmas gift for December, so we definitely can't skip that."

His hands circled her waist and over her rump, feeling the satin of the cloth covering her. "Be that so?"

"Aye." She smiled, rubbing her nose over his using her best Scottish brogue. "An I will be a good wife an let ye pick out the name."

Aiden licked her chin before stilling as her words sunk in. His fingers eased from their firm grip and he pressed his head further into the mattress to peer at her.

"Ye be with bairn?"

Knowing he needed her being serious, she sat up on his lap and nodded down at him. "I am three months pregnant."

"Ah, lass." He sighed, drawing her down and rolling her gently to her back.

He then proceeded to show her how even gentleness could bring her to wonderful peaks of passion.

Then he showed her again.